# OLD
# BAGGAGE

## a novel

ISBN-13: 978-1530424887
ISBN-10: 1530424887

Toni Kief's website: www.tonikief.com

Cover design: Heather McIntyre, www.coverandlayout.com
Cover photos: Amber necklace by Pavel V Mukhin; Silhouettes by Majivecka

Interior design: Heather McIntyre, www.coverandlayout.com

Georgia, Reglo, Verdana

# OLD BAGGAGE

## a novel

## Toni Kief

The Writers Cooperative of the Pacific Northwest
Seattle, Washington 2016

This book is dedicated to Celena Davis, my granddaughter an important part of the inspiration, and my mother Marjorie Rhoades Bass. May they argue over Gene Kelley for years to come.

## *Special thanks to:*

Connie Kreutzer Baxter and the entire Happy Hour gang. Surprising how half-price appetizers and laughter inspire. The Daily Scribes, Susan Brown, Fai Dawson, and Eleanor Orme – learning that the art of writing is easier over crepes and tea. Wina Trappen, my reader and advisor from beginning to end. Also, to Jacob Davis – and his suggestions added so much to the story. Roland Trenary, Beth Buckley, Writers Kickstart, and Writers Cooperative of the Pacific Northwest. James Johnson, I never would have put pen to paper without you. Thank you to each and every one.

# OLD BAGGAGE

a novel

# — 1 —

"What is this? Stupid bitch, you know I hate pickles!"

"Then don't eat them." And we are off; it takes so little to start an argument in this house of lies. He crawled in well after sunrise and even after all of these years, I still worry. Never am I able to completely rest, not sure if he has found a better bed or if the road and alcohol have claimed him. But the real fuel to his fire is that I know where he was at all night.

I may never know why this day, is it enough? Am I finally through with the degradation and his volatile anger? I know it isn't the kosher dills that set him off. His usual defense is to divert his guilt with an attack. Of all the people on this earth, I know how he operates.

"The dills aren't for you. I buy the groceries and I deserve a freaking pickle."

He also knows how I work to avoid these arguments and the shock is visible when I respond. The single hamburger patty continues to sizzle in the pan, and the bun sits on a small plate prepared with my favorite condiments. "This is my lunch. Why don't you go back to bed, or is it too empty for you?"

The slap to my face stings and I feel his angry fingers around my throat. His only response is a string of swear words and name-calling. I know where this ends. Soon I will be on the floor, broken and apologizing; or maybe, this time, he may kill me. He pushes me back against the counter, and I touch the cold heft of the pickle jar. I have no conscious thought about my next action. For the rest of my life, I won't remember hitting him. I hear the jar break. The juice christens his head as the acrid liquid slowly splashes over both of us. I watch the hateful look on his face change to surprise and finally to sleep as he crumbles to the floor.

I run to our room and pull out my suitcase. I dump in my underwear, toothbrush, all of the toothpaste (screw him; he can buy his own), and my makeup bag. At a second thought, I throw his toothbrush into the toilet. As I zip my suitcase closed, the smoke detector begins to wail. Seeing his wallet sitting on the dresser, I take an overdue allowance before running back into the kitchen.

I reach over his lifeless body to turn off the stove. To my horror, he stirs. His eyes don't open, and he remains unconscious.

There is an all-consuming desire to kick him, but instead, I dial 911. Calmly I request an ambulance, provide the address and promise to leave the door open.

Wheeling my suitcase to the open door, I gaze at the horizon when I suddenly hear a long-silenced voice from my childhood yelling, "Go, just go."

# — 2 —

"You miserable, mean, cheating, lying, drunken bastard!" I shriek while crossing the railroad tracks; my anger grows stronger, words directed to the weak man I left behind, "You took forty-nine years of my life, but I will be damned to hell if you get fifty!" At this moment, I recall the coolness of the jar on the counter and the uncontrolled need to fight back.

*I did it! I left.* I admit to wishing us both dead for years, and I'm sure he is still alive. I'm usually self-conscious, but I realize people driving past only see an old woman in her pajamas, struggling with a suitcase and engaged in a personal conversation. For once, I don't care. I'm grateful no one bothers to looks close enough to see the handprints on my throat and the blood staining my nose.

Blind to the beauty of the morning, I maintain a single focus, seething with anger and fear. I know I crossed the line and finally – there is no turning back. The darn wheels on the suitcase are awkward in the grass, and I'm forced to lift it over the curb and past the mud.

*How can so few belongings be this heavy?* I reach the sidewalk just as I drop the case and pause to catch my breath just for a moment, before picking up speed on the smooth concrete. My rant re-energizes, as years of frustration form into swear words. Years of humiliation, avoiding confrontation, swallowing injustice and frustrations pour out. I cannot justify a lifetime of regrets and secrets. There is no reasonable explanation for my procrastination. I straighten my jacket and wipe away the last of the blood on the sleeve. I can see my first stop a couple of blocks ahead, helping me accelerate. I have spent my entire adult life hiding. I am not ready to acknowledge the lies that have eaten away my core. For the first time since childhood I don't feel fragile, and gain strength with each step that distances me from the past.

Giddiness comes with the realization that my plan is in motion. I need to clear my head and think through the outline of my escape, but my anger keeps interrupting my thoughts.

"It was your turn to lie on the floor, and I found it gratifying, do you hear me, Bradan Donovan, proud that I put you there. Bet you like pickles now." I can clearly see him grasping his chest and collapsing covered in vinegar and dill. I have no concern for him as I open my eyes to the clear blue sky and a new beginning. My regrets are in the past as I wrestle my thoughts back to the plan.

I suddenly understand prisoners as they walk through the secured gates of maximum security. Everything looks more brilliant than it did an hour ago. I'm confident this afternoon saved both of our lives, adding a confidence to my stride. The possibility of returning to the place I called home is gone. It makes no difference if he survives or not. I am out of that life and starting anew.

There is more shame than pain in trying to understand why I stayed. I pray to understand the emotional damage caused by my inaction. The truth is probably right in front of me, but searching for it now will have to wait. It is too much to face at this moment. I prepared this escape for decades, as my personal rebellion, and it was one of the few things that kept me alive. Escape was a vague future so long; I'm surprised to be finally living the dream. I should have dressed for the road all day every day. Pajama pants and a T-shirt are not what I envisioned.

*Hello, Elizabeth, this is how LIBERATION looks.* Seeing the Mail Spot ahead, I visualize this sidewalk as the yellow brick road to freedom. I take the first full breath of a bright sunny day, noticing the smell of green grass and the vibrant color of flowers alongside the road. *You no longer own me, Mr. Donovan. This way leads to a life of my own.*

Straining for clarity, I have no control as the past replays. Everything through time and space is roiling in an emotional maelstrom. My mind reels to the beginning; tears gather behind my eyes, triggered by the old memories. As frightening as this moment is, I feel alive, more than when I was fifteen and falling in love. I shake my head, confessing I had believed that I was lucky to have found genuine love so young. *I guess luck isn't always good, and love isn't always true.*

My first stop, the Mail Spot, is now only a block away. My adrenaline flows as I again hear my daddy's deep voice just before that first date. I send a heartfelt thank you to my long gone father. He was right, the excitement of young love made me deaf, but it was hisadvice on the night of the Homecoming Dance that is my salvation. It brought me here. I can feel myself standing next to my father, ready for the game and dance.

Dad saw through Bradan at the beginning, but he was bright-eyed, handsome and a star athlete. He was popular, and I was invisible. Dad took an immediate dislike to Brad, and I fought him, confident I knew better. I ignored his misgivings and assumed it was just a father wanting to keep his little girl a child. "I never took the opportunity to tell you, but you were right. I can still hear you today." The emotions of that evening replay as I feel excitement and hope for the dance. His words play through my mind. *A lady should always carry enough money for a phone call and a bus ticket. There is no predicting what an evening will bring.*

Over the decades, that simple piece of advice became a mantra, then finally a rebellion. I saved and hid money my entire life, never sure what a *lady* may need. From one conversation, I justified my miserly way of hoarding, lying, and preparing for a multitude of scenarios. A few times, I was tempted to tell Brad about the money, but there was never a catastrophe big enough to share the hidden cache and the subsequent fight. This guilt-ridden woman turned bus fare and a phone call into a magnificent dance of mutiny. I never was able to squirrel away a large amount, but I always saved.

With a hope that a couple of dollars a week would turn into a life, I march forward. At the least, it will be a down payment on a forty-nine-year debt. Today I take my ransom and catch that bus Daddy described.

I acknowledge Bradan's attempts to dominate my life, but my spirit lit a candle. It didn't start being an escape plan, but the violence and control changed my savings from ours to mine alone. He gave me lunch money, and I skipped lunch; I picked up change from the ground, I colored my hair. He put gas in the car but made it clear it was his car. Then Brad would check the odometer to be sure the miles matched my calendar of activities. He accused me of his sins, always watching but never seeing. Nevertheless, I had my ways and kept the discount on the insurance safe driving premium too. You bought most of the groceries, but not all and I mastered the art of skimming. "Damn-it, I am angry. No, not angry – I'm furious! To you, the dear asshole of my life, Good-bye! Your hostage has chewed loose from her restraints and she is on her way toward...." I hear an evil sounding chuckle escape my lips.

I feel no further responsibility for that old dance. The ambulance call was my last act of caregiving. I stand as tall as an osteoarthritic 65-year-old woman can stand with a pink suitcase and a box of family photos. My marital duties finished and I am out of here.

Whenever I have moments where I soften, I vow to remember the worst of times. "We had good, loving times, Brad, but those counted in days and not years, not decades, not a half century." He is still charming, but I was the one knocked to the floor by the man who was supposed to love me above all others. Long absent tears well up with the visual memory of the night I lost the baby, my little girl, because dinner was late. I remember the long wait while he went back to the Hitching Post for the last call. *You rushed me to the hospital, at your convenience, after they dimmed the lights. The nurses made you stay, only because your blood-alcohol level was too high to allow you to drive.*

Setting my shoulders I lift my eyes to the horizon, all I have to do is keep walking. "Every step takes me away from him and in time, the memories will fade, too." I donated my heart for too many years and I wonder, if I weighed the tears, would I have a bucket or a salty ocean? "You selfish ass, you didn't even notice the tears dried up?" I'll never forget my thirty-second birthday, waiting for you to cash a check and pick up your winnings from the cardroom. I had believed your promise of a romantic dinner for a special girl, and I waited for hours in the sweltering car. As I wilted in the car, my mood turned to a simmer and then to a boil, that day I started to lay the groundwork for today's departure. From that moment on, I had another secret and began to dream of a life of honesty and freedom without Brad. *I emotionally left you on that day, never to return. I just didn't realize it would take me so long to physically exit.*

There is no quieting the disjointed thoughts and private outbursts. "Did I let you steal my life, or did I donate it?" I'm no longer willing to justify my existence based on his best days. No one knows him better than I do. He will never give up the drinking, the beatings, and the control. I remove myself from the role of a witness; I ponder a variety of causes or excuses to explain the man. A realization nags me: I have known the truth for years. I wasn't a partner or a wife, but his possession.

"I need another swear word to call you, you rat-bastard!" I look forward to the time he will be a faded memory, a story I survived. There will be a day when I have a complete thought that doesn't involve Brad Donovan. I snap back into the present, focusing on my escape. I count each step to quiet the narrative raging through my brain. *Twenty-three, twenty-four, twenty-five,* I block the weak rationalizations for my current circumstance. "Well, no more, done and gone. Fix your own damn lunch." *Twenty-six, twenty-seven....*

I smile with the knowledge that the silly pink suitcase gathering dust in the back of the closet had a loose lining, which I filled with savings books and bankcards. I worked one job for thirty-six years, and I smile remembering the raises I didn't share. Oops forgot to mention – got 'em, every single one. Automatic deposits to the 401K he didn't think was necessary, because he would take care of me forever. WRONG! I took care of us most of the years we were together. I worked and saved since I was a child. Mark my debt paid. I can care for myself, no matter what the situation.

I hear the distant howling of an ambulance and my step quickens. "Take it easy, fellas – these roads are treacherous." Watching the vehicle pass with no hesitation causes my heart to thump in a moment of fear. Brad's lifesavers drive past and don't even look at me. I smile at one of the small blessings of an aging woman – the cloak of invisibility. "Heroes, you will never know you are saving two lives for the price of one. You don't have to search for the second one; I'll take care of her."

I make a promise to the girl who still struggles inside. Falling back on the habit of list making, I decide to extend gratitude to the people in my life who have shown me support and kindness. So many surprising actions and good will kept this life worth living. I will send thanks acknowledging each one. The strength in my survival builds and finally leads to pride with the changing of the rules. He failed in the quest for world domination. I know he has only seen the victim in me, but his Elizabeth Ann is gone, and Libby marches back into existence. I embrace my childhood nickname, back when I was still happy. With each step away from the old life, Libby lives. The name suits me just fine.

I slow to catch my breath and try on a veil of composure. I can't allow anyone in the Mail Stop to see my panic. I pull open the door and see the smiling clerk, Rapinder. Little does she know that she is a cherished friend of a broken woman. Some days, her cheerful greeting was the only thing to keep me going. She graciously allowed me to use the computer. I extend a silent prayer for a slow business day and a promised blessing for the dear woman. The first thank you is extended like an invisible muffin basket.

I have the drive to make my life; I know I can do it. I have spent years plotting, planning, and this is the time for action. The letters are prepared, for Social Security, my job, the banks, and Medicare. They just need to be printed and stamped. An unexpected chuckle escapes my lips; I've moved so deliberately that the cost of stamps went up. A mailbox and automatic deposits are all done with the left click of a mouse and there is no turning back. I hand her a change of address forwarding my mail from our home to my PO Box.

I send a quick text to Brad's phone: *I'm finished and will never come back. Don't call me, ever. Goodbye.* I then turn off the cell phone and drop it into a bubble wrap envelope and send it to my husband. Another door slammed closed. On the back table, I open my case and pull out the savings information and guilt creeps back as I count. There may have been a hundred times when I almost told him, but Brad – life partner, jailer, husband – would always pull something that kept me in a life of duplicity. I know he would forgive an affair before he could stand for holding out money. His mistrust would have escalated to the seventh level of hell.

As I leave, I gulp back that lump that has resided in my throat for the past decade, living a lie is over. Plan B is on! Step 2, the bus stop is less than a mile. I decide to take a taxi to the Kokomo bus station and then a short ride to Indianapolis for the locker of clothes and cash I stowed years ago.

Here I come in my most profound moment of clarity. I could skip and hop the rest of the way, but that outpouring of joy has to wait, a mile of skipping could be exhausting at my age and may raise the invisibility cloak.

# — 3 —

"What is that smell! Where am I? How did I get here?" Did I say that aloud? I didn't realize how tired I was. The last I remember was gathering my hidden cash stash, buying the two-region pass and getting on the first bus out of Indianapolis. I don't remember much from then on. I lean back into my seat; the shock of reality catches up with my present situation.

I allow the panic to dissipate, and the familiar dream comes over me with the reassurance it offers. I have never understood the meaning, but the vision doesn't change with the full moon rising over a rocky horizon, and I'm telling stories to the young boy. The dream has visited me throughout my life, and I appreciate the wellbeing it offers on this night. As my mind clears, I realize again, "I left him." I will have to get used to the extraordinary.

The smell on the bus makes me think of freedom and a two-day old tuna sandwich. Not your regular delicious aroma, but on this first day of my life, it is wonderful. I'm not sure how long I was asleep, or where we are – luckily no one sat next to me. The bus is quiet except for the sound of the wheels and rhythmic breathing all around. I want to remember every minute of the first full day of liberty, so I watch out the window as the isolated black of night fades to dawn. There is too much to think about, I am hungry and still in an emotional jumble. Not a person to pray, I search my brain for some faith for assurance that this was the right action. Close to thirty-five years of planning an escape, I shouldn't feel confused. I would not suggest anyone put me in charge of any military operations. One fact for sure, I can never go back to the scene of that crime. Calmly I acknowledge the life I left was a long slow death.

I had no idea Greyhound carried so many people; until today I believed everyone flew. As morning breaks, I notice I may be the only passenger who didn't bring food. I could use a little of anything right now. I imagine I have teleported to an alternative dimension on a crowded escape craft. I look around the bus and begin to ponder the different stories riding with me. I realize there is no way to visualize what my fellow passengers may have gone through, and I decide that everyone gets a new start.

I have no doubt about my decision, but I am still distracted by an onslaught of random thoughts. I acknowledge the years of planning were necessary, but I should have tried a dry run to smooth out some of the unexpected details. I take a deep breath and release it as a sigh, knowing I may be anxious at times but not afraid. I raise my head with the multitude of possibilities. The uncertainty about every move and each word is over. I vow to discard the self-doubts and comprehend that if something goes wrong, I will just fix it. Smiling at the young woman I used to be, I allow my deepest secret to come briefly to mind. Appreciating that I am a sociological study in anxiety,

I know I haven't been completely honest with anyone for decades. The plan is underway, and there is no possibility of going backward.

The bus pulls into a stop, and I rush to the bathroom. The list of things to do starts to manifest. First, I need to stop worrying about counting money. Quash the question about why I didn't leave sooner. Thinking about it changes nothing – I can't change the past. Admit that there is only today and this moment. I check my suitcase and the hidden stash gives me confidence. It was just small deposits from every paycheck into different accounts. Always afraid of discovery, I justified the obsession, hoping if he found out, he could never find all of the accounts. Maybe if caught, I would only have to sacrifice one or two. In a stroke of luck, he never discovered any of the stashes, although I am lucky he didn't throw out the suitcase, he hated it so. The reminiscence went on for too long; I'm almost surprised my bus station escape wallet wasn't full of Confederate dollars.

I take a moment to calm, washing my face with cold water and a paper towel. Breathing in slowly, with counts of eight, then breathe out. Focus on the breath and embrace tranquility – three years of yoga save me now. I certainly don't want to appear deranged on a Greyhound bus. I imagine the authorities coming with a strait jacket. I play the vending machine as if I'm in Vegas and then get back on the bus. Tightly packed body heat exaggerates my concern about leaving my seat, knowing the rest of my life is in that silly suitcase. Now is the time for vigilance, calm, and a minimum of liquids. The thought of the bathroom on the bus is menacing. I catch the next bus going somewhere other than Kokomo.

I will just rest my eyes for a moment and ponder the next step. Hyper-vigilance is exhausting, but then again, this too shall pass.

If I jerk awake one more time, I'll be the one on the floor with a heart attack. No more fighting sleep, I need to bask in the warmth of an adventure and start another list. Number one, never again will I have to explain being late, I will just be late. Number two, no more meals without garlic and vegetables. I can eat what I want when I want, except on the bus of course. Number three, I can go to bed at seven or stay up until the rooster crows. Number four, take more window seats when traveling, and five, to be named when necessary.

Thank you, God, for the dreamless rest, I feel much better and calmer. Although it is embarrassing to have my snoring wake me. I would like to hope it was the first snore and not the 200th. The transition of menopause was full of noisy surprises and physical humiliations – I had never thought public sleeping would ever be an issue. At least everyone has the good manners not to laugh.

This morning I celebrate crossing three borders – panic, fear, and Arkansas. I can use a break to get my bearings. I just took the first bus out of town, which was my original plan, and now it is time for a destination. Today, I decide that I can go any direction except backward. There is no boss of me, and I have to remember that every day. I make a decision to get off the bus at the next stop, spend a few days, and then turn toward Julie and New Jersey. I have never traveled much, and I plan to enjoy this for the incredible adventure it is. I know I will like the next town. What is there to hate about Hot Springs?

# – 4 –

I had no idea how stiff and sore an old body can get from sitting. I used to have to do something to ache, but that has changed. I don't know if I can walk or speak, but the first thing is to find a bathroom. This depot is clean and surprisingly busy. I realize that this mode of travel lets a person see more of the country and helps to understand the real meaning of a melting pot. I have been journeying with the same people for over a day, and regret that I haven't had a conversation. I have had this endless dialogue in my head for so long; I have forgotten the sound of my voice. I've heard myself say *hello* and *excuse me*, but not much else, I have missed a great opportunity. My constant obsessing about my frightened story robs me of a lovely encounter.

Deep down I know I'm concerned that I would spill too much information, and Brad will find me. I scan the bus and don't notice any obvious spies. I need to be careful with my invisibility superpower; I think it could be addictive.

Now that I am safely away, I need to speak to my ex-sister-in-law. Brad kept me isolated and had written off most of my potential friends. He never realized Julie, also known as That Worthless Bitch, kept in touch with me. We don't call or write as often as we should, but she is an angel of a survivor from the Asshole clan. Julie is my safety net and my launching pad. Often she told me that if she could walk away, I could too. As soon as I have a phone, she will be the first call.

Enough! I must focus. I approach the ticket counter in Hot Springs. "Excuse me, sir, may I change my ticket to Fair Haven, New Jersey?"

The clerk, appearing like a security guard for the prison system, looks directly at me, "There is no problem, ma'am. Here is a schedule and just call ahead to be sure that there is a seat when you are ready to continue. Do you have friends in town?"

Pleasantly surprised, he is very kind. I hate to admit to only one friend in any city and I'm escaping my old world. "Why, no, I don't, but I need a break from all the riding. Do you know any reasonably priced places I can stay? Something clean and quiet would be great." I feel like a spectator to this conversation.

"Ma'am, if you look over at the racks near the rear wall, you will see a bunch of flyers. There should be something for you. I wouldn't suggest anything too close to the bus station. Let me know when you are ready and I'll call ya'll a taxi."

Everything is falling into place. He has no idea how important he is today, and I appreciate his kindness. "Thank you, hope to see you in a couple of days."

"I'll be here, Ma'am. Have a nice visit and welcome to Hot Springs."

I have always loved brochure racks; they seem to offer so many possibilities, and now, as a free woman,

I get to choose one. I will pick everything that makes this adventure real, adding another goal to my list. Excited about the multitude of things to see and places to go, I will pick everything that makes this adventure real, adding another goal to my list.

Now breathe deeply, focus and relax, no one cares that I'm here; no one notices how I look. I can do it myself. Hey, Brad, I'm not stupid and inept. Well, at least not so far. My new goal is to prove you wrong every single day Mr. Donovan.

OK, that is enough thought about that raging bastard today. Back to the brochures – damn, I didn't know that there were hot springs in Hot Springs. Will wonders never cease? I believe it is the perfect place to stop, and I think I will stay. Hmm...a chain motel or a low price. Oh snap, I want the Park Hotel, with a promenade and near the best springs. I know they wouldn't lie to me in a full-color pamphlet. Waving to the clerk, he picks up the phone. I gather my belongings and a sandwich, chips, and a drink from the vending machines, and head for the exit.

What a lovely day in a delightful town, Hot Springs, Arkansas. I convince myself that every day is beautiful here. I feel the warmth of the sun on my face, and the air smells fresh and clean. To make everything better, there is a cab waiting. I had no idea it could be easy, and I move with a new-found confidence. As I watch out the taxi window, the thought of a long, hot bath, clean clothes and some real food enriches my already good mood. I cast off the anxiety of my previous existence; I appreciate this journey as more exciting than perilous. I congratulate myself for my accomplishments. I have traveled, found a place to stay, and can take care of myself in the span of just two days.

The Park Hotel is perfect; it has passed its previous glory just like me. They are friendly at the front desk and seem happy to get a middle-of-the-week visitor. As I wander the lobby and halls in this classic old hotel, I know that if this place isn't haunted, it should be. I am one of the few guests, and I imagine the hotel is my palace. My plan is to use most of the hot water, wash my hair, put on clean underwear, and try on some privacy. The sandwich and chips from the bus station will do until morning, putting off the restaurant challenge for another day.

# $-5-$

"Sorry, I slept so late. Brad, I had the strangest dream. I'll get breakfast going. DAMN! Where am I?" Waking up in a strange room, I don't know where anything is, including a light switch. Slowly, the previous days returning to my consciousness. I search for a clock in the darkness wondering where hotels get curtains that could block out a nuclear attack. The red numbers to my left let me know that it is 6 o'clock. I usually sleep on the opposite side of the bed, but not this time, breaking all kinds of old habits. I am hungry and have no idea if I need breakfast or dinner, but a meal feels necessary. Flipping on the television, I see the familiar faces of the Today Show. Thank goodness, it's morning, and I imagine eggs, bacon, and clean clothes; what a wonderful treat.

*Oh no.* I realize it has been since the 80s since I began this escape. I only packed my underwear when I left the house, trusting on the escape bag at the bus station. I unfold the acid washed jeans and a couple of shirts. The pants are only 20 years out of style and as many years too tight. Luckily, I know an entire jean-squeezing dance and gyrate for a good five minutes to get into them. This is more exercise than I've had in years. I check myself in the mirror; I'm not completely zipped, but no one can tell with the right top. I don't think the bakers union would call this a muffin top, but more of a pound cake. Thank goodness, the shirts in the disco era weren't all glitter and cutouts; I have a couple of choices, and one is long enough to cover my fly. I make a vow if I ever need to escape again, I will pack elastic waist pants and hockey jerseys. Fashion trends be damned.

I find the outfit on the border of obscene, but my only other choice is my pajama pants that are soaking in the tub. Thank goodness, for the trench coat. Even on a sunny day, it will look less ridiculous than this outfit. I fight the urge to tease my hair and slather on some blue eye shadow. Instead, I'll opt for a brave face; no one knows me here, and no one will remember me tomorrow. I need food, a bank and then some shopping. Luckily, there is a café here in the hotel; it is all a single step at a time.

I have been to many diners throughout my life, but I have never gone into a sit-down restaurant alone. Recognizing I will not be ordering at a drive-through window and eating in my car today, I nervously enter, and my voice breaks as I ask for a corner table. My hands tremble as I hold the menu, hiding behind it and not reading. I catch myself listening to conversations that are none of my business. Next time I will have a book to hide behind, and I won't feel pitiful and lonely. I didn't anticipate this experience. It reinforces my determination. I will get used to the unplanned and surprise will make this adventure better. I decide to stare out of a window and continue trying to use my superpower. I wonder why I care so much what others think. They don't know me, and I know they don't give a flip.

*Chicken and waffles! Where have you been all my life?* I know that I can't make a habit out of this, but I've never been so hungry in my entire existence, and this combination is brilliant. The crispy fried chicken and the creamy, sweet waffles, there could be nothing better. Everything is hot and perfect with three cups of coffee; I'm purely happy. If this isn't the best meal I have ever eaten, it will, at least, be one of the most memorable. I lower my zipper just a smidge more.

I'm amazed how nice the people are. Is this a Hot Springs phenomenon or have I been closed down for so long that I have missed the valuable parts of society? I will learn to speak to people, not just to myself.

The server told me about a secondhand store a few blocks away. Since I have proven I can run, there will be no problem walking. There is a certain freedom in having virtually no possessions, but it would be nice to have some pants that cover a larger portion of my ass. The 80s fashions weren't kind to anyone, especially to us 60s folks. I dislike the idea of dressing like an overfed throwback to those embarrassing times. Lesson one: it is socially responsible to fasten your pants when out in public. Wearing a coat in the summer also flags me as a nutbag. Therefore, I go immediately and invest in clothes closer to this decade.

It is a perfect sunny day as I walk through the neighborhood toward the thrift store. I continue with my mental inventory. I continue with my mental inventory: money. I check the map I picked up at the bus station and discover there is a National Bank just past the store. My checking account is with National and I'm impressed that I chose so well. Then again, with a million branches. I had a good chance there would be one in Hot Springs. I also like the idea of guaranteed anonymity with such a large institution. I breathe easily knowing I need to organize my savings accounts that I'd so prudently scattered, mentally adding it to a next list. I look forward to combining them to see what I have to live on, smiling that my fear of discovery is still in Kokomo. For today, I have more than enough.

My old friend Doubt nags and I think that maybe I should wait to be sure Brad isn't looking for me. For the first time the thought he could be dead visits. I consciously put the thought aside, confident he wouldn't make it that easy. I decide to check into that possibility later. However, today isn't about him; this day is mine. I have no idea where I am financially, but trust there is enough. I used to feel dishonest about the automatic deposits to my personal account, but now I'm relieved knowing my paycheck will be in my bank in two days. I cancel the transfer to the joint account and get more cash. Sign one simple form and his gravy train ends. Damn, I am a sneaky dog, which pleases me.

From now on, I will refuse to accept my self-imposed guilt. When it starts, I have to stop and change the thought. I did the planning over years, but now I am at the mercy of details and banking hours. I tell myself that everything will work. After all, I have twenty-three savings accounts to organize. I admit my rebellion has kept me alive and now it will clothe and feed me. I make another vow to ignore the totals until I have a home base. I refuse to add another fear while I'm on the run and I refuse to ruin this sensation of plenty.

*Now quit nagging yourself and get some clothes.* Two fabulous things about thrift stores are you can buy more for less and then get a suitcase to haul it all away. Another thing is no one judges you for the outfit you wear when you come in. When I left, I had almost no belongings and in two days, I start to gather the trappings of life. The clerk appears puzzled as I check out, wearing the replacement clothes. She loans me her scissors to cut off the tags. I drop the acid washed jeans in the donation bin with the realization that I'm closer to my 80s than the 1980s.

The walk back to the hotel is full of positive thoughts and the notion of a future. Back at my room, I consider getting a rental car so I can cruise around. Then my old habit of penny pinching steps up and forces me to wait. I am empowered with the freedom of my decisions and appreciate a driver's license is a major trigger for women's equality.

Looking around the room, I notice that I'm nesting in the first bus stop on the road. The same home-building mistake I made in my teens. I refuse to fall in love with the first town that shows hospitality. *I can always come back.* I must sort out my future one hour at a time.

With a successful morning, I slowly allow the

thoughts to scatter, and I'm overwhelmed by the variety of things I should or could do. I plot different scenarios and then decide to stop adding to my list until I've checked some items off. I had outlined and planned, but life after Brad is overwhelming and will be more than only getting away. I didn't think past money, the bus, a comfortable chair, and an efficiency apartment. I must continue to follow the strategy and not get tangled in the multitude of details. I have one nagging issue still burning a hole in my heart. That decision will be the biggest challenge.

OK, things to wear – check. Next, there is a Target store in my sights directly ahead. Cosmetics, shampoo, deodorant, check – check – check. A cell phone or, as they call it on crime TV, a burner – check. I hadn't thought about a computer, but looking at the choices, not a bad idea. I can manage my money in the hotel room and not have to go to the banks. There was no laptop on my action list, but times have changed, and I think it is a brilliant idea. It will be a relief not to deal with a customer servant from a chain bank asking me questions and with it the possibility of exposure. I can also use the laptop to check the obits just to see if Brad ever made it to the newspaper.

Stumped by the choices of computer models, I stall to consider the mobile-options. They are smaller, lighter and more mobile perfect for the modern woman on the run. I hadn't thought about a tablet or the other pads. Knowing that I can take close to forty years to take action, it comes down to price every time. Although with the tablet, I have to get a phone account, and I don't need a large memory and, hold on, Today Only, I get a free carry case and a wireless mouse. Laptop it is.

I guess I don't have to justify each purchase, but that was close to five hundred dollars, and Elizabeth doesn't spend freely. I decide that Libby does.

Why didn't I get that rental car? I have too much to carry and still walk. Damn, it is as if I'm drunk, a dry drunk with power and cash. I can figure this out because I once was smart. Call a taxi, Genius – you can do it. Problem solved. Cheaper than a rental and they pick me up at the door. Hell, they even help load the bags. Kudos to Yellow Cab.

*Didn't I just eat?* This day has shot past. Fatigue barks at my legs and feet as I walk from the hotel to McDonalds for an easy dinner. Eating alone in a sit-down restaurant twice in a day is pushing my mettle.

Setting up a life is exhilaration followed by bone-crushing exhaustion. I anxiously wait for another experience that will be all mine. The smell of the budget sandwich and french fries fills my hotel room. I flip on the small television, pull the single chair into position, and kick off my shoes. A content sigh escapes my lips as I appreciate the smoothness of the remote control, coupled with the power of choice. The memory of his frustration when the controller wasn't next to his chair makes me smile. I welcome the luxury of watching anything I wish. I am not sure what I like, but I know what will never cross my screen again. Goodbye to most sports, panels of old jocks talking about even more sports, dark and violent sci-fi, *Dukes of Hazard* reruns and most of all – pornography.

I watch mindlessly for a short time. Once I finish eating, the exhaustion grips my entire body. Beginning to strip away my clothing, I walk into the bathroom. It is a little slip of happiness to find the seat is down and only one toothbrush in the plastic cup by the sink. I slide into the fresh sheets, and the coolness comforts me, another bonus of a solitary life. Sleep is begging to take over my consciousness, but I am not ready to give up this perfect day.

I startle awake after only a few minutes. Books, I can read all night any night. A plan for tomorrow manifests. I will buy a new book, maybe more than one, anything I want. I can pick a trashy romance, which is unlikely because that is what I just escaped. I had no idea that there are so many details. I look forward to morning and every day to follow as I drift back to sleep.

# − 6 −

I give up! I didn't notice all of the strange noises in this place. Every creak, whisper, and moan bring images of ghosts or painful memories. My room near the ice machine is a mixed blessing; I've learned I need sleep more than 24-hour access to cold drinks. Everything changes in a hotel on Friday night. It must be the Arkansas Tech Marching Band upstairs. Televisions whisper from every direction when all I want is rest. Why would there be traffic? It has been dark for hours. Beating the feathers out of a pillow does nothing. My body aches, my mind will not shut down, and this night is so very long. A little tranquility... is that too much to ask? I need the oblivion that dreamless unconsciousness can provide. I have never been alone; this is the first hotel where I get to use all the towels. The experience should feel luxurious and peaceful, not lonely and torturous.

If I didn't have to go to the bathroom, I would live out my life right here with my head under the blanket. I have to get busy; action will quiet my fears. Damn the clock, I will get out of bed, I've lain here for entirely too long already. A shower, makeup, breakfast, those choices will help, but I just want to lie where it is warm. I don't have yesterday's energy, and I try to bargain with myself. Maybe I'll do twice as much tomorrow. I attempt to understand the pain, every part of my body hurts, and I only shopped; maybe I'm getting sick. Sick and tired. That is probably my malady.

I know. I will walk over to the springs. One of the reasons for the hotel choice and I haven't explored to the south at all. My realization is that if I don't move, he wins and damn it, I will move.

The streets are abandoned; they hadn't quieted down until just before sunrise. All of the night creepers have stolen away while I dressed. I don't know if this is how it is in every town, but it is surely true here. I have always marveled at sunrise and this morning is promising. The stars begin to fade, and a dark blue starts to replace the night. Just the slightest glimpse of the hidden beauty is peeking through the buildings. Sunsets are your reward for staying alive, but the sunrise comes with a promise of a new beginning. You have to earn a sunrise, and here I am. All the nighttime revelers are enjoying the sleep they stole from me and are missing the best part of the day.

There are no businesses open, and I haven't eaten since yesterday afternoon. It is a sad state of affairs when I can't spot the promise of coffee. I have spent years waiting, and I don't want to do it anymore. I can do nothing about the restaurants closing. I recognize the old pattern of waiting – for my life to take off, waiting for happiness, waiting for satisfaction. Walking toward nowhere in particular, I am confident no one misses me. Once Brad was fed, my paycheck deposited and the laundry done, I had no other value. I have to keep moving; I cannot let his darkness overtake my mind.

Ahead, I spot an oasis. There is nothing like a gas station breakfast to get a girl back on the go. I don't see anyone in there, but there are lights. Muster up, Libby girl, the courage lives in you. That helps me walk through the double glass door. It is clean and bright inside, quite welcoming. *You have survived more threatening things than entering a convenience store.* I will act like a sane person and get some coffee.

Why would entering a gas station be such a challenge? I have done it thousands of times. Nevertheless, here I am, and I notice a large fried food display. My first reflex is to pull back, but my goodness, it does smell tempting. I find the coffee and remember when it used to be simple, and now there are so many choices. How does anyone know what to choose? Maybe I'll be a tea person, after sixty-five years no one knows me.

A clerk approaches from a back room.

"Good morning. Is the coffee fresh?"

"Why yes ma'am, you are the first morning customer; it is as fresh as it can ever be. I just filled the carafes, and you have a choice of five types."

It's nice to see a little customer service and friendliness. His bright freckled smile is sincere, and he doesn't look old enough to be employed. I realize he is young enough to be my grandson if I could be that lucky. "Did you do all of the cooking here? Or should I say frying?"

"No ma'am, my boss is in the back getting the food together before the travelers and truckers start rolling through town. We get busy this time of day. More people passing through than staying set." His open friendliness sets me at ease, and I decide I like him.

"Well then, I guess it is up to me to appreciate your hard work. I'll take this cup of vanilla roast. Hmm, a pop tart, and give me one of those corn dogs." I did it; I acted like a regular person. He won't know I'm on the lam. All I have to do now is to find a bench and savor my breakfast of champions in the glorious golden morning light. I will wait for the town to wake up and saunter onto the sights. I hope the hot springs opens early.

Oh, my God in heaven, what did I order? Trying to act sane, I buy crazy food. I spot a bench by a small park and settle in for breakfast. Looking at my dietary choices, and I realize this may imitate a slow suicide attempt. Tasty, though. I guess food is fuel, and this is working fine. The coffee is fresh, but a little strong for my liking. I continue to feel better; the corn dog is better than the pop tart. *What the heck is a pop tart? Is it food?* Strangely enough, it tastes like I need a second one.

The full sun clears the horizon and the morning starts to heat up. I watch the day coming to life with tentative movement. Workers arrive to make, serve and repair, keeping Hot Springs functioning. The brochures from the bus station are interesting. I didn't know that Hot Springs was the first national park; look at me, I'm learning. I thought Yellowstone was first, but I haven't been there either. I will put National Parks on my life to-do list. Nice to know our government protected some things without planning for financial profit or a campaign strategy. Oops, starting to sound like Brad, with the government this and the government that. He needs to get the hell out of my head.

Let's see, "...natural flowing thermal springs on the southwestern slope of Hot Springs Mountain." All I see is a line of tourist stops and bathhouses, all dilapidated, yet reminiscent of a grander day. There is a hint of sulphur, popcorn, and last night in the air, as the day begins to come alive. I look at my surroundings and recognize some of the places the pamphlets describe.

I am certainly not up for bathing with strangers; I can barely eat with them. I remember to repeat to myself that *I'm the stranger, no one knows me and no one cares.*

Back to my heavy reading. Begin your visit with a stop at the opulently restored Fordyce Bathhouse right in the middle of Bathhouse Row. You'll be transported back to a different time when Hot Springs literally 'Bathed the World'. *Guided and self-guided tours through this marvelous edifice will give you a quick understanding of where the thermal waters come from, how they are used and how the federal government protects the 700,000 gallons of thermal water that gushes uninterrupted from the earth every day.* Now a self-guided tour, I can do that.

# — 7 —

"Lady, are you ok? Ma'am, are you ok?"

"What? Who are you? Where am I? Oh, yeah, I'm all right. Thanks for asking."

"I just wanted to be sure you were alright and not sick or something? My buddy wanted to give you CPR, but I told him you were just snoring."

"Snoring? Oh my God in Heaven, I'm so very sorry." I gather my things and can feel the heat of embarrassment spreading up my neck, announcing itself on my face. My mind reels with questions, but the main one is how long have I been asleep on this bench? How many people have seen me sitting here with corn dog debris on my lap? They must think I'm a pitiful, crazy old woman or a drunk. "I thank you both; I appreciate your concern." I have a burning desire to hide; my veil of invisibility failed me. I can't do this – *Oh God, help me.* I need to get out of here; I can feel strangers' judgments burning through my skin. When a couple of young boys think I was one of the snoring dead, what did everyone else imagine? I have to go; I can't go to the bathhouses now! I search for a place to hide and see young couples and families filling the sidewalks in the bright morning sun. I feel their eyes as they pass. Some stare, but even the quick glances assault me. Tears begin to flood my face, as I gather the debris from my meal.

I don't know where this is coming from. It was bad enough, and now I make it worse. I can't do it, and I can't do this. What was I thinking? I am too stupid to live alone; I wouldn't accept the love my husband offered, so I traded it for isolation and humiliation? Who will love me now? How will I live and go on? I scan for an escape route, and all I can see is the street and sidewalks filled with strangers.

*Stop it.* That darn voice in my head has kept me trapped for 49 years. I have to learn to ignore that frightened self. Maybe I should name her and then leave her at the bus station. I need somewhere private and dark where I can regroup. I have to get back to my room in the hotel. I can't stand their looks of pity. Not one of them knows anything about me. The sun is so bright and harsh; I have to leave.

"No! Young man, I don't need any help." Things are getting worse. Just leave me alone, all of you. Of all times for people to act concerned. Where were you when I needed help? Go away.

A police car rolls past and slows down, and I look directly into the officer's eyes. I immediately calm down, but still feel vulnerable. I get to add freaking out to my list of sins. I walk the opposite direction, from the police. I can't be too careful.

Perfect, there's a church, and I know I could stand a prayer or two. There should be peace and no judgment there.

"What the hell? I didn't know they locked churches!" Great, now I'm swearing at a church. I didn't even look at the denomination; I guess there is a reason I haven't attended in years. I keep walking toward the hotel, still searching for a hideaway. I need quiet and rest to recuperate. I spot Madame Tussaud's Wax Museum. I consider the diversion only momentarily but have to admit it seems creepy. I decide that the hundreds of unblinking glass eyes looking back will be no comfort. I mull over the option of a massive heart failure about now but decide it would not fix anything. I need to continue to the hotel and my personal space. I try to focus on the sidewalk and start counting the steps. One, two, three – I realize I've done this ever since I was a child learning my numbers. The memory of my mother takes over, lending strength and a little bit of confidence so I can continue.

I have cried so much that the front of my shirt is wet from tears. I search my thoughts and try to sort out the crazy from the survivor and to banish the Elizabeth insecurities.

Please let the lobby be empty and help me get to my room. God, if you help me now, I will find an open church and pray every day, well, at least occasionally.

Damn, who are all of these people? The marching band must be checking out and are in formation. I pray for you kids; my hope is for each of you to fulfill your greatest ambitions. As for me, this loser needs to keep her head down and stay ambulatory. Just get to the elevator and then I can make it. Come on, come on, where is it? I reach for the button, and it glows like a simple answer. I press it repeatedly, and that doesn't seem to impress the slow moving escape route. I scan for the stairs, but they aren't visible from where I stand.

Finally, oh shit! How many people can they put on these things? Every face turning and it burns through me, and they see the frightened girl who gave up everything. I can't talk right now without sounding like a fool. Boy, nothing raises the curtain of invisibility like a meltdown in Hot Springs. I guess the promise is off, God.

The desk clerk calls over to me, "Miss, may I help you? Is everything alright?" I begin to hate southern hospitality.

"No, I'm fine, thank you. How are you?" I recognize I don't make sense as the realization hits. I may have killed my husband.

# – 8 –

Fumbling with the key card, I finally open the door. Upon entering the room, I immediately relock and secure the deadbolt. Relieved with the privacy of my room I collapse on the end of the bed. An additional disgrace wells up as I admit I haven't checked on Brad. "What kind of a selfish animal am I? I have to call. I have to find out how he is." I know he is upset with me if he is still alive. Once I face his anger and explain my resolve, then I will be able to rest. The realization that I don't know how to live without him and his demands to know my every move collapses in around my shoulders. Why me, why did this become my life? How did I let this happen? I must admit that much of my situation is my fault, that I have to suffer another disgrace and face the pain. I made horrible choices and then I ran out on him when he needs me the most. Libby Donovan, the world's slowest runner.

I collapse into the desk chair feeling a searing pain in my heart. I open the laptop and with little conscious thought begin to check the news and obituaries from home. I begin to calm as I scroll through with no mention of my name. I remove the new cell phone from my bag and touch the smoothness of the case. I weigh the options and tell myself he won't know the number. I can, at least, make the call; if he answers,

I will hang up. He needs to hear I'm never coming back home. *What if he is dead?* Will I go back to that house then? There are just two possibilities to consider, and my head hurts.

I'll call the hospital first; better yet, I put the phone back, search the computer and find a connection online. They will have a patient list, and I don't have to tell them who I am. It took only a moment to discover I can email a patient by name. Dear Brad, I wanted to check and see how you are doing. I've been worried. I'm never coming back, but I did love you for a long time. Please don't look for me. Elizabeth. – And I press send. I scold myself about the need to sugar coat the truth, but at least, it is done.

"Damn an answer already. No one by that name is a patient at St. Joseph." That narrows the options to dead or alive.

I might as well check my personal email while I'm here. I sort through the travel ads and Viagra offers ticking delete repeatedly.

In less than an hour, the panic has left, and the search consumes me. With a sudden need to reach out, I appreciate that I have no one in Hot Springs, and loneliness overtakes me. Brad always drove away my friends, but there is one he couldn't eliminate. He allowed and then tolerated Julie; I need her now. Oh, the hell with Brad, get out. I decide to send her a quick email with my new phone number.

Yikes, emails from Brenda and Mr. Offert from the office. I shouldn't be surprised; I didn't show up for work and didn't call. I'll take care of those on Monday and delete those messages too. Brenda must know something; she enclosed an emergency leave form. I'll have to find a way to print it and sign. Brad doesn't need to know anything about my job that I haven't already told him. I set up a new email address and respond to Brenda with a promise to call on Monday. Even with the years of preparation, there are many unanticipated stumbling blocks.

I have lived these sixty-five years, and I must admit I don't know who I am so no one else could either. Even the one I secretly loved the most has no idea of what I look like or if I'm dead or alive. Another decision that I lived with for forty-eight years this July. How did I allow this to happen? I consider going to another church and have to chuckle. Hell, on that last attempt God went so far as to lock me out. I ponder if it is a divine message. I was never much of a faith person, not even as a child. I only went because my parents wanted to sleep in on Sunday and I was noisy. I remember so well, my questioning wasn't welcome when I was trying to work the probability of their stories against scientific absolutes.

Then there is my job, I have seldom missed a day, and then I simply walked away from it. I call the front desk at the hotel, and they can print up the form. I sign it and fax it to Human Resources. I send a quick message of gratitude and the promise of a call to Brenda. They must know something and still wonder what happened to me. I will check in with Brenda first thing Monday, and she can give me the skinny. I wish I had her personal phone number, but regrettably, it was stored in the cell phone I mailed to Brad.

I lost much of Saturday. My freedom is so precious I will not let any days escape. I wait until happy hour to make a short call to Brad, and I'll have an answer if he is dead or home. I am sure he didn't die; that bastard would have haunted me by now. He isn't smart enough to track me down; he is no investigator like the ones on television. In this whole country, I can't imagine anything that would make him look for me in Arkansas.

I turn on the television in an attempt to control the stream of thoughts racing through my brain. Nothing helps to quash the rambling when I finally let the unthinkable come to mind. I should just be brave and go home. I can offer him money to take me back. *WAIT A MINUTE! What is wrong with that idea?* It took all of these years, and then I allow that thought to pass through my head. I know darn well, he would seize my money, beat me and then tighten the chains. I'll just call and look forward to the day that I don't know his number automatically. I tap out the ten digits and then hear it ring. The desire to speak with him dissipates, but I don't hang up. I offer up another little prayer from a desperate woman: *God, you there? The message machine will work for me. Don't let him answer. Please do not answer.*

"This is Brad Donovan, leave me a message. If this is Elizabeth I need to talk to you."

Thank you, thank you only a living person could change the message. "Brad this is Elizabeth, I just wanted to check on you to be sure you are alright. Don't try to find me. I will call you again sometime, just not right away."

Now, I have my answer followed by a burning desire to run. Then the awareness that he might notice the area code on the caller ID. I make a silent promise to come back someday when all has settled and see the springs. I have to face one task at a time. I pack and then call Julie. Let her know I'm on the next bus to New Jersey if she will have me. I like this new plan. I came in with a half empty, single throw away suitcase, and now I have two rolling cases and a laptop computer. In a single shopping day, it has become harder to run. I start pulling up my tentative roots and stuffing them into my suitcases.

What is wrong with me? I know I require more distance before I stop to rest. I need miles, many miles, thousands of them. After the burst of energy, there is a comfort knowing no one can see into this room. I lie down just for a little bit, deciding the frustration isn't going to stop until I let the emotion have its way. I don't know what I'm feeling, but I can't breathe, and the tears are guilty and hot. I'll just give up for a little while. I allow the continuing concern to pester one last time and think about how I gave my life to someone who didn't love me. He only had empty words and in reality, for some unexplainable reason, just wanted to own me. I ache to blame him for everything, but I could have done more. I dedicated years to peacemaking in a dead-end life. I gave up to the paralyzing fear, or I was just too lazy to defend myself. My rebellions were usually silent but continual, and they didn't improve anyone's life. I spent so many years in a trap that I helped construct.

What happened to the girl? Who in the world was she? One thing I do know for sure is that girl sold out. Sold out young, and then hid and compromised ever since. I wasted years denying that I was the one who screwed up. It is time to remember my principles and to dust them off and live. *No one on this earth knows who you are, Libby. That includes you.* I'm alive for a reason and for more than keeping house and a paycheck for a mean-tempered, selfish old man. I just need a little clue – something to build on.

I bought the laptop to organize my stashes of money, and I haven't done that. All I do is play mindless computer solitaire and marinate in my fear.

The details are fuzzy how I ended up in this hotel room, alone and feeling destroyed. My heart physically aches, and I can't take in enough air to regain some composure. I want to escape, and my only option is to lay here and blank out the barrage of insecurity. Acknowledging my need to let it all out, I accept I can never go back. He will kill me. Maybe not at first, but it will end with my death. I know the anger and power of the man, and he has come close before. I have to ask myself how I could still have tears for him, not just tears but gut-wrenching sobs. I have to keep the sensible dialogue running, so I don't do anything stupid. I have to remember accurately; I will not let the pain cripple me again. *I hate him.* I have never said it aloud, but I do. I continue to take the blame for my situation, but he is a hurtful, manipulative man and he only kept me as an indentured servant. What the hell is wrong with me? I was honest, loving, and true when I was young and now I'm a sneaky, bitter, old woman. I was forgiving and a perfect...doormat! I lie down on the bed and rationalize that I need little rest and then I will check the bus schedules for options.

As I sink into the softness of the motel bed, I forgave him the children he has with that woman. I realize that I have felt robbed of my own, but I can't blame her and know it isn't his kids' fault. I ponder the nature of life and chance. If life were fair, this world would be much different. I decide to accept it as my karma, payments on what I owed. I gave up children and family and "she" got it all plus a life of her own. Then again, it's all with Brad, not a real great catch. He never left me for her, which offers a personal pain. She has only heard his side of a convenient story, but her involvement took much of the heat off me, and I have to admit to owing her some gratitude.

I built a lifetime of pain on an evening of passion. I don't understand everything that karma is, but I'll learn. I believe joy and happiness existed early in this life, and I want laughter back. Even trying to be a good woman, fair and honest, I still owe – no rewards for Libby. I begin to make a promise to the universe; I will make amends and volunteer to help the helpless. I will do something to salvage the few years I have left. I want to be proud of something before I die. As a child, I wanted to be in the history books, and now I can count myself lucky to be in the phone book. I was guilty, scared, and lazy, I didn't work past my issues, but I'm not dead yet. I can do better for myself, and I will release Brad at the same time.

Taking away the option of going back, I admit he would be insane, and I wouldn't take it again. I visualize the return, knowing how happy he would be to see me until he had a couple of glasses of brown whiskey. Someone would die, and we both deserve better than that. In the quiet of the room, I ask for a sign, something and anything that will tell me which way to travel. I decide on north, south, east and west, away from the past and forward toward the unknown. The storm of emotions has dissipated, I look into the empty room and beg, *please give me a sign.*

# — 9 —

I have to stop waking up like this. It's dark, and I don't remember falling asleep. I was deep in thought and planning then suddenly, I wake up. I wonder why I didn't buy a clue when I was at Target. There has been nothing in between, either no sleep or a coma, I'm worried about losing the important parts of this journey. Will I ever be back on a regular schedule? Damn, six o'clock. What is it about six o'clock that wakes me up? I slept through much of Saturday. The darkness disappears with an open curtain, and I can see the start of a beautiful day. The sky is filling with light. As usual, a sunrise gives me renewed hope and the knowledge that everything is perfect. If it weren't for my little old woman bladder, and the concern about how much of a day I lost, I would lie back down. It had been a blissful, dreamless sleep and I feel re-energized, ready for the adventure that will let the Libby in me take control. I'm going to have to buy a clock or a calendar to keep track of my new life.

Standing at the window, a deep appreciation for Hot Springs washes over me. Once just a dot on a map, now it is real, full of people and places. I have met the nicest people with nothing but good will. Even the two boys, who thankfully didn't give me CPR, woke me gently. With my erratic sleep, I could have nested on that bench all day and been awoken by the police instead. Counting blessings and trying to recognize the wonder of the moment, I silence the pitiful voice that drags me down and pushes me to accept the unacceptable.

I power up the computer with the intention of reactivating my ticket with Greyhound. I plan to hit the bus station in about two hours. Professing love for my computer, I make another plan. I need to learn more about operating the laptop and set a personal goal for a class, and then expanded the goal to classes. OK, at 11 o'clock there is a bus heading back toward Indiana and at 11:15 there is one going north and right after that a bus to the east toward home. I am amazed, that I would allow myself the option of going back with my tail between my legs. Would I throw money at my husband and try to buy forgiveness? I am appalled that I even allowed the thought! I take a moment to question the years of pain. Deciding to stop thinking of the past as home, I realize that it was always his house, his car, his things. There, I was only another possession. Dismissing the ridiculous scenario, and I choose the bus going east and will pass Kokomo on my way to visit Julie.

"Wait a minute, *Like a Bridge Over Troubled Waters*, hum mm, hum mm." How does it go? That is the music in my head, and it is true, I am weary and feeling small. All other thought stops to work out the lyrics as the repetitive melody continues drumming of a single verse. Suddenly I recognize the message. An inner light clicks on, with the memory of singing this song a thousand times or more. Hmmm, hum mm waters. I decide to designate this as my theme song or at the very least a message from the power that could be. I'm going to sail on, because my time is here, today. There is no going back – only forward and away. Every phrase encourages and rebuilds the resolve to go east and not back. I embrace the song at the perfect moment and with a smile, I put down the phone, leave the bus website and search for YouTube.

The best thing about being alone is you can break into song and dance at any time of the day without becoming the butt of a joke. I play the song four times and dance the first three. Then I rest into the lyric.

"Thank you, thank you." A sign, I did get a sign. I will continue and never go back into that troubled water. I need to send Simon and Garfunkel a muffin basket of eternal gratitude. If I remember right, that will be two muffin baskets. I don't think they hang together anymore. My resolve is reinforced; I can't ever look back. How the song entered my dreams, I don't know, but the timing saves me. Maybe I should send them a cake too.

Pleased I never really unpacked; it is easy to prepare to go. Hot Springs served a purpose, but it is time to push ahead. Well, maybe a shower, toothbrush, food, and then leave. I realize I slept in these clothes and hadn't eaten any USDA approved food in two days. The way I look now only supports the crazy woman on the bench scenario. Deciding to blame the meltdown on the corn dog or Brad, who was just a junk food in a different package, I head for the bathroom.

"OK, Libby old girl. Let's you and I, or would that be I and I, make a pact. No more tears; banish the thought of returning to the empty existence. Forward only-stop considering the worst; nothing can be as unfulfilling as the life I left." I acknowledge that I will have some negative thoughts and promise a positive motion will follow. The thought of progress brings a smile and the hope of becoming someone special. I'm going to do away with the invisible old woman. I vow to buckle down, take care of business and decide to look out of the windshield and not the rearview mirror. "I have a little life left in me, and there are debts to pay." I am re-energized, I have moved to acceptance and stand with confidence.

Cold water and a toothbrush are the perfect tonics for a transformation of attitude. Mocking a commercial in the bathroom mirror selling the importance of clear cold water, I take a moment and honor the women who carry water and never have enough for a shower. How fortunate I am to be in this part of the world at this time. I'm grateful the wealth of this country and feel calmness take over. "There is nothing I can't do. At this moment, I know I can pay back some of my debts. If there is another life, I'm going to live it to the fullest."

Alright, enough stalling; time to check out and travel on to the next stop. Someday I can spend the time trying to understand what caused me to stash an open bus ticket when a train would have been faster. With this thought, I confirm my seat on the bus and consider the option of moving to Fair Haven, New Jersey, the home of my only friend. I feel a wave of excitement at the prospect of visiting Julie for a chance to talk it out. I know I thought New Jersey was someplace no one would find me; maybe there is another Fair Haven in another state, and I can see them all. East makes me a little nervous, but I decide I'm strong enough today to drive past the house and not be tempted to stop. He wouldn't be able to see me through the windows of the bus, so I consciously put that aside and focus on New Jersey. Julie will help me gather the scattered thoughts in my head. I know she is the perfect choice as she is the only one who could understand and not judge me. Julie has been here, right where I am now, except not in Hot Springs.

Briefly, I hope there are different desk clerks in the lobby and no witnesses to yesterday's meltdown. "Oh well, what does it matter, they will probably never see me again." I'm relieved when the clerk doesn't say anything out of the ordinary, as they print out my bill.

"Holy crap." Did I say that aloud? Surprising how expensive it is to stay in an inexpensive place. I'm going to have to balance my money and look into feeling secure. Another personal quirk to resolve, I promise to develop a different relationship with money. I have to learn how to spend now that I left my life of duplicity and scrimping. I don't have to account to anyone but myself. Just breathe in and out and pay the darn invoice. No more hiding, no more lies. My life is an open book with only one copy in print.

# — 10 —

"Nine and a half hours to the next bus! I need to start paying attention to the AM-PM portion of the days. I would think this may teach me to call ahead?"

"Well, ma'am, you can take a more indirect route, or there are some shops around here. I see you have a computer, and we do have a Wi-Fi connection here at the terminal. You will still have a long day."

Recognizing I have called to confirm the schedule to avoid this delay. At least I dodged another day of hotel charges. Time sure flies when you are crying in bed. "No, I'm okay. I'll just stow my things over there in a locker and walk around for a while. I'm feeling rather energetic."

"There is a coffee shop just down the street a couple of blocks. It is nice and has books and things. I go over there every once in a while."

"Thank you; I've wanted to get a book for a couple of days now. I appreciate how helpful you have been. I guess nine hours' worth of fluids is what I need before getting on a bus."

"Now, ma'am, sounds like a well thought out plan there."

"OK, I will see you later. Thanks again."

"Ma'am this is my job, but you are sure a pleasant change of pace. Have a good day and we will see ya'll later."

There is a quiet little corner, with no one around and I decide to take this as a gift of time to do the first thing on the list. Number one is to call the office and face that dilemma, part of my taking care of the past.

Turning on my cell phone, I'm shocked to discover seven missed calls. "How could that be?" I check the numbers hoping it was from Julie and then I see it was Brad. He must have been able to get the number when I called. Damn! I should have known better. Well, at least, I don't have to listen to voice mail since I didn't set it up; I can guess what he had to say.

Now get back to my list.

Please God, let Brenda answer.

"Accounting Associates, this is Stephanie, may I help you?"

"Yes, please. I would like to speak to Brenda, in human resources."

"Elizabeth, is that you? Where are you? What is going on? Your husband called, and he is certifiable for sure. Are you out of town, are you safe?"

"Yes, Stephie, I saw an opportunity and ran for the hills. I couldn't be with him another day." I ponder how much they know about my private life.

"Well, Miss Thing, they are talking like crazy around here. There was some thought that the bastard killed you and buried you in the woods. It is wonderful hearing your voice. I won't tell anyone anything, where are you?"

"Stephie, I can't say where I am. I just know where I'm not going to be. I do appreciate your silence. I have to be smart for once in my life. I think Brad would certainly kill me without much of a thought, especially now." Guess it doesn't matter what she knows. I have become an open book.

"I know we haven't been close or anything, Elizabeth, but if I can help in any way, just call me. I've been through it myself. I will give you my home number if you need it; we women have to stick together."

"I'm not in a place I can take down any information right now, Stephie. Nevertheless, I sincerely thank you for your vote of confidence. I sure need it. I had better talk to Brenda though; you take good care of yourself." Well, that was something I didn't expect. Sure, wish she had been a little quieter, though. It is my chance to be a legend even on a small scale.

"Human Resources, Brenda Chapman speaking. May I be of assistance?"

"Brenda, it's me, Elizabeth."

"Damn, Elizabeth, where are you? What is going on?"

"Well, I did it. Brad blacked out, and that seemed enough for me to go. You know I've prepared for that day."

"I know you have thought about it for years, but tell you the truth, I never thought you would do it. I put you on emergency leave with the boss and told him you had a family situation. You have twelve weeks of vacation and sick time. Do you need me to change your check automatic deposit? I sure don't want your money still going to him."

"Thank you, dear, I did fill out the form you sent and faxed it back. As for the checks, I have been snowing him for years. My checks go into my personal account and then I had an automatic deposit that went to his bank. He didn't realize that I had a little skim scheme going on. He hasn't known what I earn for years. Has anyone been curious or asked about me or what happened to me?"

"Oh my God, curious! You are the talk of the building, and I mean it. There are all kinds of speculation, and I just told them it was an emergency. Your dream man Brad came in on payday. He was calm and collected and within minutes, he was ranting like a crazy person. He did talk to Mr. Offert and the big cheese said that your job was secure and that there are no changes for your paycheck without your direct approval. That seemed to calm the hubby down a lot."

"What a relief. I'm sorry that Brad came in, I didn't even think of that. Did Mr. O ask any further questions?"

"Yeah, he did come to me, but I told him that I didn't know anything except it was a family emergency. He does want to talk to you if you come in. He conferred with bookkeeping that nothing was to change with your checks unless you made direct contact. He sure was red in the face; I don't think his interaction with the man of your dreams went well. They didn't like each other at all. Brad acted as if Mr. O carried you away to a honeymoon motel. It could be funny if he weren't so terrifying."

"Just remember a nightmare is a dream too. I am so sorry for all of this. I owe you my life for everything you have done." There is no way to express the gratitude I feel for her.

"Elizabeth, you would have done the same for me. It is no problem at all; everything is in order here until your comp time runs out. All you owe me is a real life and promise never – never come back as long as that man is alive."

I promised not to cry anymore, but her words touched me as my eyes became moist with emotion. There is a catch in my voice as I answer, "OK, that is a promise I will make. Maybe I'll see you at his funeral. If someone tells me when." Well, that scenario made us both laugh aloud. She is right; I would do whatever I could to help her too. I realize that I have more than one friend in the world.

"Lucky thing Mr. O isn't in yet this morning. Is there anything you want me to tell him? Like the truth or something more creative?"

"Brenda, I will leave it up to you. The truth would probably be the best. Just not all of it, please. I don't want to seem too pitiful."

"Pitiful, please Elizabeth. You are my hero. You think I don't know how your life has been. Do you think I haven't seen you survive in spite of that marriage? PITIFUL? Please, Elizabeth, you left. There is nothing pitiful about that. You are one of the most courageous women I know. I will talk to him; I think he has been suspicious of a problem for a while. You know it is hard to hide a broken spirit and a fat lip. You call me at home soon, so we can talk."

"Thank you, my dear heart, I need your home number. I would have called earlier, but left my cell phone behind. I have this new number, and I'll call you. Right now, I don't know where I'm going or when I'll be there. Just know that Greyhound has a bus stop there. I love you. I have a new email, and I would appreciate it if you would send me your personal contact information that way. I'll also need Stephie's number or email." I spelled out the information I wanted, and she guaranteed a response.

Whew, that is done for now. What an enormous pressure that telephone call was, but once I dialed, it was great. Twelve weeks of paychecks, score. People are starting to gather in the station now; I don't want anyone overhearing my mistakes and drama. Maybe it is time for a cup of coffee number two; this is going to be a long day.

# — 11 —

It is hard to believe how I know my way around a part of Hot Springs in the short time I have been here. I did notice the bookstore and coffee shop that he mentioned, and that should kill a bunch of time. I decide it is a gift to be able to spend as long as I wish in a bookstore. I have to give myself some credit, although calling ahead to the bus station may have been a better plan, but it is what it is. I just know it is time to leave; Hot Springs is a very special place in my heart, but now on to Fair Haven.

After living so much time in the negative, it is a daily battle to work on the positive, and I'm going to do it. I will decide where to live, but not yet. I want to have a few days with Julie, and I'm not sure what happens after that. I can make a permanent decision when the time is right. I will find the life I want; it is just a step at a time to become someone real.

Everything costs so much, two travel books, chai tea latte, and a scone costs almost as much as a room for the night. Money is my nemesis; I know I will have to wrestle that relationship into something more reasonable. It might be better when I have some totals. I need to relax and know there are still ten weeks of paychecks.

Seven more hours and then I'll be early for the bus. I have time to get some food to take along; learned that lesson on the first leg of this excursion. That can wait until closer to boarding time. I stroll along the sidewalks and notice another shop down a side street a couple of blocks away. I might as well try that one too. I never know where the next clue is. He used to make fun of my "looking for a sign" but I don't have to hear that again. So I'll do what I wish and look for all the signs I want.

Well, this is an interesting shop, Golden Leaves. It is perfect for someone who is leaving. Books and Gifts, Tarot –Readings, past and future lives. Whoa – I have read about this stuff, and there is a lot of it on television lately. I have always felt as if there is much more than birth and death. I have time; it can't hurt to look around, and I might learn something. Certainly, this is a step out of the comfort zone to add to my adventure. I'm finished with romance and real crime novels; this opens some new directions and maybe a little self-help. I take a moment to breathe in the clean, fresh air of Arkansas and then walk into the store.

# — 12 —

The shop smells delicious, and there is a variety of sections filled with figurines, books, cards, and stones. I've never seen any like this back home. I notice a young woman sitting near the window; do I know her? Oh, I couldn't know her. It is her demeanor; she appears so open and helpful. I can feel her eyes look into me, and it is oddly welcoming. I know I can do this. After all, this is just a store, and she wants the business. Remembering what Brenda said about my leaving, everything else will be easy. Besides I'm heading out of town; no one here cares if I try the occult. No more fear of the devil, I left him on the kitchen floor.

"Hello, please come in. I was watching you walk down the street. You have a very vibrant aura."

I'm unusually comfortable with her. "Hello. Thank you. You have an interesting shop, and I don't know what all of this stuff means." She is open and gentle. I didn't know the people in this kind of store were just regular. "What's an aura?"

"Your aura is like a light field that surrounds you."

Thank goodness, she is not in a costume or turban. She looks like most any thirty-year-old. "I have lights? That is a little disturbing. I don't want a neon billboard flashing my business." She smiles broadly. I am not always appropriate in unknown situations. I remember being witty back in the old days. Maybe it is coming back.

"Don't worry. Most people don't know how to see auras, although I have always believed that they could if they just opened up." I like that she is explaining things to me and not pushy. "Most people do have psychic abilities, but they have buried them very deeply in their socialization and religion. I'm sure you have noticed that small children and animals have a natural knowledge of good and bad people?"

"I have noticed that dogs like me, but I haven't had a pet in 200 years." Good grief, do I sound stupid? She laughs easily, and I have time to waste. I feel we have met before, and we know each other well. "I am just visiting here and have a few hours."

"This is your first time in Hot Springs?"

"Yes, are you from here?"

"All of my life, right here. Please sit down; I was just enjoying the morning and the beautiful day. Notice the nice breeze that comes through the porch windows. Would you like some more tea?"

She is good – how did she know I had tea? "Yes, I would. How did you know I already had tea?"

Smiling gently, "I saw you come from out of the coffee shop down the street, and you have a to-go cup in your hand, and it has a string and label hanging out". This time, we laughed together, I am completely at ease.

"Do you come here often? Or do you work here?" Now that sounds like an old pickup line.

"I own part of the shop, teach a few classes, and I'm one of the readers. It is still early, and Mondays are quiet. Can I answer any questions? Are you looking for something in particular?"

I have thought about psychic possibilities and the spirit world for a long time. There has been a lot more of it on television lately. I thought about readings, but I never knew where to go or what to ask. Should I mention that I was also afraid of what I might learn? "I don't know of any stores like this in my hometown." I begin to imagine a different life working in a bookstore with friendly people and interesting conversations. "Do I call you Madam something?"

"No; I'm not a madam; this isn't *that* kind of a house. Just call me Terry." Her eyes are glistening as she giggles again. Thank goodness, she laughed, I don't want her to think I am calling her a prostitute or something. Now and then things come out of my mouth that could stand some pre-editing. We sit and chat about some of the modalities of metaphysics; it is more complicated than I ever imagined.

"Let me get you that cup of mystical tea and you can look around all you like. You may wish to check out the book section; there is a lot to learn." As she leaves, I walk over to the book area, and I realize how little I know. There are rows of volumes with intriguing names and spooky covers.

Within a few minutes, Terry comes back, with two cups. "Is there anything special you would like to know about?"

"No, I'm sure you have already realized I don't have a clue. I was just wasting time before my bus leaves, and you caught me exploring."

"Well, you have certainly come to the right place for exploration. We have all sorts of books, talisman, herbs, and jewelry. I can tell you have questions, and I might have some answers." Herbs, now I know why it smells so nice in here.

I thought this would be all ghosts and woo-woo, but this looks interesting. "Auras – I need to learn about those." Channeling, past lives this is a new world, and I'm feeling overwhelmed with the multitude of topics. "I don't know where to start. What would you suggest?"

"Well, many that come in already have a particular interest. For someone new I would suggest *The Celestine Prophecy*, by James Redfield. It is a great story and a fun read. It is a story of discovery which may speak to you." Clutching our warm cups of tea, we discuss several authors and their specializations.

My ears perk up, when she mentions Richard Bach. "I know that one. I read *Illusions* years ago. So that was metaphysical?"

"You aren't as inexperienced as we thought. Have you identified any particular subjects that interest you? "

"Karma. I was wondering about karma earlier. I was also thinking about reincarnation and paying a debt. Am I using the right words?"

"You are doing just fine." She gathers several paperbacks, and we walk back to the table on the porch. I pick up one of the titles, and she adds, "There are several different theories about karma in Eastern religions. It is cause and effect. It is the sum result of our past actions and present reaction. It boils down to either paying back or a reward for a previous life."

I find comfort in the simplicity, how it breaks down that no matter what our position in life we are responsible for our happiness and our hell. I sip a cup of the sweet tasting tea, nodding and somewhat comforted about how a dedicated life can improve our next lifetime. It sounds simple and yet I see where an in-depth study could take years. I know that my recent life change may be able to counter some of the old karma.

"Sound like you are interested in past lives. Have you ever considered a past life regression?"

Coming back to our conversation. "No, I haven't ever done anything like that, but I thought about it plenty." Oh good God, do you suggest she can answer some of my questions? I'm excited at the prospects.

"If you would like a past life regression, I would hypnotize you. Are you interested in that?"

"Hypnotism, I don't think so." I am nervous about what that could expose. I don't want to lose control of myself. "I don't wish to cluck like a chicken. I thought you would just tell me what I need to do next or where I will end up."

"With a regression, I would help you relax and focus taking you back in time, and we could access memories of previous lives. The chicken clucking is not required, but optional. I am just teasing you; it is very unlikely you were previously a chicken," she says lightly.

"I have been a chicken in this lifetime, so there would be a strong possibility it had happened before." I trust Terry and feel as if she likes me too.

"With a reading, I would access my spirit guide and go into a light trance, and you would just listen. We will record it if you like."

"Yes, I would like a reading very much." I check my watch, and I still have hours to kill before the bus. "How much will it cost?" Here I go again; this may be the gateway to my life, and I want to know the price. I don't want to watch myself cheap out on anything that may help give me direction.

"I'm sure you were not nearly the chicken you think you are. I can tell you have an incredible hidden strength. The cost is $70 for either one; we spend about an hour."

"Sure, that sounds good. I would like a reading." Maybe we can find a new direction, always a good idea for a new life. I cannot believe I'm doing this. I like her, but a reading may be exposing more than I want her to know. "Will there be ghosts?"

"I can't guarantee ghosts. My mother-in-law is in the back, and once she comes out, she can watch the store. We could start in just a couple of minutes if that is alright with you."

"Great, I'm ready. You know my family had a psychic back in the 1920s. Arrested as a charlatan, and the family never talked about him very much."

"Mysticism was the rage back in those days; do you know his name or more about him? There could be a possibility psychic sensitivity runs in your family."

"I don't remember his first name, but the last name was Mattern. My grandmother suggested he was a fraud and kept the story brief. I still have an aunt who is alive in my mother's hometown where this all occurred. I'll have to call her." She is one of my only living relatives and I need to make contact with her. I let the thought drift away because of my shame.

"That could be a fun search for sure. Have you ever tried to make contact with him or anyone else?"

She is losing me again. "Make contact? He died before I was born and even my mother never met him." I'm starting to get a little twitchy now. I always thought he was just some crazy story, and now I feel like there could be a real life there. Am I falling for everything I hear? I think I will just be open and maybe not jump to any more conclusions. That's the plan for today at least. "I can browse around some more. I don't want to interfere with your business."

"You are the reason I'm here, so don't you think for a moment you are interfering with my time. Momma Jenkins, are you busy back there? Can you watch the store? I have a reading to do."

An older woman enters from the rear of the store, and her face is flushed and friendly. I begin to believe that working in a bookstore is the key to happiness. She greets me and goes to a stool by the cash register. Terry leads me down the same hallway, into a small, welcoming room.

The simply furnished room has a table covered with a weaving and two adjacent chairs. The lighting appears like candlelight, but I don't notice any candles. Terry sits down and points to the chair opposite from her. As I look around the room, she lights a small incense burner and turns back to face me. While Terry shuffling a deck of regular playing cards, I'm intrigued. She continues handling the cards, stacking and unstacking, then shuffling again. I expected a giant crystal ball or mystical cards with markings I have never seen before.

*A reading, I'm having a psychic reading.* I have wanted to do this for a long time, but I was short on opportunity and nerve. Now I see that it doesn't take nerve at all – just time, $70, and curiosity. I suddenly feel naked and exposed, that I am giving this woman permission to enter the most private part of my soul. I didn't think this through, but for some unknown reason, I trust the feelings Terry inspires in me. I must have come here for a reason, and I can only wait and see if she can get past my fear and access any truth or if this is all crap, like Brad used to say.

I make the decision if this is too silly or uncomfortable I will leave. "Is there anything I need to do? Will the Jack of Clubs mean something?" I hope she doesn't think I'm stupid.

"You don't have to worry, just relax and breathe calmly. Close your eyes, if that helps you relax and clear your mind. I may ask questions or mention something, but I don't need explanations; just yes or no answers are fine. I use the cards to help me focus, and they give me direction, but mostly they are a tool for concentration. Many readers use a Tarot deck, but I like playing cards because of the familiarity. If you prefer, I can use the Tarot?"

"No, I am fine with what is easiest for you. I'm quite anxious; I trust you will do what is best."

"You are cute. There is nothing for you to do except relax, and listen. You can't make any mistakes, and I will record this for you so that you can listen later. Sometimes things go past so quickly, and I miss some of the details. There is no need to be nervous; I work as a conduit for the other side. The information is all yours. I would like to ask your first name."

"My given name is Elizabeth, but I go by Libby. I'm sorry, but I need to ask. Could you explain more about my vibrant aura?"

She stops shuffling for a moment and looks directly into my eyes. "I could see the colors around you, and there was a lot of red, yellow and green. The major color is red, which is life force and brilliant; this tells me that you are in a time of raw passion and survival. It has some yellow around your head, which is alertness and analytical thought. It can be more childlike, but with the red, it convinced me that you are making changes, and they are huge. There are just little touches of green which is healing and new growth."

"Is this where I explain things or just say yes or no to you?"

Terry chuckles quietly and goes back to shuffling the cards. "Yes or no is just fine. I don't want to be influenced by your story, so let the information flow through me."

"Yes, yes, yes." Wow, she is good. I am fascinated and recognize this is much cheaper than a trip to the liquor store with Brad. Damn you, Donovan stay out of my brain. Today is about me, not you.

"Libby, I see you have a lot of spirit around you. It is almost like a crowd, and it feels as if everyone wants to talk to you. Do you ever just know some things?"

"Yes, I do."

"That could be one of your guides, but you have several spirits around you. Have both of your parents crossed over? I feel a strong male influence pushing to the front."

"Yes, they both died some years ago, within six months of each other." Shoot, I'm not supposed to explain. "Yes."

"Then I think this may be your father. He says 'You will be helped when needed. You have a ticket or a pass, something of that sort, and you don't need anything else.' Does that make sense?"

"Yes, that is him."

Terry doesn't open her eyes and continues to turn cards. I'm not sure what to think of everything; I'm relieved she doesn't stare at me. I need to pay attention and quit pondering all of the questions I have. I can ask later. She lays the cards out in lines that seem to have a pattern.

"He says 'turn the other direction, get on the trolley – train – something and go the other direction. Don't make the same mistake again.' He is proud of you and is confident you are capable. He seems satisfied and is stepping back. He adds 'I love you the mostest'."

"He used to tell me that as a child." The emotions flood my eyes with longing and joy. "I love you, Daddy."

"Now we have a feminine energy. Her name starts with an ah or a vowel sound. This female essence is an equal to your Dad. I believe she could be a mother figure. She is quiet but formidable."

"Yes, that is my mom. Her name is Anita."

"She gives an okay sign. She wants you to know everything is fine, and you don't need to worry about them. She has asked me to tell you that you are never alone. Anytime you need help call, and she will be there."

"Just like when she was here. I could always count on Mom. I love you, Mom, take care of yourself some of the time." I am so glad to hear from her; she always stayed in the background, but she was like an iron rod down the family's spine.

"She is holding up one finger, number one. Does that make any sense to you? She says remember number one; it is never too late."

"I don't know for sure. It could be a couple of things, other than the obvious." My mother was always a bit of puzzlement to me. "She did tell me once not to forget who I am, but she was often cryptic."

"No, that is not it. She is pressing – she is wrapping her arms around herself – no, it is more of a cradling her arms and says 'never too late.' She is firm on that. Does that make sense? She slipped back quickly; it is almost like it was a trial for her to speak. They all support that you are in a major transition right now. It is not clear if it is work, relationship or moving, but significant change is the theme."

"Yes, each and every one of those is accurate." Well, I feel exposed and yet intrigued.

"Do you know a woman; she is strong and tall or, at least, puts forth a feeling of substance, and is commanding."

"Yes, I do. I know a couple of them."

"This one would have crossed over a long time ago. She is comfortable in her spirit and position. Her name is mmmm, M? Ok, M like from the Bible. Martha or is it Mary?"

"I had an Aunt Marian; she was a hoot."

"I don't know if that is her, she seems to disregard the name, she says there have been many names in many times. One is the same as another. She has the demeanor of a teacher of someone giving the orders."

"I'm not sure who that would be if it isn't my aunt. My mother had a friend, and there was also a teacher that I was close too, but I don't know her first name."

"She says you know who she is and don't worry about it. She wants you to know that you have had many lives. It is your turn to stand proud. Don't be afraid. There is a lot of time, and you will accomplish new things." Terry seems deep in conversation with herself. "She sees you as a young person and says you can go back, but there are no do-overs? You stalled for a while, but she has faith that you have much more to do. She shows me a soldier."

"Yes."

"She is powerful and domineering. Others are pushing to talk to you, but they all defer to her. She is going to allow someone else to speak, but she will maintain the control. Ha-ha, she is kind of funny. She promises she will manage the rabble."

"I can tell I like her. To remember her will be great." I am thrilled to think I have such good mojo around me.

"It is clear that you have had a large loss, after a long sickness. Have you recently lost someone?"

"No, not since my parents years ago, even though it feels more recent than it was. I was an only child. So no siblings."

"She is clear it is a recent loss and that you are grieving, that your heart is sad. Don't worry the pain will pass sooner than you can imagine. Everything will work out the way it should. A long, sad story ends here, and life begins anew. Does that make any sense to you?"

"Yes, very much." There is an urge to elaborate, but I guess it isn't necessary as long as I understand.

"She wants you to recognize you have been off track, but your universe is shifting. You will make up for lost time, and soon you will enter a golden era. You have a lot to learn and even more to see."

Terry's demeanor has changed as if a dark cloud has spread over her face. "I see a woman; I don't know the connection. She seems close to you. She is resting among rocks; I can see her, but I don't see a face. She doesn't move. There is a golden glow near the face. She wears a necklace, and I can't tell what it is, but it glows. It feels as if she has been waiting for peace for a long time. The scene is peaceful and yet I feel sadness. She is young; she cradles her arms, and two babies are resting with her. Does this mean anything to you?

"No, I don't have children or real jewelry."

"Surrounded with tears, she is resting and very still. Now I see what looks like a building, no it is a complex of large buildings. It might be a city, and you are crucial in the activity. You do not admit to your position and are reticent about the tremendous service you have been asked to provide. She has gone now, but additional images are coming quickly. There is still a line of people waiting to speak, but the boss is telling them they must wait. Your male guiding spirit has stepped in and announced 'we will talk to you soon.' He is concerned that you will miss the crucial message that love surrounds you, and there is support from many. You have felt alone, but it was never true. Everything will all work out the way it should. Happiness and adventure lie ahead of you. They all are touching their hearts and fading away. The two women are the last to go and want you to understand that they are always with you. When you talk, they will hear. To have an answer, you must be quiet and listen."

I have been watching Terry, and her face is tired, all energy appears drained.

"Bye Ms. Mmm, I love you, Mom." I feel a warmth and comfort. Maybe I do have friends, only in a different place. "Terry, are you OK?"

"Oh, yes, I'm just fine. There was a lot of energy there, and it was intense. I feel as if we only had the tip of the iceberg on your connections."

We sit and chat quietly as Terry recovers. My family has always been small and with my parents' passing it almost disappeared. I think of my aunt and regret never staying in touch with her. After this reading, I no longer feel so alone. I am full of disjointed thoughts and emotions. I know who the babies are, and their secret is my personal pain. Events in my life had stolen them from me and I feel the familiar emptiness. "Do you think I was supposed to have children? Were they the babies I could have had to make a family? I am sure it is too late to start now." Tears sting my eyes with the onslaught of emotions of love, sadness, and confusion. There is a lot to think about, and I will have time on the bus.

"I can't tell you. It could be symbolic. The answer will come to you as everything settles in. Let's go back to the shop; I have somethings I would like to show you." Terry leads me to a counter in the center of the store. "Many of these are tools to help balance your chakras." Terry continues to talk while I dig through the brilliant rocks. I'm surprised she can still speak after what we just went through. "Are there any stones that would be good for me?"

She points me toward an even larger display filled with multiple bins of rocks. "Chakra? I swear you speak in a different language. With the break in the reverie, we begin to talk about the variety of rocks, and I study a chart just above the shelf. These are brief descriptions of the properties of each one. There are also cards with each bin explaining a variety of energies. I pick up a sample of malachite as if my hands have a new sensitivity. I know I need this piece; it is for transformation and clearing the way.

I decide on a little larger bag to hold my new treasures, a blue one with the embroidery. I'm thrilled about everything. Besides the malachite, I buy onyx for a little self-control and, of course, a quartz crystal for healing. I search through the smoky quartz, which is to eliminate negative forces. I decide on a large chunk so I can throw it if he ever finds me. To my pile of stones, I add turquoise, mostly because it is so darn beautiful and makes me happy. I decide my choices are perfect as I wander toward the books. My sadness and confusion have dissipated, and a new confidence is pushing me forward.

Terry returns her eyes are moist and sparkling "Libby, look at this and tell me what you think." She places a transparent stone into my hand. "This is a special piece of amber. I think the necklace the young mother wore was similar to this." She places a yellowish rock into my hand. It has warmth like no other, and the golden clarity draws me in. Terry's voice breaks through my trance. "Amber is ancient fossilized tree sap. Sometimes you will discover amber with something in it, like leaves or insects. I saw a piece with a scorpion once, but that was large and not only rare but exceptionally expensive."

"You have so many rocks, but I believe I love amber best." The soft smoothness is a texture I have never felt before as it warms my hand. It is silkier than any stone I have ever touched, but still obviously a rock.

"I love it too. Amber helps with healing and protection. It has the power to pull out disease.

"Oh my, Terry, this is beautiful. It is so translucent and golden. It has something on the inside? Looks like a bug, or maybe two." This piece is different from all the other amber she has in the store.

"Yes, I have had this pendant for a while in the shop. I moved it to under the counter as the customers would handle it and they weren't right for it." She talked on about how she felt this piece was unique and knew to save it until the owner came in to claim it. "This piece needs to *belong*." She spoke about the people who looked at it, and it bothered her knowing it was waiting for someone. "I would like you to have this."

Tears flow freely down my cheeks; her kindness touches me. "I love it. It is so, so beautiful and comforting, I can see back through time when I gaze into it. How much?"

"It is a gift. Just take it with my blessing and remember this day."

"There is no way I can ever forget this day." I proceeded to buy a gold chain for my new gift. I stand by the small mirror on the counter and fasten it around my neck. It feels so familiar and completes me.

"I knew it should be yours. It is perfect and comes alive against your skin. I will get your recording of the reading ready, and you can keep your things right here on the counter if you want to look more."

"Thank you, Terry." The words seem to fall short of the feelings that are so close to the surface. I place the selection of the small stones on the counter along with the spirit bag. Finally, I add two books, one on the spiritual power of rocks and another on auras.

"I'm afraid to look more. I want just to move in here; it would be easier."

"I'm certain you wouldn't be happy with the bathroom facilities after a few days."

Terry adds the reading CD to my pile of purchases and Mrs. Jenkins starts adding them up with a hand-held calculator. I have so much to think about. I'm anxious to listen to the CD when I'm not so excited. There is a deep warmth, almost a joy in knowing I have another friend. I don't remember ever connecting with someone so quickly. "Since I'm traveling, I don't dare buy more. I need to remember who has to carry everything. All finished. Let's see the final bill."

"Libby, I would like it if you would sign up for our newsletter."

"I don't have an address, Terry. I will take your card and let you know when I settle somewhere. I see you have an email address on here; I will truly be in touch. This is not the last you'll hear from me."

"We send the newsletter by email. There is no need for a physical address."

I happily sign up for the newsletter, adding my new email address. Everything feels right, but now even I can hear how silly I sound. I need to find a rock for calming the hell down and maintaining a thought.

# — 13 —

This day has been a gift. I am so far out of my comfort zone I may need to buy hiking boots. There are still four more hours until my bus, but I feel as if I could fly down the street. There is so much to think about, but Mom's message that it is never too late keeps replaying. I know what she was talking about, and I need to find a way to listen to her. I know I can never amend my mistake, but I can maybe offer some healing.

As I walk back to the bus station, even the air seems to have changed. I still feel anxious, but there is calmness, and I'm comforted to know that though I am alone, I will never be lonely. The sadness has lifted. I'm going to sit for a few minutes and watch everyone else running off to new adventures. I realize half of them are leaving, and the other half are returning. The sensation seems to be exhaustion if that could be an emotion. Maybe I'm harboring a fragile hope that life could be simple. I wonder about all of the different stories and decide that everyone over the age of fourteen has a secret, and silently bless a second bus station with new beginnings.

A bus has pulled away, and the station quiets down. I decide to call Julie again to help fill the time as I wait for the bus to New Jersey. I am a little surprised she didn't call back, but then I remember turning off the phone. I hope she is home. This trip could be a mistake if she isn't there. I take out my cell phone. I'm utterly amazed that the phone shows four missed calls. A cold chill passes through me. I refuse to allow the thought of Brad to take away my wonderful day and tell myself it must be telemarketers. I punch in Julie's number.

Beep..."Julie, this is Elizabeth. I was hoping I could catch up with you. I finally left him and I'm not sure where to go. Call me at this number it is my new cell phone...." My phone clicks with a call, and I hope it is Julie; it would just be like her to call back while the message is still recording.

"Hello, this is Libby."

"Elizabeth! Is that you? I just picked up the phone and redialed. Where the hell are you? What is going on? You email, you don't call, and you leave a number with no voicemail. You use the same fingers for dialing as for typing. What is this area code? You better get answering Missy; I have questions."

"I left him, and I'm at a bus station in Hot Springs, Arkansas."

"WHAT! You are rattling my mind, Lizard. What happened and why are you in Arkansas?"

I had almost forgotten how she always called me Lizard. It aggravated Brad; he always used my full name and she would have none of that. "I finally had enough. He was unconscious on the floor, so I grabbed all my underwear and ran to the bus station."

"Bus station, what the hell! Where is your a car? Quit punishing yourself and get your ass on an airplane. Time to get up here and tell me what is going on. You have some splaining to do, Lizzy."

I try to explain that my only destination was out of the house, and I've let everything else take care of itself. She stays relatively quiet as I give a brief breakdown of my last day of marriage. I assure her I will give the complete down and dirty tale of woe when I get there in two days. I knew she was my first destination and then maybe on to Omaha.

"Omaha? Omaha, Nebraska? What's in Omaha? You know where I am, and it isn't Nebraska. Do you need me to come there and pick you up? Did he hurt you again? Oh, Lizard, I am so sorry, I will let you answer in a minute. I'm so excited; we will work things out when I calm down."

"It is so good to hear your voice, Julie. I'm not someplace that I can spill my sordid story of life and despair. You already know most of it."

"You guys have been together since dinosaurs roamed. How long was it?"

Forever curious, I always love her enthusiasm. She makes me feel like she is on my side no matter what the details are. "We started dating forty-nine years ago and our forty-seventh wedding anniversary is in August."

"Holy crap, you did give him plenty of time to man up and do right, didn't you?"

"I guess I did. Has he called you?"

I hear her snorting laugh as she answers, "I have heard nothing and don't worry; that man doesn't have the balls to call me. He knows I would climb through the phone and kick them into his throat."

"Now back to today, would you mind if I came to see you for a little while?" Wow, it's hard to ask for something, especially since I have already reserved a seat on the New Jersey Express. I hadn't even considered she might have a life."

"Damn girl, you better not think of going any place else. Quit with the stupid bus, get a plane ticket and get here."

"Alright, calm down, the bus leaves in three hours." I haven't traveled; I mostly have been locked in the house or at work for so many years. He had the cabin, but most trips were Brad and drinking buddies. "I have enjoyed seeing some of the country." I feel gratitude for this brash woman and grateful that I have a real friend he couldn't drive away. "Julie, honey, I don't have your new address, I only know your town. Let me get my notebook so I can write it down."

Julie pauses a moment. "I will text it to you if you like."

"I don't think I can do that. This is a throwaway phone I bought at a mini market."

"I'm sorry Elizabeth, I was distracted, and I'm on the computer and booked you a plane ticket. Did you know Hot Springs has an airport that doesn't fly anywhere in New Jersey?"

"No, Julie, stop. I will find my way. I'm excited about the bus or maybe a train. There is so much to see, and I've never traveled before, other than for fishing. Is there a train station in Fair Haven?" I don't even know if there is a train station in Hot Springs. I thought things were moving, but once Julie is involved, you are on hyperdrive.

"Too late. You need to get to Little Rock. I booked you a ticket on American Airlines. You just pick it up at the reservation desk. This way you will be here by morning instead of two days."

"How am I going to see the country on an airplane? I've never flown before. I can handle the travel, Julie; I'm in charge of me now."

"Get a seat by the window and it will be night time anyhoo. Would your husband approve of your confidence? Hush up, let me do this one thing for you and get your skinny butt to Little Rock."

Damn Julie is taking care of business as usual.

"Blah, blah, blah. Tom will be happy to finally meet you. Don't you worry about the ticket, I'm sure Brad didn't let you out with the family fortune, and I owe you so much more than this. I need to see you as soon as possible. You know I will die if I don't have all the bloody details."

"I do miss you, and I'm anxious to see you again. It will be wonderful to talk to someone who understands my truth. There are buses to Little Rock every half hour, and I'll call you when I know the arrival. Are you sure this is a good time?" I begin to gather my belongings from the locker and pick up a shuttle service flyer on the brochure rack.

"Hell Liz, I don't have any bad times when I think you are on the way. You are my sister in arms, and I will be there. I have retired, so what else do I have to do, buy cats?" She snorts a raucous laugh.

"It's wonderful hearing your voice. I almost forgot the sound of your laugh. I can't wait. I'm excited about telling you about today, too. Let me go for now and I'll change my ticket and get to Little Rock. I will see you soon."

"Damn soon, Lizard, you better haul ass because I'm waiting. You don't want me coming to get you."

"Yes, Boss, soon." I'm relieved. She didn't have to buy me a ticket, but it sure makes me feel special. It is comforting to have such a friend, and I feel a sincere gratitude for two gifts in one day.

# – 14 –

Things change quickly; I walk to the reservation desk clerk, and he places my bus ticket on hold and calls the shuttle service.

I'm rolling to Little Rock within twenty minutes. My life has been a blur since meeting Terry, so much happened when I thought it would be hours of sit and wait. It has been years since I've seen Julie, but we kept in touch on my office email. I'm looking forward to a real, honest, face-to-face conversation with her.

Before long I'm rushing through the airport, I thought bus stations were busy. Many people are traveling in this world and most of them in a hurry. I haven't had enough time to get worried about a flight. I keep repeating to myself *this is the safest mode of transportation*, but damn when airplanes fail, it is spectacular. I have no idea what Julie concocted to expedite everything, but the attention I'm getting is remarkable. Greyhound never once had me remove my shoes, throw away my water bottle and x-ray my whole body. It is hard to believe that I'm sixty-five in the modern era, and this is my first complete shakedown. I notice a different vibe between airline passengers and bus riders. As much as they are different, they are the same – each carrying bags of food. The biggest difference is the travelers at the airport have to buy snacks on the business side of security.

The books I bought at Golden Leaves allow me to isolate and fill the wait time. I read and reread, due to my anxiety. I'm still not ready to talk to fellow travelers, but I can see it in my future. Luckily, there aren't a lot of people traveling from Arkansas to New Jersey in the night, and I get a whole row of seats to myself. The takeoff is exciting and after a few minutes, I can stretch out over the seats and sleep most of the flight. I awaken to see the skyline start to lighten as we travel east. The flight is almost over when I see the massive sight of Newark. The population in this country is staggering, and I think of my small town home. The landing is the most worrisome part of this whole adventure, but through the skill of the disembodied voice over the speaker, we all survive. Knowing I will do this again, I decide next time, I will be sure to have a window seat and daylight hours.

Endless possibilities rise with the sun, and I'm invigorated. Even though sleep has been fitful, the anticipation trumps exhaustion as I gather my things. I'm excited and ready to see my friend. My mind reels as I travel further away from Brad. I wait to deplane, which sounds more sophisticated than getting off the bus. I relish the thought that I'm in Newark, another new place I have never seen. My self-reliance is delicious. Although I acknowledge I'm not ready for Paris; I have moved around okay in Arkansas and good morning, New Jersey.

My one public breakdown is less traumatic as time passes and I make a silent promise to return to Hot Springs, my first city love affair. Now I'm ready for a metropolis.

Recalling the momentary consideration of going back, I am thankful I thought it through. The price I would pay is too high; I know it was only fear. Everything I have accomplished would be gone, including my private rebellions and a future. I know his patterns well enough that he would be sweet until he had a couple of drinks and then the tab would come due. With this thought, I decide to be honest with myself as my primary core value. Second, I will be authentic with others and not try to please them with empty words. No more guilt when I make mistakes, I will work things through. No more traveling backward – I will be fine, my mother promised. I finish my slip back to Brad thoughts as the groggy passengers move me toward the ramp.

The Newark airport is enormous and crowded. I continue to follow the flow of passengers. I don't want to ask what to do next when I see the overhead sign for baggage. The building is huge and brightly lit. There are little cafes on each side, and I smell the coffee and baking bread. The colors of the sunrise shine through the windows along the ceiling, as I try to keep focused on the baggage signs. I know it is early but privately hope that Julie is here somewhere as my confidence wanes. I begin to walk as if I belong and saunter down to baggage.

I usually would have overthought this, but things moved too fast to worry. I will just have to act like who I wish to be. The massive room is full of tired travelers and baggage delivery platforms.

"Lizard, Lizard is that you?" My friend's voice cuts through the din of the crowds.

"Julie, I'm here." My goodness, she has aged, but it has been years. I would know her anywhere, and the voice is still familiar.

"Lizard! You are an incredible sight. Do you have your things?"

"Not yet, I haven't found the right luggage area yet. I'm surprised I found baggage; this place is huge."

"Well, give me your baggage tags, and we will find them. You look exhausted and yet beautiful."

"We won't need the receipts; my suitcases are distinctive."

We stand near the carousel for a while, and everyone crowds together waiting for personal belongings. Eventually, it begins to spin, and each item slides down the ramp and to the eager hands. I have to squeeze through a crowd bunched together inches from the conveyor. I am able to muscle my way in to pick up my pink bag and hand it back to Julie. She stares at it with a devilish glint in her eye. By the time I pick out the plaid one, she is beside herself.

"I can see you still aren't shopping at Macy's. They don't have cases with such panache."

"That case has been my salvation, and I love it." I think it will be with me forever, so the memory of my life before never leaves. "So don't mock my choices."

"I didn't mean to insult the case, but you must admit it is one of a kind." Julie continues to giggle as she turns toward the exit doors.

I can't help but smile knowing that the plaid one isn't much better. "Did Tom come with you?"

"Hell no, I told him you were coming, and he said we needed time together. He borrowed his friend's condominium on the river for us. Tom is a great guy; I don't know what I did to deserve him."

"I would guess that you survived, and he was your reward." I love her snort and laugh; it fits her, as the sound erases years.

"Damn Liz, I have missed you. I got out but never understood how you stayed. You will probably end up with Prince Charles."

We continue laughing and chattering about life's penalties and rewards as she expertly ushers me to the parking garage.

The thought of a private condo on a river is almost too perfect. My adventure gets better and better.

I'm frightened and amazed how she maneuvers through the aggressive morning traffic and after a half hour of hell, we slide into a private parking garage with a key code entry. Once parked, I sit for just a moment to let my tired legs rehabilitate. She opens the trunk and again picks up my pink suitcase.

"Don't mock, Missy. That is where I hid my secret stash of money. It has been my secret escape route for thirty years. It is so girly I never had to worry about Brad using it." I have forgotten how silly that case is; it has just always been there. "I did notice that the majority of travelers have black, blue or tan luggage, and none of those choices suit me."

Julie smiles kindly, which is contrary to her nature. "So you had this suitcase when I was married to Brad's brother. Were you planning a trip then too?"

"I have planned my getaway for years. I am great at planning, not so much with execution."

We enter the locked entrance to the condominiums, and I can almost hear her thinking as we pass through the lobby and into the elevator.

"Speaking of execution, what finally set your jets on fire?"

"Tell you the truth, the more I think about it, the less I know. I try to tell myself he passed out on the floor, but I did encourage that with a pickle jar."

"Was he dead? Did you finally kill him?" Julie seems concerned.

"No, and no again. You are not harboring a murderer, if you were concerned." We both laugh a nervous chuckle, knowing how easily it could have ended that way for any of us.

"If you killed him, I would have to buy extra groceries for the hideout." Julie's cheerfulness returns as she unlocks the door to the condo. I am in awe of her command of life and the beauty that has come in the passing years.

"Hey, a woman on the lam has to be able to pack and roll; that I can tell you."

"Well, let's roll. I know there is a lot of information I want from you, and I would prefer we were warm, shoeless, and holding a stemmed glass of wine. You still drink, don't you?"

"Ah Julie, I still drink a glass of wine every few months, need it or not. Maybe I'll have coffee or orange juice and wait until later in the day." Nevertheless, the thought of no shoes and a comfy chair sounds heavenly. I have been on the road all weekend and haven't had many conversations.

# – 15 –

It is an elegant place, two bedrooms, sparse furniture and clean. There is no question a man owns it as there is almost no evidence of personal items or human habitation. The beauty of the river with an outline of the city takes me away. "Julie, you said a friend of Tom owns this, right? Is he married?"

"Tom said he has this for business clients and family when they visit. He bought the place during the real-estate boom and then, after the crash, he decided to stick with the investment. It doesn't give the impression that anyone has ever been in here before." I walk through the main rooms appreciating the Spartan and yet elegance of the spacious rooms.

"I like it; I don't feel like I am interfering in someone's personal life."

"Nice view and we could play golf or use the exercise room," Julie said.

"You don't play golf."

"And you don't exercise. Guess we will have to entertain ourselves another way. There is nothing like a 70 inch TV for watching the Food Channel. You need to unpack. I have already moved into one of the rooms; yours is the one on the left. I'm going to change my clothes and unload the groceries."

I had no idea how much I missed her strength and spontaneity. She makes me feel comfortable and safe as if I don't have to battle alone. I haven't felt protected since I was a new wife. I open the door to the left and enter the bedroom and discover a suite, "Julie, why is your stuff in the small bedroom? Please take this room."

"Hell no, I came over early so I could choose. You are granted more than the big bedroom – check out the bathroom. It is such a surprise compared to the simplicity of rest of the place."

I'm touched to have her spoil me. In my rush to meet the rest of the day, I decide not to unpack and just open the cases and set them on the shelf in the largest walk-in closet I have only experienced in magazines. I decide it is more important to utilize the sunken tub than to hang up my meager wardrobe.

I look at the sunken bathtub and choose to save that luxury for later. I couldn't resist the multiple head shower with the transparent glass enclosure. I need a hot water massage to energize my aching back. In the warmth of the vibrating warm water, I think of the woman on the other side of the wall; I appreciate that our connection is deeper than friendship. Our lives were forged in a Donovan fire, and there is a security within our wounds. Even though we haven't seen each other for almost fifteen years, we never lost contact. My mind sinks into the luxury of having her near. As I towel dry, I faintly hear the clanking pans. Refreshed, I slip on clean, comfortable clothes and wrap a plush towel around my hair. The enticing smell of brewed coffee draws me to the kitchen.

I hold a warm mug, we fall into a comfortable conversation, and she begins to crack eggs into a bowl and slide them into a hot omelet pan. She adds cheese and a few chopped vegetables and reaches over to push the lever on a red toaster, pre-loaded with English muffins.

We have years to catch up on, no time to waste. We have traded emails, cards, and notes, but I haven't had time with her in so long. Even though she still has family in Indiana, she never came back. We fill our plates and sit at the breakfast bar. She looks at me intently and restarts the critical part of our conversation. "I didn't know when we met that we were both tangled into an impossible situation. The Donovan boys have so many issues that call for psychiatrists and possibly drugs. Ever since you saved my life and helped me escape, I have worried about you. Elizabeth, you are the friend of my heart; I owe you my life and the big bedroom."

Both of us are wiping tears from our eyes before we take the first bite. Julie is full of surprises and never had a filter for what she has to say. That is probably the reason that she got out years ago, and my armor kept me trapped. It feels good to be here and I decide to unpack my few belongings.

"Time is up, Lizard. No more excuses, it's story time. Are you ready for wine or something else?"

"It is still too early; I can't imagine wine with the taste of eggs still in my mouth." I know if I had a glass this early, I'd fall asleep by 4:30. We decide on more coffee as we clear the dishes.

We talk of our beverages of years gone by and estimate the numbers of Diet Cokes we have shared. She shows me multiple six-packs of soft drinks and juices in the refrigerator along with a giant box of wine. Clearly, she has a need to hydrate with a multiple choice of caffeinated beverages and alcohol.

"How much did you spend on the groceries? I want to give you some money for all of this."

"Shut up, Lizard. I know who you are and what you came through. That bastard didn't let you escape with much of anything. The least I can do is to buy a few groceries. Don't mention it again."

"You also paid for my flight."

She looks at me with an exaggerated pout. "Zip it. You are not the boss of me. Now sit down, put your feet up and talk."

Pulling up one of the stools at the breakfast bar, I take a serious stance. "You underestimate me, I have been planning this for a long time, and I have money."

We talk and laugh over the training from my parents, and how I saved living the lesson. She ushered me back into the walk in closet and we sit on the floor pulling the pink case to the middle of the floor. I extract the bank accounts from a slit near the edge of the lining. We roll on the floor with the joy of my rebellion and the complexity of my financial situation. Instead of guilt, we celebrate my daily existence of little rebellions. We decide that she needed to be a bit more like me with money, and I needed to be more like her on getting the hell out of a dangerous situation.

Another snort and a pat on top of my head, "You are fantastic. I thought I knew you, but you surprise me. I have been so worried, and I had forgotten that you are no one's fool. How much do you have?"

"I don't know, but several thousand."

"What do you mean, you don't know how much? Count it, Liz, how can you stand not knowing about your nest egg? Oh, I'm so sorry; I don't intend to bully you, I just know that miserable family takes everything they can. His brother put me out with nothing. If it weren't for you, I would have been in the streets. He even kept my mother's china. I had to take him to court to get it back. The jackass shipped it thrown in a box with no packing, and it was all destroyed."

I raise my fist in the air. "That rat bastard! I didn't know about this, but I'm not surprised. They demand the last word, don't they?" We share ugly memories of the brothers dedicating years to revenge for some minor infraction and never allowing anyone to have the smallest victory. We talk for over an hour seated on the floor of the closet as we share stories and Julie stacks my account books and bankcards on the empty shoe rack. My revenge had become a daily deceit when I hid money from Brad. She thoroughly understands the purpose of my miserly ways.

Leaning back against the wall she sighs, "That's right, little *miss I'm at the bus station*. I always blamed Brad thinking that he had you accounting for each nickel, dime, and minute of time."

"He did, but I found ways around him. Maybe his behavior encouraged me to make it a monetary retaliation. Often I only saved a few cents, but I always had a stash. He knew about the change basket on the top of the chest of drawers. He never noticed that it stayed about the same. Occasionally he would empty it for some minor purchase, and he would then add a change for a while. As the years passed, I became more proficient in the battle. I honestly believe that his iron control of the purse strings caused me to devise more creative ways to steal."

"OK, Mata Hari, you were married and legal partners. I don't think you took anything that wasn't yours."

"You will love this one; you know I worked at Accounting and Associates for thirty-six or thirty-seven years."

"Of course I remember. That's where we email. You were the bookkeeper or something, right?"

"Well, they are an accountants and an inventory service company, and I held several positions over the years, mostly in bookkeeping and customer service." I went on to explain how cunning I became. How he had been thrilled with the automatic deposit system, believing it was a 100% immediate deposit into his account on payday, not a day after. He had no idea this afforded me some control; I had my checks deposited into a private account and then I have an immediate transfer to his account. "As long as it was what he expected he was happy. Every couple of years I upped his deposit up a few dollars as if I had a raise, but I was able to make skimming a science. Bradan James Donovan talks a big story, and he is so sure of himself, he doesn't realize he isn't that smart."

Julie notices that none of the twenty-three account books is up to date. Some of the accounts are quite old, and there are no details on the bankcards. With a snide smile and a shake of the head, she announces,

"You buried all hope in the lining of a sissy suitcase. Twenty-three accounts, why so many?" She continues to study and shuffle the stack of booklets and cards with her mouth slightly ajar, I could almost see her mental computations. "I guess we need to move you from cheap to frugal and contact some banks."

I smile back. "I felt devious most of the time. Brad believes money is power, and he was blindly confident of his position. I just appropriated a little for myself, and always feared he would find out what I was doing. I decided that several small pots were a safer bet. If caught, I would confess to one maybe two, but not all of them. I make rotating deposits in different accounts every paycheck. As time passed, they grew. I started saving for a personal reason, and that afforded me some dignity. Occasionally, I would feel ashamed, but he would always do something that kept the secret."

"I'm incredulous, but I do understand your position. My life with Shawn destroyed me and after so many years, I no longer struggle, but the scars remain. Your courage and good sense impress me. What about tax time? Did he notice the discrepancy?"

"I did the taxes. He only signed and waited for refunds."

"To hear him say it, he was the brains of the operation. You are my hero. You played with fire; I know him and if he found out, you would be dead. I mean that literally."

Our conversation continues, and I feel relief to speak of my life in safety. We discuss the fears about finances, retirement, and survival. Julie shares her personal regrets of spending more than she earned and not building for her life now. Gratitude for her husband shines through her tears and laughter. I can't help but personally recall the weeks of arguments for my 401k retirement plan. He argues against any deductions, and I claimed it was mandatory. He tried to act hurt that I didn't trust him to take care of us, but after weeks of friction, he relented.

After two hours of serious discussion of dollars and cents and the cost to fill this closet with designer shoes, Julie reminisced, "I remember you picking up pennies from the street, announcing them to be lucky and put them in your shoe. I thought it was a cute quirk. I bow to you, my Queen. I left with nothing and you walk away with a financial empire. What is the most surprising part is you don't know how much."

I may have left with money, but I paid a toll in years, and I'm exhausted with this exposure. We consider the trade-off of time or money. She opted for time and rebuilt a comfortable life. I stayed and now may have some financial security, but my clock is ticking. Time is something that can't be retrieved, and I feel sadness for the loss of years. We sit in silence, and as I begin to stir, I discover my leg has gone to sleep. We laugh and try to rub the pins and needles into submission. We help each other stand, recognizing age and stiffened old bones. The thought of a chair and sunlight motivates us to leave the closet and resettle in the living room. "By the way, I will still be paid for ten more weeks. It is my sick time and vacation; job loyalty pays off."

"Of course, it does." My friend snorts with amusement.

I make a mental note to call the boss and officially quit.

Julie continues, "I have thought about the reasons I stayed and there were many, but it took the time to realize how they slowly broke us down to accept the violence as our fault. With the isolation and constant chipping away, we accepted there was nothing else."

She is ahead of me on the recovery. I hadn't put much thought into the reasons I stayed. There were times of happiness; it took years to convince me of my failures as a human. I'm confident no one would ever want me now, and there is sadness in that realization. I left him emotionally years ago and was afraid to walk out the door until now. "I have to admit the afternoon I called you, earlier that day I was considering going back."

"Get out! Whenever you think about going back to that bastard, you will call me. I'll be there with money and a gun, and then I'll talk you down. Those brothers are mean, selfish bastards, and you are better off living in a box down by the river. Remember that as long as I have a home, you do too. So don't worry about that box scenario."

"My life with Brad taught me to lie. I don't like it, but I'm good at it."

Julie looks solemn, and I can tell she remembers her pain. "You had to lie to survive; he felt justified controlling you. I have never understood Brad's need to own you. Maybe he had a feeling that he never completely had you, and that is what drove him."

"Nice diagnosis, Dr. Julie. Why didn't you prescribe medication?"

"Speaking of medicine, I think it is wine time."

She carries the empty juice glasses to the kitchen, and I overhear her order a pizza. I head to the kitchen planning to help and within thirty minutes, we are settling back onto the couch with stemmed glasses and paper plates. We watch the sunset and the lights of the city appear, as we share the New York style pie. We also share our lives and doubts, trying to understand the complexity of our relationships with the Donovans. We search for answers and make amateur verdicts on everyone involved. I can't believe we almost talk through the night. Julie shakes me awake, and we watch the light creep towards morning. Only then did we both pad off to bed. I haven't slept much since leaving Hot Springs, and it finally caught up with me.

I can't deny I was looking forward to bed, fresh, clean sheets and the comfort of a safe sleep. After a couple of hours of complete unconsciousness, I awaken with the recollection of the bathtub.

At this moment, I extend gratitude for the sunken tub and discover a lovely set of bath salts waiting for me. Julie is a beautiful friend, and I wish we lived closer. Then again, if she did, I wouldn't have a hideout. I settle into the warm, comforting water and doze until the water becomes cold.

# - 16 -

"Hey, Lizzy, are you going to sleep all day? Are you hungry for breakfast or lunch?"

"Whatever is easiest, crazy woman." I feel as if I am emerging from death. No dreams, no sudden starts. "Julie, I would like an aspirin sandwich, please. Damn your wine."

"You ungrateful wench, you are not allowed to criticize my choice of beverages. It was the finest big box available, and we didn't even drink half of it, Lightweight. Let's get moving. We are going shopping. I want you to own an outfit that has not been previously worn by strangers. You need something to go with that beautiful pendant you are wearing. It doesn't want someone else's cast offs."

"Now look who is the critic. What is wrong with my fashion sense?" I rush to dress in my second best thrift store outfit. As I leave the bedroom, I can hear her starting to rattle around in the kitchen. "Jules, stop. Don't start cooking. I want to take you out for brunch."

"I like the way you are thinking. We keep this up and I'll be hauling groceries home to Tom. He loves me when I have food."

"You know that man loves you with or without food. You are a lucky lady." I like seeing Julie comfortably in love. It gives me hope. "I am ready to roll, old woman."

What a day. We take a couple of hours, but I have a new outfit that comes with machine printed tags. We find a tiny beauty shop for facials and haircuts. New makeup on top of it all. I had no idea how run down I was looking. Now I know what it takes to be marvelous. Right this minute. I feel fabulous for any age. No, wait a minute, mentioning my age compromises everything, so I'll just accept that I'm gorgeous.

We decide to move to Julie's house tomorrow morning, and I will meet the man of her dreams. I hope he likes me. I worry that his opinion will cause me to lose my friend. Then the voice of reason whispers to remember that not all men block and control. Julie is anxious to introduce us and shows no concern.

We make it back to the condominium in time for dinner. I feel like we have been eating and laughing all day long. I sigh, recognizing one of the best days of my life. I decide to acknowledge and honor all of the great days. We still have most of the food she bought. The cabinet looks as if she stocked up for winter. I am amazed that I have hardly thought of Brad all day. "Hey Jules, how do you feel about soup this evening?"

"Sounds fantastic. I couldn't eat anything too heavy. I'll be right there, and we can toss it together. How is the wine doing? Do I need to get more?"

"The wine is fine. That box is amazing and it never runs out. Although, I don't think I will want any tonight. I haven't had more than a single drink for a couple of years, and my tolerance is low. Last night seemed to have knocked me over."

"Bull! You will want wine; I will see to it. I'm pretty sure that you need fluids."

I'm looking forward to this evening; I am still a social animal. The days alone were important, but being with someone I trust and can be open with is golden. Last time I was this happy I was a kid. I feel great, look tolerable and now I'm going to build something new for dinner. I start gathering a little of everything and begin to sauté the mishmash of ingredients in the largest pot I can find.

"Hey, Libs, what are you making? It is starting to smell unbelievable in here."

"I tore up that roasted chicken, added the cans of soup and when it blends, the bag of frozen vegetables will go in. Then I think I'll roll out the canned biscuits. We will be having a chicken pot pie."

"You are freaking brilliant; I never thought of making anything with soup except soup. Then again, you were always a kitchen wizard. I remember you would make fantastic meals out of a can of tuna and a box of marbles."

"Oh, quit it. I seldom cooked with marbles."

"You know what I mean. He imposed restrictions on you; every move watched, but in the kitchen, you seemed to soar. Often something new and exciting came from the simplest ingredients. That talent of yours has always amazed me. If I were you, I would be fat."

I had never thought of the kitchen as my freedom, but it was. I am self-taught and loved cooking ever since I made my first homemade soup. I never thought of it as my art and domain. "I hadn't considered it as anything other than the challenge of a new dinner. Brad liked staying out of the kitchen, and as long as pans were clanking, he was happy. He knew he could escape to the bar while I washed the dishes." He loved his evening cocktails; I can't remember a night without them. Shawn was more secretive about his drinking and Brad was the social one.

"I remember, early on I wished he would stop drinking. As time passed, I longed for him to pass out so I could breathe for a little while. I will never forget the dread of those nights when he didn't get sleepy and would dive into mean." Julie and I share stories, but our individual hells are personal.

"I know for sure that Shawn was similar, only I swear that bastard never slept. You know that after years away and a multitude of self-help books I finally accepted that we married them for a reason. I hate to admit it, but there were some good times."

"WOW, Julie, you have changed. I remember the days...."

"You mean years."

"Yes, I remember the years that you could not think of a kind word about any of the Donovans."

"I spent a lot of energy questioning those times and the relationship. After meeting Tom, I started reading in earnest. I was broken and could not heal until I understood. Shawn was charming, funny and friendly, especially with a buzz. I did love him and yet I tried to blame him for everything. The hard part was realizing I was instrumental. Shawn could have been one hell of a man, but he had a fatal flaw when it came to beer, vodka, whiskey, rum, and me. I couldn't let the anger and frustrations go until I honored his good parts and acknowledged my involvement."

"You know Shawn has never remarried."

"Yeah, I know."

I had to stop and think about what she said. I blamed myself for decades and then I just attributed all the misery to Brad. "Not standing up, not walking away and not being honest that is on me. The pickle jar to the back of the head, that was all me. I focused on guilt and blame for so long; all that is left is my shell."

"Elizabeth Ann, you stop it. You are no shell; you are a vibrant, smart woman who has been hibernating. If you have breath, you have a life. Every day is a new beginning. I'll pass, no thank you on the pickles, they don't go with potpie."

I wander back to the kitchen and begin to add most of the limited spices to the pot. Julie comes in and pre-heats the oven. She hums and tears open the box of cornbread mix. I flatten the biscuit dough, put it on top of the potpie and slide it into the oven next to the cornbread. Julie takes down two dishes, and I start cleaning up the cooking mess. Ten minutes later, I open the oven to a golden display of dinner. It all looks delicious, and we realize how long it has been since we ate. I can't help but smile about cooking together; it was fun, and I have missed that most of all. We move to the counter, dish up the steaming rations and crack open cans of iced tea.

We sit quietly and eat as if it were the last meal, no – more like a first meal. Everything is lovely and warm, the perfect comfort celebration.

Julie looks at me with her dark eyes, "OK, I've given you some time, and I want this story told. Realize I will be dragging you out of bed at sunrise tomorrow for your birthday. You have given up happiness while searching for happiness."

"My birthday? What is the date today?"

I always loved this woman, but she has changed, and I like her even more. It is clear it took her years to move on, and I'll have to get a list of those books she keeps mentioning.

"Sunrise – give me a break."

"I know you will be up and peeking out the window in spite of yourself."

The thoughts keep digging deep into my core; I don't know who I am other than how I reflect off others. I'm Robert's daughter, Brad's wife, Mr. Offert's bookkeeper. Every part of me is a reflection. My life has been wasted by burying an unknown and possibly the most important part of me. I can't believe how long I have lied and tried to live up to someone's expectations. Who am I? I need to know.

She only knows me on one level, but I have pain that has eaten away at my heart, and I can never recover. My lies extend beyond my little life with the big man; I have been unforgivable, and I can't blame Brad for all of it. I know I can never make it right.

"Lighten up, there is no such thing as a perfect life. It is not possible since we share the earth with imperfect beings." Julie pushes her plate back and looks incredulous "My God, I've read the papers, and I know you didn't kill the Pope. You can't change the past, but the future is before you. Are you living under an assumed name and on the run from an organized crime syndicate?"

"Almost: I do have one thing I must do before I take care of me."

# — 17 —

With no warning, the decades of tears begin to spill as my initial sin assaults my heart. My friend clears the dishes and returns to wrap her warm arms around me. She stands behind me making no sounds, just offering comfort. It is a long story of a secret and regrets that are decades old. I have never spoken of this since it happened before I married him, before I learned to lie. I was young and a fool. I had no plans to share this, but it is pouring out of me with the hot tears. "I have thought about it every day for the last forty-eight years. I've held it for so long, but this is where the largest part of my heart resides."

"Holy crap, bring it, and I mean that, Liz. Confess this is the only way you can move to the next chapter. Secrets are cancer to your soul, and you did mention it. I need to know your story. The weight will lighten as you share the pain." This woman has more clichés than a Poor Richard's Almanac; it must be the self-help reading.

"I guess it is time, and there is no one else in the world I can tell." I have not allowed myself to mention this since I was sixteen. I feel a wave of nerves pass over me and a certain excitement. "You are right; I do want that wine now."

Julie gathers the food and the rest of the plates, then guides me to the cozy living area. Gut wrenching sobs envelope me. She leaves me to my humiliation, and as the emotion begins to subside, she reappears with a plate of cornbread, two stemmed glasses and the box of wine. "Start from the beginning. Settle in and don't conceal a single detail."

The low evening sun lights the room with a golden glow, and the shadows have already grown long. I hear the air conditioning kicking on. The scene seems appropriate. We each have a glass of courage, and we are both full of warm, comforting food. Still snacking on the cornbread, Julie chews quietly allowing me to tell the story on my terms.

"The beginning was in high school. My parents had a rule, and I wasn't to date until I was sixteen, but one of the big deal football players asked me to the homecoming dance. My birthday was only three months away and so with begging, crying and teenage theatrics my parents gave their approval so I could go, with a strict set of rules."

"Was that Brad? Don't tell me it was Brad. I need you to be with someone else in your past."

"Yes, it was Brad." I can feel the embarrassment creep up my neck and spread across my face.

"Oh my Gawd, you guys do have no other history. Is he your only guy?"

"Yes, my whole life has been wrapped around him, ever since I was 15. I should describe it as warped around him. I never had good sense when it came to that man."

"Lizard, I'm so sorry I don't want to interrupt, I promise to be quiet."

"No, you won't be quiet, I know you. I can't hold this any longer, and I'm hoping that I can gain some clarity too."

I take my friend back through the years to my teens. Starting by explaining my youth as an only child and the love, I have for both of my parents. Smiling at the memory, I clarify my dating requirements and the list of rules. I had to be sixteen to date, and that was the primary restriction. When I was fifteen, Brad asked me to the Homecoming dance. I begged and pouted until Dad allowed me a possibility. Brad had to come to our home and talk to him first. To my surprise, he met them and Dad was impressed by his good manners and courage. Dad was the first to cave, and Mom never did like Brad. She said he was too smooth, but it was two against one, and she gave in.

Mom swallowed her objection, and she helped me find the right dress and set up an appointment to have my hair done. I didn't know how to dance, but luckily, it was the 60s, and you could learn by watching and jumping around the living room with Dick Clark and The American Bandstand. I also went to my friend, Darlene. She didn't have much experience either, but we danced the afternoon away. Thank heavens for Chubby Checker and the simplicity of the twist. The tension diminishes with the memories of the music of those years. Julie turns on the radio and finds a *classic* radio station. We laugh and dance reminiscing our years of innocence.

Falling back to the couch, I can see the questions on her face as we sift through our youth. I have no choice but to return to the memories. Looking at those days from the knowledge of a greater age, I can see clearly the excitement, youth and hormones were equal measures of fear and love. Boys my age and older were a mystery to me. I knew the kids around the neighborhood, but they were all still children or dipshits. I was confident that this date was the turning point of becoming a woman.

Julie moves slightly in the darkness; I hear a knowing harrumph, and she patiently waits for me to go on. She takes a sip of wine and then clasps her hand over her mouth settling back into the couch.

We don't turn on any lights, and the darkness gives me the safety of solitude. "I had to meet him at the dance after the football game. Dad picked up my friend Claudia and drove us to the stadium. The game was exciting and a big win. We laughed and talked with other students as we walked up the hill to the school gymnasium. Claudia didn't have a date, so her mother picked her up out front. I had to go into the dance alone and wait for him. My main memory is of the insecurity of the wait. I was afraid he changed his mind, and I would be humiliated. I sat in the bleachers watching the others dance, talking and laughing. Even then, I didn't know how to mingle. How would I tell my mom and dad that he stood me up?"

"You have always over thought things, can't blame that on him." Julie then covers her hand back over her mouth and snuggles back into her corner of the sofa.

"Finally, Brad and three teammates made a big, noisy entrance. The energy of the dance changed.

They entered, oozing confidence with shouting, bringing the victory with them. I don't remember much else; I was focused on him and the date. Damn, I was already whipped." My mind flashes with the handsome, seventeen-year-old superstar. He had to shave and knew everyone at the school. My memory is so clear it is as if I am still at the dance. "I was just a quiet girl, a student; I knew people, but only really had two friends. I didn't belong to any of the social cliques that developed at that age. I lived in my dreams from my bedroom and looked at high school as a springboard into a fascinating and challenging life of education, travel and exploration."

"I like that girl, bet she still lives. What did you want to be when you graduated? I have several ideas, which don't seem to fit you anymore."

"Julie, I don't even think I'm related to her anymore. She wanted to be a history teacher or work in government. She had a Peace Corps application hidden in her room. She wanted her name in history books and dreamed of writing scholarly articles for literary journals. I think she died that night."

Smiling gently, Julie interrupted "I don't want to sidetrack the story, but I want dessert." I sit for a moment and curl my legs under me, pulling the afghan from the back of the couch. Julie re-enters the room, with two Ben & Jerry containers of Chubby Hubby and spoons, she looks directly into my eyes. "That Libby still lives, and you have tons of time. Now back to the story. How was the dance?"

"Really, Chubby Hubby? You couldn't resist." She shrugs with a wink.

We share memories of school dances gone by and agree that it was as if there was glitter sprinkled around the edges. All of those previous years seem to have been ten minutes long. In the darkness, we both feel like young girls again. "He had a car, which might have been a deal breaker if Dad realized that fact. He and two of his friends drove me home. We arrived a few minutes before curfew, and he walked me to the door. The first kiss under the porch light was the perfect ending to the ideal night. I assumed he went home after dropping me off, but learned that they went to the liquor store and got drunk under the bridge. I believed for years that he was the boy I envisioned."

Julie added, "Fifteen to seventeen is a wide age gap in those days. Fifteen is just coming off of Barbie dolls."

"I was so in love with the idea of love. The girls today are not nearly as innocent; they seem more sophisticated and informed. At least, I hope that means they are."

"You are right; fifteen was a lot younger then than now. I blame television." Julie looks quite satisfied with her revelation.

We continue into a deep conversation about how things have changed. Digressing into the messages of the TV shows we watched. We can't summon up any shows about sex crimes supporting the television industry in 1963. We share out favorites now able to see the lessons with Fury and Flicka on Saturday morning sand Sid Caesar and the Honeymooners in the evening.

The two of us take the empty cartons into the kitchen and then with no discussion, finish the cleanup. Knowing we are leaving in the morning, we polish the kitchen to its previous pristine condition and settle back onto the couch each taking our corner.

"Now, now I have gotten you off topic. I'm sorry, I will stay quiet."

"More wine, please." We giggle and feel as if we are young again, breaking the law with illicit alcohol.

"Brad called the next day and asked if he could give me a ride home from school on Monday. I was completely thunderstruck. He liked me; Brad Donovan, number 23, liked me. The next weekend he took me to the movies. The weekend after that, he came over for dinner and visited with my parents. He never budged from the perfect gentleman with them. He even helped my mother with dishes. By the end of the second month, the full court press was on. I thought I was blessed to find the perfect guy so young, and my life plans changed from that first night. I learned later that the football team had a deflowering-virgin bet. They were sharing details and keeping score. I had no idea he was on the leader board and had a regular girlfriend who was away at college."

"He has been with you ever since. It can't be completely for the bet."

"That would have been one hell of a gamble, let's see who can do fifty years. There was a short break between my Junior and Senior years, but I guess bitterness can play tricks on memories."

"Within two months of movies, Coca-Colas, kissing we had worked up to a fevered pitch."

"Oh, I remember fevered pitches. Is that what they called it in those days?" Julie can diffuse the emotional aspect of my story and makes it easy to explain the decisions that became the foundation of a lifetime. I continue to wrestle with the raw emotions of my antiquated shame.

"You know exactly what I mean. The first time is critical to every girl, and my details are still vivid. Ol' Jackass claims he doesn't remember. He had several first times under his belt by the time it was my turn."

Julie snorts and under her breath, I hear her whisper "Under his belt."

"I was just another sophomore in the back seat for him. We were at the drive-in movies, back row with all of the other high schoolers."

"What movie?"

"Well, it is kind of embarrassing, *The Parent Trap*."

"With Hayley Mills or the one with Lindsay Lohan?"

"Stop, if it were the Lohan one, I would have known better. Considering what happened next, I always thought it was prophetic."

"Happened next? I'm visualizing the sheer romance of the back seat of a car with a Disney movie. Were there Jujubes involved?"

"Junior Mints. It was terrible; he swayed me with candy and a box of popcorn. Ah, the gritty side of young love. I remember we had to move his dirty gym bag to the floor making room." I'm amazed by details flooding back as I gaze at the city lights from this elegant condo. I can still hear the tinny voices from the speaker attached to the window and the bitter smell of the dirty clothes. All of it burned into my brain. "I fought him off for two months, but the kissing and the first three bases were so delicious. He had been patient and would stop when I asked. But, you know teenaged boys; he would just pause and then persevere. We had been close to the homerun for about a week, and he just kept telling me how much he loved me and that there was no one else for him ever."

"He told the truth that time."

"Therefore, I gave it up, and it hurt. Where were the music and the little blue birds that are supposed to show up?"

We both sat wordlessly until Julie broke the spell: "Liz, didn't Hayley Mills sing Let's Get Together in that?"

"Julie, you should be a diplomat. You can break tension better than anyone I know. Do you want a salad?"

"No, I do not want a damn salad. The potpie was more than enough and we are working on more important issues than a salad. Lettuce continue."

Genuinely smiling, I resume. "I have never had the heart to watch that movie sitting up and missed most of it that night." I can feel my face redden with the memory of the passion and anxiety.

"I'll never watch it the same again." The grimace on her face exaggerated the scene, but her laugh was all knowing and full of her experiences.

"That night opened a door, and old Brad was not going to allow it to close. The next morning I dashed off to the library trying to learn more than the talk about periods my mother gave me."

"Those were different times; we were all ignorant. Now that you bring it up, everything I knew, I learned from some sweaty teenaged boy in a car. Where did they learn it? I remember that I knew more about a frog's reproductive system from biology class than my own. Never realizing it was supposed to translate to us mammals. So you went to the library. That is brilliant."

"The girls now have the internet instead of the library; I can imagine the pictures they get when they type in sex. Those images would be an indecent deterrent." We both shudder and take another sip.

"Not brilliant enough. I got pregnant and to this day, I think it was the first time we did it. I had no idea how it all worked."

"Oh honey, I didn't know. What did you do? How did you cope? You know I heard about that happening lot of times."

"I didn't realize it for over three months. I was irresponsible, but I hadn't had periods for that long, and each one had been a surprise." Old emotions well up and release in more tears. "I put off talking to Brad and a month or so later I told him that I might be pregnant. He was livid, his face was bright red, and I swear steam came out of his ears. He said I was stupid and wrong, that it had to be someone else's and that I was not going to ruin his life. He had a football scholarship and accepted at Purdue.

No matter what I made up, I wasn't going to steal his future. He called me a whore and, well, you know the drill, da ta da ta da."

Julie has tears on her face and moves closer to me, and we both wrap the afghan around our shoulders. "I am sorry, Liz."

"It was a long time ago, and you were not responsible. Now I know that was my first real clue to who he was, but I didn't understand." The sharp pain of shame still stings with a paralyzing fear. Julie reaches over and holds my hand. "You know those were the days of no birth control or sex education for girls or single women."

We divert to the stories of illegal abortion and shotgun weddings. We deliberate how things have changed for the better and how in our day, boys were celebrated for their exploits. When it came to girls, they could be marked for life if there is a whisper about her sexuality. The memory of how I loved him comes over me like a familiar fog. "I thought Brad was my safe place, and he threw me under the proverbial bus. I only wanted his love."

Looking out of the sliding doors, we move to the patio and silently stare blankly at the stars and the night sky. Julie drapes her arm around my shoulders and looks deeply into my eyes. "What did you do?"

"I walked out. After the fight and name-calling, I knew I was on my own. I did everything I could to hide the obvious. I quit the school activities, avoided my friends and stayed in my room when I was home. My plan of action was to ignore it and hope it went away."

"How did that work for you, genius? From what I've read, they don't do that."

"Tell me! I was about seven months along and showing when I told Mom. She had been suspicious and one day when Dad was playing golf, she came to me. By then it was evident, and I was aware of the mistake of avoidance. I stopped eating with them and was to the point of suicide as my only way out. She delayed in a hope that she was wrong, but it was beyond that stage, and she came to me, taking charge of the situation. My dear, dear mother was there for me. I think she had already run the possibilities through her mind and ruled out a tumor. She hunkered down and together we made a plan. As we talked, I discovered that I had been the reason for my parent's shotgun wedding. Even though I admired their partnership, she understood it was no way to start a marriage. She had been there, and when I thought my life was ending, she brought hope. I told her of Brad's response, and she was relieved that option was out. My mother believed in me and was confident I had a life to live, and some jerk wise guy should not steal it. In the plan, I was never to mention the pregnancy again especially not to Brad; it was not his business." On some previously unrecognized level, I am always trying to measure up to him and believed I fell short of his approval.

Julie speaks up "I'm in love with your mother. I keep putting myself in your position. I had a couple of scares myself. I will always remember the options my young mind built. With that and societal expectations and I'm surprised that we made it through."

"I think that teen mind is an oxymoron. There is so much going on, trying to be an adult and still a child. At least, kids today have information and the same curse for being sexual have changed. They need to thank our generation for sex education and Planned Parenthood. Although I hate to break it to all of them, oral sex is sex." I divert to another topic easily, and relief washes over me, but I can't stop the story once it started.

"Mom planned some shopping trips, but she was taking me to a doctor in Indianapolis. She contacted her best friend, Madeline. They had been friends since birth. The families were neighbors, and they were born two days apart. Even though Maddie moved away, they stayed close and talked every Sunday. I am still envious of their lifelong friendship. Maddie had moved to Omaha, and they decided I could go there to have the baby. We put together a cover story about my aunt in Atlanta being ill and needing help."

Julie smiled, "Damn, sounds like Mom should have worked for the CIA. I know you have always been close to your dad. I'll bet he was ready to murder Brad, what did he have to say about it all?"

"Mom made sure Dad never knew, he didn't pay close attention and he may have chosen to simply not know. She was amazing and the best mother ever. She told me the disappointment and rage would not help and could only make things worse. She assured me I was going through enough and we just didn't need man drama." I appreciate to this day that turning to Mom was the best place to go. She is still my superhero; she threw on her cardigan sweater, cat-eye glasses and took care of business. There was a cover story, and Mom taught me once you have a lie, believe it and live it. Every possible detail was worked out. I was to call regularly, and Dad would be okay. We decided if he wanted to speak with me, she would do the dialing. He never questioned her and accepted everything as fact. Mom was an honest woman, and I was shocked how complex she was and how quickly she lied."

"I'm sure it wasn't easy; she lied to support her daughter. Ninety-nine percent of mothers would sell Frigidaire's door to door in the Arctic Circle to take care of their daughters."

With another sob, I recognize how she was there for me. "I have never been there for my son." The emotion steals my breath and Julie holds me until I begin to calm. Then she takes our glasses to the kitchen for a refill but brings back cups of chamomile tea and a box of tissue instead. She hands me a cup and then sets her shoulders. I can tell she has something to say.

"You were sixteen years old, in a small town. Finding your son a suitable life was taking care of your boy! I remember those days and your child would have been marked a bastard, you a whore and life would have been nothing but a struggle for both of you. With no diploma, series of low paying dead end jobs and cheap apartments he would have started life with two strikes and no hope. Now think clearly, Liz. Did you adopt him out, or what happened?"

"I stayed at Madeline's for a month before he was born forty-eight years ago the 27th of July. Mom and Madeline arranged an adoption. They told me they found a young couple that had been trying to have a baby for years. I was able to hold him, and I named him Andrew after my grandfather. Mom and Madeline took the baby the next day from the hospital neither of them telling me anything more. I only got to hold him twice, and I can still feel his perfection in my arms."

"I can't imagine being able to hold him and then let go. Do you know where he is? Do you know the family? Have you been in touch with them?"

"No, Julie, the dynamic duo blocked all information. Those two crazy women told me they accepted full responsibility and guaranteed his care. I am sure he was somewhere near Omaha because they weren't away for long. Mom said she would keep in touch with the parents, but my responsibility was to let it go and move forward. I, for once, listened to my mother."

We sit through the silence looking at the lights of the city. Julie's eyes brighten "Do you think he is in Madeline's family?"

"I don't know. When I came back home, I was a wreck. I was depressed and physically spent. I felt the scarlet A on my forehead as I went back to school. I kept my head down and stood by the story of an ailing aunt. I didn't maintain any friendships or activities and started taking some college courses.

There was gossip around the school, but I wasn't popular enough for any full-scale chatter. Since I had the nerve to show my face, it all blew over. My mother and I were the only ones in Kokomo to know the truth. Brad was seeing a couple of cheerleaders after we broke up and had graduated in June. So that connection was broken, and I dodged him as best I could."

I had been back a couple of months when he called again. Initially, I refused to speak to him, but he was back to being the patient sweet boy I had loved. He didn't push too much, consistently checked in, chatting with Dad. One day he was at the door and caught me face to face.

Neither of us ever mentioned the pregnancy again. I justified his action that he probably thought it was a false alarm and was ashamed of his behavior. We entered into an unwritten contract of 'don't ask, don't tell' that still stands. I remember going to lunch with him when he was home from college one weekend. I can still see the young man he was, although college matured him. I could tell he was frightened of being a small frog in a big pond. He liked being a local hero in his hometown and college wasn't for him. By the end of the first semester, he had washed out of the football program, and never a scholastic contender, he was back in Kokomo. He needed high school sports to sustain his ego and when that was over, he was too."

"Well, I know you took him back. Otherwise, you wouldn't be sitting here drinking tea and full of potpie."

"Yes, by now I was in my senior year. My grades were good, and I was starting to dream again. I applied to a couple of universities, but figured I would go to IU. It was near home and not expensive."

"Were you dating anyone, Liz?"

"No, I was still so stunned from that year that I was just a student and bookworm. I would spend time with an odd group of mismatched outsiders, but I was not ready for another boyfriend. I saw all men as walking time bombs, and I still loved Brad. To this day, I don't know why. I just did. When he came back, he got on with Chrysler. It was a good job in the factory, and he has stayed there all these years. Even the Kokomo college graduates come back to get engineering or desk jobs with them. Brad moved back with his parents, worked hard, made good money, and settled into a day-to-day Midwestern life. It took him a month or so to call me after he was home for good. No longer a high school star, but had become a college washout. I was a senior, and he asked to take me to the Homecoming football game. He said it was our anniversary, and he would like to just hang out. I met him at the stadium, still apprehensive about getting into his car again."

"Of course, you went. I hope he paid."

"I guess in the overall scheme of things we both paid. He seemed so alone and searching for a way to recover his expired fifteen minutes of fame." We laughed in unison. "I was engaged and then married just five weeks after graduation."

"WOW, he does move things along when he has a goal in sight. Did you tell him what happened?"

"No, never did. By then we had a year of my lie and I was afraid. I continued to support my story until today. You are the first I have told. As time passed, the fear lessened, and it was just too late. I still think of my baby every day. When I lost our daughter, I had a breakdown and a difficult time recovering. I still didn't tell him about Andrew. My shame turned into a fear that he would go after my son. I didn't want Andrew anywhere near the hell of our lives." As I look back, I comprehend Brad blamed me for his sins and never once did he ask if the pregnancy was real.

"Honey, I remember when you lost the baby, it was a horrible time. Shawn kept me away, afraid of what may happen. Was it because he was beating you?"

I could only nod my head, "He never thought of me or the babies, just himself. I justified the inexcusable for so long and lied to myself more than I lied to him. I have never forgotten that night. Oddest thing, he showed me who he was repeatedly, but I let love deafen me."

"I am so sorry, Liz, why didn't you tell me sooner? I could have been there for you." Now Julie and I are both crying as we both reach for a tissue at the same time. I never knew how it would feel to let my deceptions out into the light and to have someone I trust to release the tears.

This part of my life was something that I buried; I honestly believed I would go mad if the story got out. Keeping it between Mom and me was a way to save my son. Andrew was always my son; never did he belong to Brad. I was a goofy kid, but believing my son was safe and loved; I could go on.

"Mom said that Madeline told her the couple kept

his name out of gratitude to me for letting them have him. That little act of charity permitted me to believe they were marvelous and loving. I found comfort knowing that Andrew existed, and I did right by my boy. I understood before his birth that I would leave and never see him again. I felt lucky on one level and devastated at the same time. We had signed papers before he was born and my final signature was the day they took him away. I never got to meet the couple, but I trusted my mother and never doubted that I did the best I could for him. "

"Liz, have you heard anything about him since?"

"Mom used to give me little pieces, never very much; like he is healthy, he started school, played soccer. I thought she was getting information through Madeline." The ache of her death and the loss revisits my battered heart. "I would have done anything for a picture or a glimpse of his face, but I didn't want to ruin his life. I honestly believe that I had to go home and live what was left. Any chance of a future depended on that story. I convinced myself that I kept it buried to protect Andrew; I could never allow one of my children to live in Bradland."

The night becomes cold, and we return to the dark the living room. Julie turns on a small lamp near the wall and quietly asks, "Why did you stay so long? You had a right to leave too."

"I can't explain it. I don't understand it myself. I have a whole list of maybes. Maybe fear of making him mad, fear of failure, fear that I was as stupid, lazy and as useless as he tells me. When the barrel of death is staring you square in the eye, it is amazing how powerful the need to live becomes. Brad seemed to need me so desperately. I gave up everything for him."

"Excuse me, a barrel of death? He threatened your life. That bastard, did you go to the police?"

"To wake up with the taste of steel in your mouth, that is a real convincer. He had made it clear that the police wouldn't believe me, a stupid worthless idiot, and he had played football with the chief of police and drank with half of the officers. Small towns have some bad points too. You know it would have been a swearing match, and I believed I had no credibility."

"Elizabeth, I didn't know that it had gotten so violent. I learned so much since I pulled out of the insanity with his brother. Shawn's violence was escalating and getting more vicious. I too blamed myself until one day it was just too much. I had gone to a lot of counseling and support groups before I understood the gradual brainwash. Step one is isolation and they both mastered that. Even when I lived in Kokomo, we had limited time together. It is as if they knew that friends would weaken their hold. I could have easily stayed with Shawn, but I had my sister, the lawyer, to fall back on. When he fractured my collarbone, I knew it was not going to end, and I had kept my sense of injustice intact. There was something about you two; I thought he kept you under his thumb, and you were half robot. No, a *Stepford* Wife. Remember that movie? I remember the day he wouldn't let you leave the house unless you had a destination and a return time. You were afraid to be late, and I should have realized things were worse than they appeared. My own drama blinded me." Julie looks pensive. "I often wonder what their mother went through that taught both of the Donovan boys to build these abusive relationships with women they obviously love."

"No one could be sure. Momma Donovan has been gone a long time, and I doubt she would tell the entire story."

"I've wondered how mean the old man must have been." I was complicit in my situation keeping the truth concealed. It was terrifying, but the worst part was the humiliation. "I learned to take it and from time to time it would get better. Whenever he had a girlfriend, my life improved. He would avoid me, and that was a gift. I never knew if I should thank them or warn them. This last one he has been with around, at least, ten years. She gave me the freedom to turn up the heat on my escape plot." As long as he had an extra paycheck and if he showed up a dinner at 6:00, life was relatively smooth.

"Why do I feel surprised that he had mistresses? Does Brad have any redeeming qualities? Oh, yes I remember he is good looking, charming and tosses cash around. Qualities that attract a wide variety of hoochie mommas."

"After the first couple of years, he always ran around. He would be so sorry, and I was the only one, blah blah blah. It worked for years, Julie. I always tried to believe in him until one day I just didn't care. I feel foolish that I didn't realize how easy it was to leave."

"I'm sure you still hate him. Women often wait too long for a man to behave the way they did once on their best day."

"Shit no. I know it isn't just women, but some romantics don't give up until there is nothing left. They stay for that last particle of hope. I don't hate him; that passed a long time ago. I don't care; the opposite of love is indifference. I had more faith in him than he deserved. Which supports his allegation that I was stupid?" We both laugh and go to the kitchen for fresh wine glasses and the rest of the cupcakes.

"Elizabeth, I would like to take you to my house tomorrow, you will like it there. We have an extra room you can move into, or I can help you find a place. I'm going to make sure that you never go back."

"Now that I've had this therapy with you, there is no possibility that I will ever consider going back. I only contemplated it for a short time while crying alone. I decided tonight that I need to see my baby first and only then will I decide where to live. I have ten more weeks of paychecks, and I will organize my money. The first account, the oldest one is for Andrew, I opened it when I got my first job."

Julie nods knowingly. We then pack up, leaving food in the freezer and a thank you note to Dave, the condo owner, and go to bed.

# – 18 –

"Happy first birthday, Lizard! Time to get up. We have places to go." It isn't the crack of dawn, but it is still morning. She catches me soaking in the tub one last time.

She notices my laptop is still on a banking site, as I tried to do a little money counting after our time last night, but it didn't work out too well. It is going to take bankers hours to figure that mess out. I have account numbers, but never had statements sent; there are years of interest and unrecorded deposits in all of them.

"You amaze me, trying to do accounting at three AM and after so much emotion and wine. I left Shawn with my purse and the clothes I had on, and you leave with the First National Bank in your underwear. Have you slept, Lizard? "

"I dozed a little in the tub, but my mind is just reeling."

"Dozed in the tub? Good thing you didn't slip under the water. I don't think it is safe."

"Julie, what in life is truly safe anyway? It is just part of my new plan, no more living safe or up to someone else's expectations. Every dawn begins a new day in my life. I will never do one more day of the same. Today's first step is to get out of the tub."

"Have you thought any further about finding a place in or around Fair Haven? My offer still stands for the extra room."

"No, thank you. I am not ready for a home base yet. I am going to find my son. He may not want to see me, but I have to do it. I have saved for him since his birth, and I have ached for him since I was barely sixteen years old. This is non-negotiable. I have to do it."

"I understand, Liz. Did you find anything about him last night?"

"No, I only have a first name; I didn't even try. I don't know where his parents lived when I gave him up and a lot of time has passed. I know my mom's friend Madeline is the key. I hope she can help."

"I have done some research on my last job. I would love to be part of this. Do you remember Madeline's last name or her husband's name?"

"I was counting on you. We will do this in order, first breakfast, Fair Haven and money."

# — 19 —

As soon as I dress and pack, I wander into the kitchen. She has my laptop set up on the kitchen counter and has Madeline and Omaha typed into the search engine. I laugh and type in E. Fornier plus Omaha NE. We have several hits with a variety of first names. I want to dedicate some time to this search and convince Julie to wait until we settle at her house. The fear of failure is unyielding, and I want to live today in hope.

I load my few things into the car and help with four bags of groceries. We leave for the one-hour drive to Fair Haven. We make it in two, stopping at the first pancake restaurant we find. Most of the trip we are quiet, letting last night marinate. Being comfortable in silence with her reassures me of the genuine friendship.

We are about to enter Fair Haven and her cell phone rings. She is unable to reach it in time and pulls over. Never one to let a telephone call go, she plays back the message on speakerphone. "Julie, this is Tom. There is a man here at the house; he said he is your first husband's brother. He seems very anxious to talk to you. Call me as soon as possible." We sit in a stunned silence, and finally, she screams. We were within minutes of her driveway. My first reaction is to get out of the car, but she grabs my arm. I can see the gears in her mind cranking.

"Calm down. I'll call Tom before you go running down the street." By the conversation, I can tell he is aware of the situation. She told him that she is only a couple blocks away, and he answers, "Newark, you are still in Newark?" By the end of the conversation, he has given us an hour window. He would ask Brad to come back then.

She puts the car in drive, makes an immediate U-turn and gravel sprays from the rear tires as she pulls away. She drives to a coffee shop nearby, sends me in with my laptop and instructions to contact banks and she will be back as soon as possible.

I'm so grateful for Julie and the man she married. They didn't ask to be part of this mess.

Sitting at the rear corner table, I have a view of the entry and notice everyone coming and going from the shop. I feel trapped, with nowhere to run, except maybe the restroom. I try to lose myself in the banking pages and continue to gather financial numbers. Many of the banks have changed hands or been taken over, but with the account numbers and Google, I find the answers. Three of the accounts are now at the same bank, and I can combine them and arrange for email bank statements. I think about a new job in a covert government agency. I realize he never had the brains or the interest to piece it all together. He just assumed that I behaved.

Two hours pass and then three. I had to move to an overstuffed chair by an outlet so that I can plug in my computer. With the passage of time I have calmed down and with my third chai tea latte, I order a tuna bagel. As I calmly gaze out the window, I see a small blue Ford pulling into the drive through window. "Shit. It's Brad, oh my mother in heaven, don't let him come in. I want to run to the restroom, but I don't want him to notice any motion. I turn my head slightly and keep my eyes on the computer screen. He passes within a few feet of me, but he never looks in. I breathe a shaky sigh of relief. At this moment, I see Julie's car park in the lot, and a good-looking older man get out and walk in. As he cleared the door, I saw Brad's car pull out, taking a tentative sip of his drink, and he drives away.

The man walks directly to me with a welcoming expression, "Hello, I assume you are the Lizard, I'm Tom. The coast is clear, and I'm taking you home."

"You don't know how close we were to the coast catching us. See that car? It's Brad."

"He didn't see you? That was way too close for my old heart."

"Mine too. I'm so happy to meet you, Tom. Where is the wild woman?"

"Thank goodness she wasn't with me, he would have heard her. She will love this close escape. Guess your guardian angel is watching out for you." He is a quiet, confident man and he sat down next to me watching the parking lot. In a hushed voice, he starts to give me some of the details of the morning, "Brad showed up at our house around ten this morning. I knew what was going on, but I feigned ignorance. I had the best time getting his name wrong. I tried to get him to leave, saying Julie wasn't home, but he refused until he could speak with her. That was when I called."

"It was another close call; the timing today has been incredible." I want to apologize for Brad's behavior as if I had not raised him well. "I know that determination. I hope he had some manners."

Our conversation continues as he gathers my computer and I throw away the last of my cups and sandwich wrapper. He described Brad in a way I never imagined, saying he appeared broken and desperate, almost frail. He went on to tell me about Julie's handling everything. I'm impressed how he is unashamed to show the love in his eyes. We both laugh aloud when he describes her walking in like a hurricane and called out *Bradan Donovan, what the hell are you doing in my house, you sorry old dog? I haven't seen you in over a dozen years. How is Elizabeth?* As Tom drives, he is animated with the activities of the day. He brags how she never faltered, comforting Brad with feigned concern and empty promises. A few minutes later, we pull into the driveway of an impressive home with too much yard. The conversation ends as he shuts off the car, he adds, "I'm a little concerned about the woman of my dreams incredible ability to lie so convincingly." He has no idea.

# — 20 —

We enter a Better Homes and Garden decorated household that is so perfect it shouldn't be inhabited. I'm nervous to be in their home, and I'm ready to catch another bus. Tom walks me through the entry and turns to a room off the kitchen where Julie sits at a computer. She looks smug.

Tom is visibly relieved that I am not moving in with them. Although he seems to be all right with anything Julie wants. Her confidence and bravado give me a familiar sense of safety. She is sure that Brad is gone, adding he was going directly to the airport to catch a plane. We tell her of the adventure at the coffee shop, and she understands my need to keep moving. I ask about the closest bus station.

"I want to give you the financial update. I worked on my homework assignment when I wasn't dodging bullets. You will be surprised how money grows when you hide it for a zillion years."

"You and your darn bank accounts, I wish you would have taught that skill to me back in the day. Oops, I forgot, how did you do that again?" Strangely, Julie seems embarrassed asking, but I know her well enough that she can't stop herself.

"Blah, blah, blah, my parents started me out. My mother always had us save part of what I earned. Therefore, with thirty cents allowance, I saved fifteen."

"Fifteen cents, that's harsh. I hope they let you spend the rest foolishly!" Julie squeals with joy.

"Hey, those were different times. We could go to the movies for a quarter and take a nickel to spend. Not like the $8.00 ticket now with the $10 bucket of popcorn. Don't forget this was the early 60s, Sister."

"True enough, Liz. I never learned that lesson and promise I never will. Maybe I should sue the parental units for neglect. Even if I saved, I'm sure some emergency clearance sale at Macy's would come between me and my good intentions."

"You have to notice the only times I have shopped at Macy's has been with you." We giggle like little girls.

"This afternoon, I have moved ten of the newer savings accounts together, and I have $62,007. I lament the interest rates; they used to be golden in the good old days. I have a dozen of the older accounts left, and some of them have changed, they will take some work. I found emails for them and made inquiries and requested statements. I don't have to be careful now unless you drop me off at his car rental office."

"I don't know about you Liz, have you thought of medication? Maybe you can get some with your Medicare," Julie says teasingly.

"You know darn well I would have gotten the generic to save the difference in cost." There is that snorting laugh of hers.

"I emailed my office to arrange a time to speak to the boss. It wasn't fair to leave them hanging, and we all know I'm not going back." I'll call my boss again on a less eventful day and thank him for everything.

"Shouldn't you wait until closer to the end of six weeks to quit? You don't want to lose the time you earned by speaking too soon, Liz."

"Good point; I'll confirm the emergency leave. My Social Security kicks in today. I'll get my first check next month. I almost forgot it is my birthday. It is nice, having money I can use without permission. Cash lasts longer when you aren't giving the majority to a thirsty fella."

"No joke on that account. This afternoon he hid his loss of a paycheck, but the laundry and catering service was too much for the poor boy."

"Stop, Julie, you are filling my head with a vague sense of value."

I need more information on Andrew. I'm frustrated I have to sit and wait for Madeline; I'm sure at eighty-plus she won't be out late. What time is it there? They may have gone to the early bird special. I've waited over an hour, and now I'm frustrated that Madeline isn't home. I open my laptop and turn it back on to book the train ticket.

With unusual timidity, Julie stands up from her screen and asks, "Is there anything I can do to help? I have a decent knowledge of searching out truth and justice."

"No, I'm sure there are things you have to do for your own life. You have been gallivanting the past few days."

"What part of retired did you not understand? I don't play golf or bridge so what else do I have to do? I'm a busybody, and I honored to help. This is a project, and I love projects. I've been working on a family tree, and I have all kinds of search options saved. Two computers are better than one, and we have work to do. Besides, I have a head start on you."

"I can't argue that logic and I do appreciate the help." I hand her the oldest savings book, from a bank that has been bought out more than once. "This one I opened when I got home from Omaha forty-eight years ago. This one is for Andrew. Have at it."

So there we sit with National Public Radio in the background. I didn't remember that we developed that addiction so many years ago. I'm comforted to hear voices I recognize.

"Alright, Mata Hari, I'll make you proud."

# — 21 —

"Here is a fabulous idea, Lizard. There is a room upstairs on the left, you take a shower and try on some makeup and clean clothes. Dress like who you want to be. I have some ideas, and I will keep at it."

I exit the room and lock myself in the bathroom. I wash the tears away with cool water and begin to brush my hair trying to calm my pounding heart. I'm afraid I might have a stroke over all of this. I had no idea how easy it is to tear open an old scar. Julie has been quiet out there; I have no idea what is going on.

Once dressed, I sit on the pastel chintz chair looking out over the deck onto the manicured lawn, finally feeling all the nights of limited sleep. There is a quiet tap on the door and Julie whispers. "Liz, are you alright? I have some information for you."

Oh, my dear God, my heart leaps to another level. Please give me the strength to open that door. Once I open it, there is no escape. "Yes, Julie, I'm coming out."

"I found an Edward Fournier in the phone listing, so I called. I talked to Connie, their daughter-in-law. Madeline is still alive and doing very well. Mr. Ed is in a nursing home. Connie is a character; I told her I was you and she knew your mother and was so friendly. She extended her condolences and said Madeline misses her dearest friend."

"Keep going Julie, I need to know every detail." I should have known she was up to something sending me off the way she did.

"Sit down, you look like a ghost. She will drive over to be sure Madeline gets the message, and I gave her your cell number. She knew who we are, well who you are. It didn't sound like she knew the whole story. Connie was aware that you are Anita's daughter. She seemed anxious to talk to me/you at length. I mentioned to her about your leaving that no-good rat bastard and that we were casting about trying to build a new life."

"No, you didn't." I'm alarmed now. "How could you?"

Julie hands me a little notebook with flowers on the cover; the first page is Edwin and Madeline Fornier, an address and phone number.

I stare at the number and then rush to my cell phone buried in my purse. Once out, I begin to dial trying to put a script together at the same time. Julie reaches over, takes the phone from my hand. She disconnects the call, I count to twenty, after I calm down, and she gives back the receiver. I'm much cooler now, and I know by punching in the numbers, this action has me leave Brad's life and start my own.

It rings three, four times and then a recording of an elderly woman's voice that sounds so familiar. After a long beep, I speak "This is Libby Donovan, Anita's daughter. I'm sorry it has taken me so long to call, but I would love to see you and Mr. Ed again. I'll call back in a couple of hours." My new wait begins.

# — 22 —

From here on, I keep close to the phone. I know that this is going to work. About two hours later, my cell phone rings and I race to answer it. It is Madeline and she told me Connie had come over and helped her get her messages; she told me there were over twenty and mine was the last. She has expected my call for a long time. My face burns shame that I didn't contact her sooner. Julie is hanging over my shoulder, her face pressed to the backside of the telephone; she is not going to miss any of our conversation.

Once I hung up the phone, I repeated everything I could remember to Julie. "Madeline has kept in touch with Andrew and said that he is an amazing man. Her cousin Lorene raised him, and he has known about the adoption for years. When Madeline heard he was thinking about trying to find me, she prepared the contact information. He hasn't followed up yet. Lorene told him when he was ready, the first step is to contact Madeline. He works for a large high school in Colorado and is married with three children. Julie! I'm a grandmother. I'm a grandmother. I don't have the right to be a grandmother."

"You dog, you are a grandma! You goof. You deserve every good thing that comes to you."

"I promised to call tomorrow to work out details for a trip to Omaha."

Julie jumps in, "I'll pull up the airline website, and we can get some prices."

"She was excited about having company and was so sweet and doesn't appear to think poorly of me."

With the repeated late nights, it is this call that finally exhausts me. "There is a reason Mom and Madeline kept their friendship through their entire lives." My eyes are swelling from all of the emotion and tears. I need to lie down, but I also need to make a list.

"Don't worry Liz; you know she stayed in touch with your mother her whole life. They both knew you and your situation, probably better than you did."

"Guess you are right. My mom kept secrets from everyone except her Maddie. The friendship was what sustained her. I have to remember I know some women, and they all like to talk amongst themselves."

"Yes, we do! I know for a fact that I'm fabulous and I like her daughter. It seems like a great family. I'm going to love Madeline. I can't wait, I will get tickets, but I wanted to run that by you first."

"I will buy my ticket."

"Damn Skippy, you will! I will put things together, but then we can go in a day or two. "

Silencing the room, I appreciate everything but recognize one thing for sure. "No, dear woman, I must do this alone. I have a need to step up and face my past. I have hidden in shadows too long and didn't want to hide behind your Macy's skirts. In fact, the next call to Madeline will be tomorrow morning. You can join me once I have some control."

"I do understand Liz, but please call me every day. You are heading into the most exciting adventure I can imagine. I respect and care about you. I can be there within a day or two if you need me. Put this on one of your damn lists, turn that cell phone on and leave it on. Charge it and keep it close, I will need hourly updates."

"All right, all right, let me do that right now."

I enter the phone book app with Julie and Madeline's numbers. I don't know what my number is until this moment, and I try to commit it to memory. I had only used the phone for out-going calls, but circumstances are changing. "OK, here we go, my number is... aw shit, and I have twenty-eight missed calls. How could that be? I don't have voice mail, but someone has my number. I hope it is Publishers Clearing House with a winning ticket."

"We both know who it is; somehow Brad has gotten your number."

"It must have been the time I called to check in to see if he was alive."

"Liz, you have only been free for a week and a half. Do you think that possessive drunk would let a meal ticket go that smoothly?"

"You remember him well. I guess I will have to talk to him at some point, but not today."

"Good girl! Now let's get things moving."

# — 23 —

We spend a couple more hours on the computers, laughing, swearing and getting my life into one pot. I go to bed with savings combined and Andrew's account brought up to date. My 401K transferred to an IRA, I don't have to take any payments until I'm seventy, so it can hold for now. For the first time, I feel secure. I speak to my boss and in four short weeks, I am officially unemployed. Mr. O approved my vacation time and will have a check issued; he also allowed the emergency leave time to continue. He thanks me repeatedly for nearly four decades of service and we reminisce about me being one of his first employees. He thinks it is time I use his first name and honors me with such kind words. I guess meeting Brad on a rant brought him up to date on my private life.

My Social Security automatic deposit is set to start today on my birthday. Jules should have been a financial planner. She gets on task and stays there. I finally realize how crippling and time-consuming over-thinking each step is. She finally agreed about the train and in three days, I will be in Omaha to see Madeline. I have a need to see the country and we agree it is also a stalling tactic. I can identify my shortcomings as I take these necessary steps.

Tomorrow, we go shopping, so I can show up with gifts. I don't know if an 87-year-old woman needs diamond earrings or not, but she is getting something wonderful and glittery. I haven't seen her or Mr. Ed since Andrew's birth. Julie thinks I should set up a fruit of the month, so maybe both. However, right now, I need to lie down for a few minutes before dinner.

I missed dinner, sleeping straight through the night, and woke up still enthusiastic and finally rested. Trying to be quiet while everyone else in the house sleeps, I dress and creep into the kitchen. I settle at the breakfast bar for a couple of cups of tea and a muffin while looking through the folder.

After adapting to the time difference in Nebraska, I dial my cell phone. I'm happy when she answers, "Hi Madeline, it's me, Libby. I wanted to call and confirm my visit.It is. Great. I bought a train ticket and will be there in three days. I need your home address, so I can find you once I arrive. I will call before I come over. No ma'am, you don't have to pick me up, I'll come to you. See you soon."

Well, I am on my way, and find it scarier than leaving Brad. With that move, I had nothing to lose. Now I have everything to gain. There is a strength building with the decision to tackle my greatest regret. I put aside the fear that Andrew hates me and acknowledge the possibility I never existed to one of my two living relatives. Omaha, here I come, with a two-day ride, I will go back forty-eight years. I pick up the folder Julie has left on the counter with my name on it. Inside is an Amtrak ticket, rental car and hotel reservations, all purchased online. I love the Internet. I wish Julie were coming, but I know that this is my journey. I must face it and handle whatever comes next. I appreciate everything she has done, but this is so deeply personal I must go alone.

On some level, I know this trip is necessary for me to become whole. It would be wonderful to have a pushy, get the job done kind of fairy godmother with me, but she would have to return to her life, and I would have merely delayed my stepping up to responsibility and healing. I smile in the knowledge that I will return a hundred times to sleep in this welcoming home.

# − 24 −

Julie and Tom insisted on driving me to Washington DC to avoid the first connection. They are going to go sightseeing and stay for a couple of days. I am dumbstruck by the buildings I have only seen in photos or on money. The city is surreal as I add DC to my to-do and see list. Awash in history, the stories come alive while we push through this commanding city. It is still early, and Tom drives us past the Mall and the White House. When we arrive at the Amtrak station, I still have time before boarding. My friends continue to chatter, but I'm numb to the next leg of my journey. Every breath is conscious as I calm my pounding heart.

Anxiously, I wait as Julie and Tom continue to chatter about dinner and the Smithsonian. I hear their words, but I can't put together sentences. Tom checks my two bags, and it is finally time to leave. I hug them both with tears and sincere gratitude for what they have gone through for me. I'm relieved to board as I again take charge of my destiny. The afternoon light fills the windows and I soak in the warmth. There is no one in the seat next to me, so I use it to set up my carry-on and laptop. I tilt back the seat only slightly and gaze out the window, soaking in the noise of the other passengers settling in for the long ride.

I am pleasantly surprised at the splendor of the northeast. There are the expected factories, but there are also farms and incredible colors rushing past the window. I have brought new eyes to this journey as I cross half the country. I become an enthusiastic child seeing the world for the first time. My experience was all in the Midwest, and the diversity and size of this country stuns me. The long afternoon hours slip past as I watch patches of other lives. Admiring homes and choices of people, I will never know as they speed past my window. I bask in the wonder of the infinite possibilities. I try to store the sight of the Blue Ridge Mountains to revisit any time I need them. My choice to sit next to the dining car is a mixed blessing, but there is regular activity and people to watch. I look into the bag of treats Julie packed and munch on some grapes as I appreciate the country where I was born. It seems to have the best of everything. The mountains and forests leave me breathless. I have so much to see, and cheerfully work on my to-do list that has been forming in my enthusiasm. I am thrilled to choose where I will go after this. I write down Yellowstone, DC, the Rockies, both oceans, Florida and my itinerary grows. I have so much to do and see before I set down roots. This seat serves as all of the home I need for now. I notice that I nested near the emergency escape exits on both the bus and the train. I smile at the irony and know that I will probably never have to use them, but a quick getaway offers a sense of wellbeing.

This trip has shot me from the cannon, and I refuse to worry about where I will land. In error, I had thought the hours would spread out and give me time to wrap my mind around the magnitude of the expedition. As darkness envelopes the car, it slowly quiets into the regular rhythm of the sleeping passengers. I realize over forty years of obsessing exaggerates the tension. Secrets prepared me for nothing; all the suppressed emotions demand attention. The insecurities return to nag: I stalled too long, he won't want to meet me, or he wishes to meet me to express his hate. My mind bounces back and forth with numerous scenarios. I work to calm the damn conversation in my head. Wasn't I going to leave that frightened voice in the bus station? Thinking is too intimidating; I click on the overhead light to read and hopefully to build some positivity.

I nap, worry and read as the night passes. Watching my reflection on the window, I can't help but see the child, the girl and the young woman who have all become me. We four meld together and I know I would never have gotten here without them. I slip into the warmth of childhood memories of watching my reflection from the back seat as my parents sing folk songs on our way to Michigan for a rare vacation. Like tonight, my sleep is elusive with the excitement of the new adventure.

I keep my face away from the window as we stop in Indianapolis. I know he wouldn't be watching trains, but I want to avoid looking at the familiar land of my past. After an hour at the station, a young man takes the seat next to me and nods hello with a tight smile. He immediately focuses on a cell phone and a variety of games. I discover comfort with each rhythmic clack of the track taking me closer to Madeline and my Andrew. More miles pass, and I begin to see the magnificence of the heartland that I had taken for granted.

I awaken to the slowing train, as the man next to me rolls over onto my seat, cuddling to my side with a slight mumble. I don't have the nerve to move him away. I have to admit the human contact with this man/boy motivates my maternal instincts, and I develop a desire to protect him. As I bury the inappropriate urge, I try to make myself smaller and withdraw toward the window. He has been quiet, and I can only imagine the embarrassment he may awaken to. I smile and remember my youth filled with hopes and dreams, all of the incredible possibilities.

He awakens and excuses himself to the restroom. Once back, he speaks for the first time "Almost to Chicago, is that where you are going?"

We enter into a brief, very polite conversation, about his attending Northwestern and plans for his future. I listen and encourage finally offering him a half of my turkey sandwich. We eat the snack, returning to quiet. We are in Illinois and I steel myself to the train change; it is one-step at a time. Breathe. Gather my belongings. And off the train. I collect my suitcases from the loading area and move to the final train, the California Zephyr.

The name takes my imagination to the 1930s, and I am a femme fatale traveling with secrets and danger.

This train makes frequent stops, and I venture into the station for a bathroom that does not move and decide to leave behind my finished books. The first one is in Galesburg, Illinois and the second in Ottumwa, Iowa. I wrote a note in each to enjoy and pass it on. I hope that the books each have their own adventure and end up on someone's shelf with a long story of adventure the owner couldn't imagine.

# — 25 —

Omaha, finally. It is too late to call anyone, so I gather my luggage, pick up my rental car and find the hotel. I was worried about finding my way around this unknown city, but the rental employees gave me directions and then programmed the address in the GPS.

Once I settle into my single room with two beds, I savor a long overdue shower that also steams my good outfit. I set up the second bed with my cases and belongings, which is much nicer than keeping them on the floor. I try to nap, but my nervousness causes me to keep an eye on the clock, slowing down time. Eventually, I doze which makes it possible for daybreak to arrive and I can take the next step.

"Good morning, Madeline. I hope this isn't too early to call. Oh good, do you have some time today that we can get together? No, I have a rental car. I'll come to you, any place you want. Okay, that would be perfect, I would love to buy you lunch. Great, see you there at one thirty."

OK, Libby, you are doing this. Don't over-think, you have hours to get ready. I check Julie's treat bag one last time, and there is a note of encouragement wrapped with a muffin. I am touched as I tear open the packaging for the sugary breakfast. It should hold me until lunch. I dress in my new outfit and apply makeup. I want Madeline to like me and to make my mother proud with a good impression. It is a beautiful summer day, which is a good sign.

I begin to worry about a map and remember the GPS; all I need is an address. With my computer, it took less than a minute to get, a map and directions to Applebee's. I write down the address for my GPS feeling smug and very modern. Confident in the knowledge there is no making up for lost time and the past is the past. Real changes are in front of me, right now. I will face each of the upcoming days one hour at a time. Once I have the address I need, I search the internet for a bookstore. That is always a good decision. Okay, I just have to remember, the sun is out, and that is my positive sign.

# — 26 —

Not wanting Madeline to wait for me, I arrive at Applebee's a little early. After I tell the host who I'm expecting, I settle into a booth. My first thought was damn I could use a drink, but iced tea will have to do. That would be the perfect plan, start out with a buzz: *How to impress people in one easy lesson, show up with liquor on your breath.* I am nervous, but I know I can probably outrun her. She is in her late 80s and I'm only in my mid-60s, so I have an edge. Damn, Libby, shut up. Are you planning to fight this woman? She is Mom's best friend. She is the safest person to meet in the entire world. In fact, I think I see her. I'm stunned by how fantastic she looks and decide it is questionable if I could outrun her. She has changed, but only around the edges. I still know her warm face and sparkling eyes.

"Madeline, over here!" I can't stop myself; I have to go to her and wrap her in my arms, holding her close. This woman saved my life, took me in when I was in trouble, and I have forgotten how much I love her. "Madeline, you look fabulous, I would know you anywhere."

"Libby, my dear, you have changed since you were sixteen."

"You are right there; I was just a garland, now I'm an old broad." Thank goodness, it is still easy to be with her as the years dissolve.

"You silly girl, you are still slim and sassy."

"Well, slim is so much better than skinny." My favorite way to defuse any situation is an inappropriate comment. "How are you doing and Mr. Ed too?"

"I knew it was you on the phone; no one else ever called him Mr. Ed. Kids today don't get the joke. I'm doing just fine, a little trouble with my eyes, but I've stayed healthy. Now for Ed, he has been in a nursing home for a couple of years. He has the sixth stage Alzheimer's and it has been slow moving. He is in the last phases of the disease and hasn't been lucid for a while. I spend every day with him. When he is coherent, he flirts with me, no telling from day to day who I might be. I pray he knows how much I love him."

"I am so sorry. You two always seemed so perfect." My heart breaks; they were my idea of happily ever after.

"Honey, with the passage of years, things change and remains the same. We had some hard times too. How are you? I'm so glad that you left that asshole."

"Madeline! Language, missy. You are right, though. I dedicated so much of myself to someone who didn't appreciate me."

"Oh, he loved you as best he could, just not the way you deserved. He wouldn't have kept you around if there were nothing there. Don't put yourself down. You have made an honorable life considering the beginning."

After we order, Madeline looks sadly at me. "I miss your mother so much." I can see the emotion flood her eyes.

"I do too, Madeline; I do. I know you may think I'm crazy. I went to a bookstore in Hot Springs and a psychic let me talk to her. I didn't know I was a believer until then."

Madeline looks pensive and answers, "One thing I have learned in this long life I am blessed with, is there are things we know that are wrong and things we don't know that are right. I might have thought you were crazy years ago, but no more. Too many unexplainable things have happened and with Ed's disease, I have opened to all kinds of possibilities. Did the piesick tell you how Anita is doing?"

"That is psychic, and she is with Dad and seemed to be as happy as I have ever heard from her. She pushed me to follow up with you."

"Libby, your mother was a wise woman; she only ever wanted the best for you."

"I know, I know. I feel I have disappointed her in many ways. Ever since I told her about the pregnancy, I felt like a failure. I questioned that decision since it happened, and on many levels, I wanted to change my choices for a long time."

"You made the right decision, honey. A cousin in my family has raised him. I've been able to see him grow into a good man."

"That is wonderful news. I was so afraid that he was just out there with strangers and no one to watch over him."

We both pick at the food we ordered. The server removes the plates and packages the leftovers.

"Libby, your momma followed with Andrew and the family since he was born. I know she never told you. Your mother came out to see him a couple of times. He knew her as a great aunt, although it has been years since she could come."

"What, I didn't know that. She never said anything to me." I have no jokes now; I can't help but let tears flow and ruin my amateur makeup application. I am relieved, a little angry and happy at the same time. "I wish she would have told me. I knew nothing about the adoption."

"Your mom thought it was best, to give you a chance at the life you deserved. Do you think your mother would let her grandson slip away? Let me take care of this and we will get out of here."

"Madeline, I'm paying, and there is no question. I invited you, and you have been so kind as to meet me. I could buy you food for a thousand years and never repay you."

"From what I see, you have paid for a long time, Libby Lou."

Thank you for everything, it helps me get my balance and pull myself together. I understand Mom's friendship with her; she is open, listens and doesn't seem to judge harshly.

"Madeline, if you are not busy I would like it if we could go over and see Mr. Ed for a couple of minutes."

"Honey that is where I am off to after lunch. That thrills me that you would do that; don't be disappointed if he doesn't know you."

"I don't care if he knows me or not, I know him and I want to see him. I love Mr. Ed."

"Ed always loved you too; he thought you were a great kid, with all kinds of promise. He will know on some level that it is you."

"That's right Madeline; I'm a sixty-five-year-old girl. At least this way, he won't know how I've thrown my life away."

"Silly girl, you haven't thrown anything away, and you still have years ahead of you, so don't talk like that in front of me."

# — 27 —

I thought it would be sad to see Mr. Ed, but his eyes light up when I walked in. He smiles when I call him Mr. Ed. He is frail, and his eyes appear innocent. I pray he has no pain. A lifetime of memories must reside in his head; he reaches for me as I stand next to his bed. Madeline and I sit in his room and continue with a hushed idle chatter. I decide not to give him the box of cigars I brought, but Madeline says they would please him. "Don't worry, honey; the nurses would not let him have a fire." When we open the box for him, he makes happy sounds. He takes one out and lifts it to his nose, and we watch memories flood his eyes.

I plan to see him again. It feels necessary and the least I can do. I'll bring a book he might like next time, and I will read to him. We leave quietly, and I follow her home.

I won't worry about dinner tonight. With lunch and Madeline's snacks, I may not eat again for days. She loved her emerald earrings I brought for her. She deserves beautiful things.

The day races past, just like the years since I was here last. Tonight I look forward to sleep and feel satisfied that I'm doing what needs to be done. I turn on the TV and watch the news and an entertainment program. The noise is aggravating, so I turn it off.

It is still early, but I won't be out anymore today, so I slip into my pajama pants and t-shirt, glad to remove all elastic bindings. It is seven o'clock when I settle into bed with a book and my phone. Now that I'm comfortable and cozy, I punch in Julie's phone number. After five rings, I know she is busy and leave a brief message. They are probably out for the evening; she had mentioned wanting to see a movie.

I want to be up early to explore Omaha before I meet with Madeline again. I am going to buy a camera and a journal to keep all of the information. I think about the times I thought about journaling but was too lazy. I have no more excuses; this is my time to do all the things I imagined. I can feel the comfort of my mother's presence.

Madeline has promised more information about Andrew, and she will search for some pictures. I have a strange feeling of peace now that I know Andrew has been in her family. If the cousin is anything like these two people, I know it was a good life. I yearn for some pictures and wonder if that will satisfy my craving. I know it doesn't matter what he decides. I am glad I came.

Lost in my musings, I start to drift off when the phone rings. I almost don't hear the muted song from under the blanket.

"What do you want now, crazy woman?"

"Elizabeth, its Brad. I'm so glad to reach you. Where are you? I miss you, just tell me where you are, and I will come and get you. I need you at home."

"Brad?"

# — 28 —

"Yes. I've been calling, and you didn't answer. Are you all right? Where are you?"

"I didn't expect to hear from you." Damn, I can hear a quiver in my voice. I want to sound confident. I don't want him to think there is any chance I will return.

"Why is that? Of course, you would hear from me. I'm your husband. I have a right to know where you are. I am coming to pick you up and bring you home. You belong here; I need you."

"I'm sorry, Brad, I am not coming back. You need to make other arrangements and don't call me anymore."

"I asked before, and I'm only going to ask one more time. Where are you? Elizz..."

I hang up and wish there was a slam app for a cell phone. *Oh, my dear God, help me, I need Julie, and I need her now.* The phone rings again, and I don't answer. I know how he works, I have to calm down, I am confident he can't track me. I still have an Arkansas area code. Even if he could, it wouldn't be tonight, and then I begin to anger over his stealing my peace.

Even though it is late, I call Julie and get her voice mail. "Brad called, and I'm going to shut off the phone until morning." The timing for her to be out with her husband is less than perfect. The receiver beeps and I click to answer.

"Julie, I didn't even get a chance to shut off the phone, I was leaving you a message. Thank God, you called. I'm sorry, I'm quite upset, and there is so much to tell you."

"Lizard, calm down. Is it about Andrew? Is he OK?

"Yes – no, it isn't all about Andrew. Brad called."

"Don't worry about Brad; he was going to talk to you at some point. What did he say?"

"He sounded so sad at first, and then I could hear the undertone of anger in his voice. He probably had been drinking, and I know how the dance goes. He wanted to know where I am and wants to come for me. I just kept ignoring his questions about my location."

"Good for you. What did you tell him?"

"Nothing, I hung up after only a couple moments. But he said he would find me."

"Perfect, just keep hanging up. You know this isn't a television show. You have a phone from Hot Springs, Arkansas, and you are in Nebraska. All he has is that number, and there is no permanent address. Even if you had an address, there are a thousand more places to hide."

"I'm starting to feel better; you are right. I had used my home address in Kokomo to get the phone, so he doesn't even have the hotel in Hot Springs, I've been several places since then, and I still don't have a forwarding address."

"Liz. Use my address if you need one, I will forward your mail wherever you are. I'm cool with that."

Julie brought sense into my panic. I have to get him off my mind. Andrew is so much more important. "I do have a P.O. Box, but that is back home, I can do a change of address."

"Now tell me about Andrew. Did you see Madeline yet?"

It felt great sharing the day with Julie, just talking about it helped me wrap my mind around everything that is happening. We have set seven PM, Eastern Time for me to call her tomorrow, so I don't have to risk leaving the phone on. I can't have Brad calling me I have to maintain control. I know there is no way he could find me; he can spend his time searching Arkansas. I have no close connections back home, and my only family is my aunt in Illinois that I hardly know. I don't even have her phone number. He would never find anyone that knows where I am. There is no connection to Omaha he could know. I don't think he will waste much of his precious time looking. Now the droning of the television quiets my mind, and I welcome sleep.

# — 29 —

Amazing how much I think about eating and sleeping now that I don't have to take care of someone else. When I do sleep, there are so many crazy dreams that make little sense, like a bad movie channel. Glad Dr. Jung isn't here to give me a diagnosis. I make a conscious decision worry less about any meanings. I'm sure they are trying to tell me something. For now, I will just accept the dreams as cleaning my karmic house. I'm no longer afraid of the monster in the closet. After a long hot shower and clean clothes, it is time to hit the brochures in the lobby. I pick up a newspaper, get some breakfast, more cash and buy a couple of notebooks. One journal for my search for Andrew and the other I'll write out some of the dreams. I don't have to be at Madeline's until two-thirty, so plenty of time to explore Omaha.

I am pleased how being alone has ignited a newfound sense of exploration. I am part of an amazing world, and I regret living so small. The people I met have been helpful, and no one has tried to rob or abuse me since I left Kokomo. Not every stranger is a crook, another thing that Brad had wrong. Next time, I will choose my guru much more carefully. Yup!

I drive around to some of the sites on the brochures, checking out Joslyn Castle, Old Market,

Zoo, several museums and Fort Omaha. I spot a little café, have lunch and begin my list making in one of the new notebooks in earnest. Thrilled and nicely distracted, I make plans for more exploration. Thumbing through the brochures, I find a senior tour and decide to take Madeline. With newfound energy, I start for Madeline's and stop at a little neighborhood grocery for some snacks to take with me.

# — 30 —

Once I arrive, she meets me at the door. She has on her new earrings, which pleases me. They make her green eyes sparkle. "Hi Madeline, how is Mr. Ed today?"

"He is doing great; he was very present. We had a long conversation, and he had a great idea."

"He did? That is fantastic."

"Now, Honey, come on into the kitchen and sit down. Would you like some iced tea?

We enter the kitchen and sit at a simple round table. There is a feeling of comfort seeing the out-of-date appliances and evidence of feeding one family for decades. Their home hasn't changed much since I was here before.

"He decided that you should have his car."

I'm shocked and can barely respond. The idea just stalls in my brain. "Now Maddie, not to be rude, but how could he decide this? I couldn't accept something like that. It is too much and how would you get around?"

"Honey, I don't drive much, and I have my own car. I wouldn't use that beast and he certainly won't drive it again. It has been in the garage for, let me see, going on nine or ten years."

"But Madeline, how about your kids, don't they want it?"

"Wait until you see it, Libby, you will understand why they don't want it. They always called it the T-Beast. He thought it would be an investment as a collectible car, probably one of the only uncollectable T-Birds ever. When you see it, you will understand so much about Daddy's financial strategies. I called the garage, and they picked it up, to get it running."

"I don't know how to thank you. You don't have to do this for me; I don't deserve it."

"Libby, just stop. You deserve a lot; it is about time you learned to say thank you and let Ed do this for you. You know you need it."

I can hardly contain myself, such a kind thing to do and so unexpected. "I'll gladly pay."

"Honey, it is a 1982 T-Bird, an automotive monster. Its top value was when he drove it off the lot. It solves one of the issues I was going to face. The shop will call when it is ready to go."

"I don't know how to thank you. If it is as big as you say, I can live in it and continue to travel, the best of both worlds."

Madeline still sounds mysterious but looks so proud of herself she almost glows. I notice how slowly she moves as she brings two glasses of tea. "Libby, I couldn't get our lunch out of my mind. I dreamed about your grandmother last night. At first, I thought it was you, so familiar even though I had not seen her since I was a first married. Then it dawned on me you look just like her. She was a resilient woman, and you are proving you inherited most of her qualities."

"My grandmother, I never got to know her. They lived so far away, and I was young when she died. Mom often talked about her; it was generally how Nana wouldn't put up with my foolishness. Everyone deferred to her; she was quietly in charge."

"Oh, your mother, I miss her so; she was part of my life since we were born. We were together every day until I married Ed. She was one of the best people I have ever known."

A great pride wells up with the love of my little mother. "That is so delightful to hear. I miss her too and then Dad died six weeks after Mom. That was a tough year, and yet it helped motivate me to leave. I didn't want them to be ashamed of me any longer. They seemed to have lived in love, and I am envious."

"Libby, Libby, Libby. Your mom also had secrets, and we kept them for decades. Your dad was a good man, and she was happy living in his shadow. I am pleased to see you break a cycle. She was so smart and capable, and she pushed her plans aside to take care of you and your father."

"I never thought about the possibility. She seemed satisfied and was always just my mom."

"Honey, she was happy being your mother, but she was like every human. She had aspirations." Madeline's eyes light up with that gleam of treasured memories; she pauses fingering the moisture on her glass. "Yes, your mother, my dearest friend, always wanted to be a teacher."

"I wanted to be a teacher, and she did too? She drove a school bus for years; I should have guessed."

"Anita loved education and kids. She wanted to be surrounded by children. With the war, her education stopped. Everyone had to work. Then when she had you, she was lucky to survive. She couldn't have more children after that. She was never ashamed of you and thought you were perfect. You are so beautiful and smart; she moved her dreams to you. She worked for you to receive every opportunity to be your best self."

I feel devastated; I have failed my mother and myself. "I had to be a disappointment to her."

Warming our almost untouched tea, Madeline reaches over and pats my hand. "Not one moment was she disappointed in you. Your mother was a brilliant woman, and she understood how life changes everything. She bragged when you took classes and often talked about your job and how you were the sole cause of the success of the business."

"I see so much of her in you, as well as your grandmother. You are a perfect blend, just in case you didn't notice it."

I begin to cry with no control to stop. "I was their only child, they gave me everything they could and then I throw it all away on someone who isn't worth a flying damn."

"Now, now, Libby. Stop it. Your husband loved you in his own broken way, and you would be surprised how many people in this world care. You have survived; your momma hated that man, and I know he was mean to you. You will be surprised how many years are left, and you will have more stories to live. I was impressed when you were here before and, as young as you were, the focus was what was best for the baby. You had a certain maturity beyond your years. I know I haven't seen you in decades, but your momma told me how you volunteered and worked to make a good home. The trip you are on now is beautiful. I thought all night about what you have told me. It takes incredible courage to come back here to find your son."

There is a knock at the door.

Thank goodness for this reprieve. I am again overwhelmed. I don't know what I feel. Madeline and Julie encourage me, and it is hard to accept. I know I walked away from my baby and never told his father. I need time to fix my melted makeup and let things soak in. It has been almost fifty years since I was here before and that is comforting. Best of all, I remember where the bathroom is. After all the years, I am still a sixteen-year-old girl in trouble. I know my biggest mistake wasn't having the baby; it was waiting so long to find him. Madeline acts as if it is no big deal, but it is huge. I have spent my life hoping to make up for the night at the drive-in and burying myself in shame.

I can hear her speaking to someone, and it sounds like a man. It's probably the guy with the car. I can hear them from the bathroom enter the kitchen; I splash cool water on my face and reapply mascara.

# — 31 —

"Libby, are you here? I have someone for you to meet."

"Yes ma'am, I'm in the bathroom." Oh my lord, I have to pull myself together; I should pay the garage for the work on the car. I'll just stay in the dark corners, so they can't see what a wreck I am. A couple of deep breaths and here I go.

"Libby, this is John Scortino. He is married to my cousin Lorene. He has driven over from Council Bluffs to meet you."

I look at a dark, older, compact man, a little bent over with dark brown, dancing eyes. He is in a suit, and I'm sure he isn't the mechanic. "How do you do? It is very pleased to meet you."

"John and Lorene adopted Andrew." Madeline's eyes are sparkling, and her smile fills her face.

Where did the hours go? I am back in the motel room, and it is still a blur. The last clear memory was when Madeline introduced me to John. We sat and talked for hours. He is a lovely man, intelligent and well spoken. Most important, he dearly loves his wife and children. I rest assured that I did the right thing.

We all laughed as John told me how Andrew learned about the adoption since he was a teen. He said that when Andrew hit a growth spurt and grew to over 6 foot tall, blonde while living in a family of five-foot dark Italians. He shared cherished photos of Andrew's childhood. I'm stunned how handsome and happy Andrew appeared. About this age, he announced that he was adopted, and that is why he is different. They never tried to deceive him, and he has known since then. John and Lorene were also foster parents and later adopted two girls from Korea making a home full of children. John described them as a blended family. They never had much information about me, just that I was young and in trouble. They knew my mother, and she kept in touch and sent a birthday card with $3 and a stick of gum every year. John thanked me for sharing my son with them. He said that getting Andrew was the beginning of the busy, noisy lives they had visualized.

John promised to call Andrew and provide my contact information. We all agreed with my plan to leave any meeting up to him. He bragged about how Andrew is a high school teacher and a soccer coach in Boulder, Colorado. I mention it took three generations for my family to produce a teacher. My eyes drank in his childhood image, and they ache to just to see his face. John brought me up to date when he added, "Our boy is married with three children. He has two boys, twenty and seventeen and there is a little girl, Lilly, two and a half years old with his second wife." I lost some of his words with the realization that I might be considered a grandmother.

John kindly avoided asking about my life. He never probed the question about who the father could have been. I am confident I can live the rest of my life with the joy of this afternoon, but on another level, I yearn to see Andrew just one time.

I sit in my hotel room with carry out pizza, and I calmly replay the afternoon. Right now, I am happy and secure I made the right choice. He had a family of good people, and I send out more gratitude.

I took photos with my phone of the pictures that John had and emailed them to Julie. I have to call her at seven. Tomorrow I pick up a new 1982 Thunderbeast, and I am a giant step closer to seeing my son.

I can't remember ever feeling so alive; this day opened many possibilities. My mind is just roaring with excitement, but for now a long, very hot shower.

# — 32 —

I slept ten hours, which is outrageous. I've lived on six to seven hours a night for most of my life. Then again, all my old sleep habits have taken a hit since I left. I don't have to get up to make breakfast, clean the kitchen and rush to work. I realize how busy, yet empty, my life has been. I've been alone for a long time, working two jobs, one for pay and one for shelter. If it wasn't for years of plotting an escape, I had nothing other than the thought of my son. I don't remember what love was all about; life became an empty day-to-day thumping, almost as if I was merely waiting for death. Today I wake up full of love, and I recognize what I have missed.

I was right to leave. I will never go back to that existence, but why do I feel the need to call Brad to inform him about our boy? I can't disclose where I am, or why. I have maintained the secret of Andrew for so long; I'm afraid to expose him. However, it is no longer an option. Oh, my great auntie's panties! I know I would hate me for taking forty-eight years to tell the truth. I allow the shame to boil to the surface and decide that this is the last time. I will never know all of the different possibilities and need to accept what happens. It is outside of my control and obsessing over the worst case has no value.

At some point, I will settle down and find a home and maybe a job or something to do with my days. Hell, I have the tendency to face one issue at a time with the damn list-making habit.

I still want to call Brad, which means I need to call Julie instead, I decide to try and shut down the internal dialogue and just call.

"Talk me down, girlfriend. I want to call Brad, Jules. I feel this burning need to tell him everything. I have kept his son hidden for so long and doesn't Brad have a right to know?"

"Hell no, Liz, he has no rights. Think now, how would he react? He is mad enough, and then you add this. You would have to give him a location for Andrew, and then, he would track you down and beat the fear of the devil into you. This man sent you running and hiding from the start. He has beaten you, degraded you and cheated. You cannot make contact with him until you have wrestled your insecurities to the ground. That man wasn't your partner; he was your jailer."

"I hate it when you are right."

I turned the television on to fill the room with chatter. There is no changing what happened in 48 years ago, nothing that can change it. He is a mature man, and he will opt for what is best for him at this time.

Instead of preparing a catalog of conflicting thoughts that are outside of my control, I unplug my telephone and confirm the ringer is on. Everything is in motion, and my job is to wait. If he does meet with me, I vow to answer all of his questions. If he wants to talk to Brad, I will give him the information. He doesn't need my protection; he is not a child. No longer planning on the day after tomorrow, I leave for a day of action, breakfast and the Lewis and Clark museum.

As I wait for my oatmeal, I think of Julie pressing for a home decision. I smile replaying her dialogue. *New Jersey. What are you going to do with Elizabeth? New Jersey. I thought about you yesterday, and there are some nice places if you don't want to live with me. New Jersey. They have some volunteer spots at the hospital or find something else to do. You have a good twenty years left in you and don't you think it is the time you became what you wanted?*

I have been defined by my reflection my whole life, as the weight of sixty-five years bears down on my shoulders. After a brief emotional stumble, I shake off the insecurity. I finally look to myself for encouragement and strength. I am free and in control.

At the landing, I consider the audacity of Lewis and Clark to take on such a journey. The sun shines on my face as I look over the river and wonder what they saw standing in the same place. I walk around the park lost in a time travel adventure, camping, hauling and hunting. I commune with Merriweather about the changes in the country since he was here. I don't hear his answer, so I continue to listen and wander caught up in the magnitude and pure insanity of a trip to the Pacific Ocean by canoe, on foot and clueless. Slowly returning to my own time, I snap a couple of photos, and I apologize to the explorers for some of the abuses of progress. I had been anxious about sightseeing alone, but it is easy, and I like it. The luxury of lingering over exhibits, meandering through history, moving at my own rate and spending in the gift shop all new experiences. I would have never been able to visit this park in my past life, as Brad would have no interest. I buy a book by Stephen Ambrose called *Undaunted Courage*, confident Mr. Ed would like it to read to him.

I check my phone and find there are no messages. It is after lunch as I decide to see Mr. Ed. I will spend tomorrow with Madeline, and I recognize the burning necessity to see Andrew. It doesn't matter if he wants to meet me or not. I start a plan, knowing he lives in Boulder. John and Madeline both have my cell phone number, and that will take care of a face-to-face, but the day after tomorrow I will take the T-Beast and go to Boulder.

Once I see him and know he is alive and well, I will make a decision on who I want to be and a place to live. I can't make any permanent choices until I see Andrew. For now, I will not sit in silence repeating the same worries. Then it dawns on me; I ran with pictures, Madeline has more of my mom, dad, and grandparents. I will put together a family history notebook that I can give to Andrew. I refuse to consider the alternative.

"Well, from what you say, you can live in that car. It sounds about the size of a two bedroom condo." Thank goodness for a joke, we both laugh, and I feel myself coming back around.

After an hour with Ed, I rush back to my room. I think I can access my computer at home, if Brad has it turned on. There are more digitized photographs there. I pull out the old picture box from my suitcase. This project is great; I find a couple of pictures from high school and my childhood. Mom and Dad's wedding picture, I also have some ancestor photos that I will copy when I pick up a folder for Andrew.

I will have this ready for when he says yes. I am out of that old life. *Chin up, things to do.*

Spending the evening putting together the book for him and laying out the materials I need to have copied. I type up some labels with names and dates if I know them. He will want to feel his family in his hands. When I come up for air, I discover I'm famished, and it is late. I consider room service, but instead I go to bed hungry.

Just as I climb under the covers, the phone rings. I freeze and then check the number, and it is Julie. "Hello."

"Adoption Anonymous, this is your triple A sponsor."

I laugh. "When did Automobile Club hire battleaxes? I think you mean AA, but either way. I'm glad you called." I spill out about the park and museum and then explain my photo book plan. Not allowing her to answer, I prattle on.

"First thing tomorrow I'm going to the office supply store I found to buy one of those memory stick things that save computer files and a photo binder. I can check out cameras and get things copied."

"Okay, girlfriend, breathe a moment. You don't need a camera. You have been taking photos with your phone. Those stick things are called flash drives; I don't want you asking for a stick thing." I take the conversation back on and chatter on about my project, and she encourages me.

"I also did a little research on Andrew, now that I know his last name, and he works at a high school in Boulder, Colorado."

Julie goes silent. "For someone who waited for most of her life, there is no stopping you now."

Once we hang up, I get out of bed and reboot my computer. I break down and eat a six-dollar bag of peanuts from the mini-bar. I check my Facebook page and see that Brad has been there, no surprise. I am relieved that I haven't visited the page since I left. I am aware of my tendency to say too much; luckily, I haven't even thought about it. I read his message – You are gone; I never believed you would ever leave me. There was one constant in my life, and now you are gone. Please come home. I love you, and I can change.

Interesting. He got four likes.

It is hard not to respond to his post. My first reaction was to type *You couldn't change.* I understand it is best to stay silent; thank goodness, I just spoke to Julie. I don't need to engage him; he is a master at manipulating me. I couldn't resist and change my relationship status and the password. Before I sign off, I unfriend him and enter a new the password. I slip back into bed for a fitful night. My brain is reeling with possibilities.

I'm up at six AM and bring the laptop to bed with me. I try to stall the investigation, but I know I'm going to do it. I read the email newsletter from Golden Leaves, but that only stalls my obsession by a few minutes. I begin at some social media sites. I search Andrew Scortino and don't find anything that I can be sure is him. So I search high schools in Boulder and two schools in, there he is. My heart swells with emotion as I look at his face. I see Brad in his appearance, but he is not a chip off anyone's block. In no time, I have to leave to pick up Madeline for breakfast and tell myself I can search more this evening.

# — 33 —

It has been three days and no word from John. All I can think about is meeting Andrew. I go to more tourist sites and spend time every day with Madeline and Mr. Ed. We have read almost a half of the book. I am enjoying it and hope he is too. Sometimes it appears he isn't in the room; I decided he is traveling with the explorers, and he is meeting Sacajawea. Everything I wanted to do has been checking off the list.

I am so anxious about Andrew; I have become a cyber-stalker. I continue in my wait for John to call. I'm sure he hasn't forgotten, but I don't know how much longer I can wait.

I make what seems to be a reasonable decision. I've gas and the T-beast. I'm going to Boulder.

I explain my plan to Madeline, and she invites me to stay at her home. It is tempting, but I have inhabited someone else's life for too long. She has done so much for me; I already owe her and explain how for the first time I need to stand alone. She understands as we set up an email for her, on one of the oldest unused computers I have ever seen. I promise to stay in touch with a guarantee not to ever slip away again.

I wind my way to the interstate and settle into a comfortable rhythm. The only destination

I have is Boulder, and I hope for some interesting stops between here and there. None of this escape has been what I expected. I justified my inaction with the worry about the unknown, and I was wrong. The unknown is fascinating and often beautiful. I realize that not everyone is honest, but the people that matter have been. I walk out on a baby, a husband, a job and a life; I'm the least honorable person I have met. There will be some harsh judgment to pay, but today I don't have to tell anyone my story. I am the mysterious stranger I wish to be. Now there is a plan to open up some exciting possibilities.

I have lied for so long I am anxious to discover who I can be. Therefore, I resolve a false identity won't help when I didn't have one to start. As my mind continues to build and deconstruct different scenarios, I drive on. Instead of creating a new self, I decide to tell only the truth about this Libby. I won't offer any information, but if asked, I will opt for truth. I am surprised how much I like the quiet time alone; I thought it would be the most difficult part. I have no explanation for it, but I adore the silence, with no expectations. My thoughts and conversations are often redundant, but I'm gaining confidence. I notice the change in my emotions and thoughts from a couple of weeks ago. I am free.

As I drive west on Interstate 80, there is almost no other traffic. Draped in the solitude and rhythm of the road the miles click away. My mind for once is blank. The beast offers the comfort that only a big old American car can offer. The scorching sun beats down as I face hours of a straight highway and scenery consisting of uncountable rows of corn. The vibrant green stretches are beyond my comprehension, only broken by a few farmhouses with dirt driveways. I peek down the rows as they pass organized in an unnatural pattern of human control. I see evidence of life on both sides of the road, and I'm wondering about the generations of choices that provided for life on the plains. My personal angst raises its doubtful head, and the same old questions reverberate "What am I doing?" I push it aside and drive on.

I have labeled myself by relationships, job titles, politics and a few accomplishments. I stop questioning who I am, maybe for a moment and anticipate the days ahead. Instead of the constant questions, I start to put together some answers. I visualize a small home and begin to decorate it with vibrant color. I picture a couch and a chair just for me. I toss away the eternal questions of self and destiny.

Over the years, I recognize how my life has been an internal dialog. Today, I study the metaphor of the highway. My story changes from day to day avoidance to something as straight and level that narrows like an empty road racing to the horizon. I don't know when it will meet the setting sun if it is even possible. I can see my life as a series of stories, usually starring someone else and not a single hero. I mull over the multitude of possibilities spiraling in and out from the interstate, but no exit calls to me. I chose the road most traveled. I have worked hard to fit an image designed and sold to women of the 1950s. I have fashioned myself to be the good girl, the loyal wife, the honest employee. In reality, I have only disappointed myself.

I turn my back on the missed opportunities and the dread that I wasted into a sad older age. Defined by our secrets, our dirty little secrets, I begin to sing. The songs from my childhood filled the car and I realize I'm a walking Woody Guthrie songbook.

Suddenly it dawns on me; the truth is what breaks the rules, and personal honesty leads us to our authentic self. I can't bemoan the wasted decades and understand I can't change them. The sins I committed in haste and confusion didn't go away; they expanded in the dark recesses of my humiliation. I have exaggerated and fed the lies as they linger, poisoning and causing the same destruction as a slow moving cancer.

It is impossible to cut them out, as they have roots that can enslave the heart. From this milepost, I will no longer blame others for the crimes against me. I was complicit in allowing it to go on. I have begun to set the secrets free, and I will leave the guilt and shame at the next rest stop. My salvation is this moment, as my escape becomes a journey.

Damn, I'm starting to sound like the books Julie tells me about. I read enough of the same type over my years I should have earned credentials.

My bladder is my guide, and it is making an 8-hour trip into an adventure. I am learning that the journey isn't the destination, but a means of arrival.

I acknowledge that I'm stalling, but I will savor each day for the small gifts it offers. No more fear, no more lying, just openness and keeping my eyes wide open. It is hot and with the windows down, and the rushing air everything seems full of possibilities. I decide I will allow my mind to visit the past, but my body keeps facing forward. I will eventually throw away the regrets. I am excited about today. This is a risk, but there is nothing to lose. I resist the trap of expectations.

I will see my son. I don't know if I will be lucky enough to meet him, but that doesn't matter. I will not consider the day after that. Right now, it is just to find my son and rest my eyes on him. At least from meeting John, I know Andrew knows I care. I have spent hours rehearsing conversations that seem ridiculous now. I only confuse myself with fantasies and dread. I can't write a script when someone else has the lead.

# — 34 —

My phone, where is it? I hardly recognize the ringing as I float along in my mental reverie.

"Hello, hello."

"Hello, Libby. This is John."

"Hold on, let me pull to the side of the road." I pull off the interstate onto the shoulder. "John, how wonderful to hear your voice. How are you and your bride?"

"We are both just fine. I'm sorry it took me so long to get back to you. Andy was out of town for some coaching thing and just got back. He sounded like he has been expecting to hear from you."

"I feel terrible that didn't come years ago."

"Libby, don't you worry. He has called, and I told him about meeting you and the time we spent together. He wanted to know what you looked like and what kind of person you are. He has asked for some time to think about everything. I have tried to give him the little bit of the history that we talked about and what I thought about you."

"Yikes, John, you weren't honest, were you?" I answer.

"I was honest, very honest. I like you, and he would like you too."

"Andrew was a lucky man to have you two in his life. I would love to meet your wife sometime."

"Lorene was broken-hearted she missed the visit and wanted to get together soon if you have the time. Lorene trusts me and agrees wholeheartedly with your plan. Andy is a bright man, and he will make the right choice. It may take a while he is so busy with coaching and his family."

"I'll make a point of visiting you two. I'm indebted to you."

"Did I give you my email address? I want to be sure you have every way to reach me when he decides."

"Yes, I have all of your information. I hope it is alright – I gave Andrew your number and email?" John sounds sheepish.

"Oh, that is perfectly fine. You can give him everything I own. I'm so pleased that you have done this for me." I can feel the emotion starting to pour from my eyes.

"We weren't clear about this when we met, but I hoped you would be OK with that. I will do anything for my son, and I hope that you keep us in mind."

"I will never forget, John. You and Lorene did what I couldn't and 'thank you' feels so inadequate."

John sighs. "Libby, you gave us the life we wanted by sharing the son we couldn't have. There is no debt there we owe you for one of the greatest joys of our lives. Don't get me wrong, he has been a challenge but every day it was worth it. I wouldn't trade it."

"I have to go now, good luck, and we hope to see you soon. You are right; the thank you does feel like an inadequate gesture, but thank you."

I sit for a while on the side of the highway. There is not much traffic, and I need to get out of the car. I pull into the Colorado Welcome Center near the interchange of 80 and 76. There aren't many vehicles in the large parking lot so I can park close to the entrance. I sit at a picnic table for a few minutes as I regain my sea legs. I am surprised how weak I feel. There is no place for dinner, but I don't think I could eat. I walk into the center. They offer free coffee and have a smorgasbord of vending machines. The volunteers are closing down, and they give me one of the last cups of coffee. Not ready to leave yet, I walk around aimlessly sipping the bitter brew; I can almost taste the bottom of the pot. There are racks of brochures, and I feel stunned by the incredible history of the area. Realizing how much has been built on brutality and the only evidence is a historical marker and a brochure. I gather several booklets for future research and recovering my clarity, I buy a candy bar and a bag of chips. I am confident I am on the right path.

# — 35 —

It took me ten hours to reach Boulder. It is a lovely city, but I can feel the elevation, and my breathing is labored. As I drive through town, I stumble across the University. I like watching the young people walking around swaddled in promise. I search for a motel nearby.

The view of the mountains in the distance and the campus nearby is so new to my eyes. It feels like the opposite of Hot Springs, but still perfect. Then again, I didn't know Boulder was such a large, vibrant city, at least twice the size of Kokomo. Life is certainly more exciting and challenging than it was a month ago. Difficult to believe in such a short time I have adventures to journal about and an entirely new life. Thinking of the items I have to document I consider Brad and the postcard I could send him. *Dear Brad, I'm having the time of my life. I have seen parts of Arkansas, New Jersey, Nebraska and now Colorado. Having a wonderful time, glad you aren't here.*

Finally hungry, I spot a Denny's Restaurant for a quick dinner and check into the motel next door. Going to bed early, I am gifted with a good night sleep full of the familiar dreams of my childhood. Even though it is a new place, my constant apprehension has dissipated.

Waking up early this morning, I lay in bed listening to the television news. After an hour, maybe a little more, I pull myself together and think about the breakfast special at Denny's. Today will allow for exploration. I consider buying a GPS for the beast, knowing how helpful it was in the rental car. I write down the address of the motel, to avoid any embarrassing problems. Then I remember exactly how frugal I can be; I plan on a GPS, but will pick up a free map at a gas station. Hot Springs was easy to move around in, but this is a larger city.

Dressed and ready to explore, I start to leave my room. Oh, fantastic, they deliver a newspaper to the room, and there is a free breakfast in the lobby. I cancel the restaurant plan and find a little table adjacent to the lobby. I put the batter into the hot waffle iron and check out the brochures. I have a quiet chuckle remembering how nervous I was the first breakfast on the road, and now I'm comfortable sitting alone with a book and the paper.

Having no schedule, I bask in the sweet smell of waffles and coffee enjoying the morning. There are families and couples wandering into the breakfast room. The children show the excitement over all of the choices, and I enjoy watching them put together their perfect meal. The adults are mostly after coffee and the specials. I appreciate the luxury of no plans.

I like where I have settled, most everything I could want is within walking distance. I prefer local diners and try to avoid the big chain restaurants. The food seems authentic and not a formula menu planned at a corporate office and shipped in by a fleet of refrigerator trucks. Sorry, Denny's.

I feel sophisticated and worldly, such as it is. Boldly, I leave my room, talk to people and explore new places. It is easier than I ever dreamed. From my favorite information source in the lobby, I join in for the Banjo Billy bus tours. After I leave the bus, I consider the walking tour of Boulder on Friday. As long as I stay busy, I'm not waiting.

A significant benefit of staying in a nicer motel, besides the higher price, they have events and a bar. This weekend there is a Psychic Fair and Jewelry show. A couple of weeks ago, I would never have gone to a Psychic Fair, but after Hot Springs, I'm ready to check it out.

Knowing Andrew has received my message, I open up to the world around me. The age-old pressure is inching away. After decades of guilt and hiding, I am stepping from the shadows. Glad I have the journal, I am filling the pages with new discoveries.

# — 36 —

"Hey Jules, sorry I missed you. It is Friday morning, 9:30 or so. I'll check back tonight or tomorrow. I am going to the Mystical Winds fair at the motel. It starts at ten and runs all weekend. Hope you are doing something fun. Love you."

My fourth day in town and a week since I met John. Still no call and I can't complain. I made him wait forty-eight years. Every morning I tell myself this is the day, and it encourages me to continue. Running out of tourist things to do, I decide against a rock climb or white water rafting. In the early afternoon, I take myself to a movie. No action adventure, no killing, I enjoy my bag of popcorn and a light comedy. Silencing my phone, I put it on vibrate and keep it on my lap, just in case. Surprisingly, I was not embarrassed to laugh out loud while sitting alone; it just happens. I can't believe I was worried about laughing. At least I'm not sitting in my room, moaning over Brad or Andrew. I have become the star in my own expedition.

I am not who I was less than a month ago. I was eating and hiding in a room to cry. Now, I smile over the freak-out on the bench in Hot Springs and am relieved I wasn't arrested over that display of crazy. I thought just seeing a picture or knowing Andrew was doing well would be enough, but with each step,

I want more. Who knows what I will want next? I am so near to him I watch the streets for a familiar face. I resolve to tell Brad about him at some point soon. As much as Andrew has a right to know about his birth parents, Brad has a right to know about his other son. Just not today. Coming to terms with my selfishness in trying to own Andrew and hide him from his father, I have a lump in my throat as I plan to contact Brad after he calls, if he calls.

Returning from a morning walk, I double-check the times for the Mystical Wind's Jewelry and Psychic Fair. They are setting up, and my curiosity is piqued as I look into the busy room. The thought of talking to Mom or Dad again crosses my mind. It could be interesting since there is no particular future at this point. The realization that Andrew will not want to meet me revisits my ongoing insecurity. *Tomorrow I will start to come to terms with that possibility.* I head back to my room and go straight to my computer. While it powers up, I take a deep breath, I resolve to stay here another week and only then will I decide where to live.

I look at the dark blue folder I have been making of photos and history every evening. I will deliver it to John and Lorene before I leave. They can give it to him.

Aware that it is summer vacation, I check the high school website again. I am connected to him as I stare at his photograph. I copy and save several pictures to the flash drive for my personal album. I will have them printed, and I'll frame the one with him with the soccer team. Continuing to surf aimlessly through the internet I stumble on the Boulder, Colorado website. There are rentals and let the thought of settling here visit my mind. There is an Events heading, and I spark up with the possibility there will be something new for tomorrow other than chasing meals and thrift stores.

I go for an early lunch and chat with the waiter. I have become recognizable. Eat a couple of meals a day in the same café, you start developing friendships. I'm finished shopping the boutiques and the gift shop. There is nothing I need at this point; I have no one who wants a souvenir. I swear I have spent my entire life waiting, and this is enough. I enter the double doors to the Fair at the hotel; it is late enough for them to be busy.

There are colors and laughing voices; it is very inviting. I'm interested in a variety of booths and I'm swept along with the activity. There is a wide assortment of things to do and learn. I'm stunned by the diversity. I guess my one visit to Terry didn't make me the expert I thought I was. Some of the people appear to be in costume like there is a New-Age hippie dress code. Surrounded by chatter, and welcoming from every booth I feel no pressure to buy. The community is open to visitors and offers unending possibilities for no extra charge. I shake many hands and pick up some business cards and flyers. The whole experience is so bright and pleasant, and the worries leave my mind. The event is going on all weekend, so I vow to come back. The rooms are full of positive energy; I don't notice any judgment other than me sniping at the dress code.

Since Terry mentioned my aura back in Hot Springs, I have a picture taken. I was curious and this way I can see what she meant. I stare at a photo of myself looking more like a mug shot, but there is a gold and green light around me. The photographer mentions some concern about the red streak and then she asks me about stress. Ya think? It is a vast improvement over all the red Terry had described.

There are several rock displays, and I get to see some larger pieces of amber. Terry was right, they do get expensive. I study the jewelry available and most appears to be unique and hand-made. Some of the tables have the materials so I could make jewelry, but that I decide to put off for when I have a permanent place to live. I have had a couple of compliments on my amber pendant that I wear every day now. Not drawn to anyone for a reading, I prepare to leave. I might later, as they are going to be here all weekend. Just being here has given me a message. I need to stop waiting and move. Time is a-wasting.

# — 37 —

I go back to my room for a nap, one of the benefits of retirement. I give Madeline a call; she makes me feel as if my mother is still with me. She is excited I went to the fair and admitted she has never done anything of that sort. She will watch the papers, and if there is one in Omaha, I will drive over, and we will go together. At least, she doesn't laugh at me. Julie will, but she laughs all the time. I haven't admitted to either one that I have started web-stalking my son.

Madeline tells me she has spoken with John and Lorene, and she is as excited as I am. She shares that Andrew has been away for part of the month and now, he is busy with summer soccer camp. He knows I'm here and may be open to meeting, but needs time to prepare.

Thanks to the morning newspaper, the internet and my impatience, I learn that the University is hosting a statewide soccer camp. Excitedly I read the schools from all over the state will participate, including Andrew's school. Justifying a plan that is starting to build, I acknowledge to myself the University keeps drawing me. Using this as a premise, I study the campus web page and especially the map. There is a list of classes and a job fair this weekend. That is all the excuse I need. In reality, I know exactly why I am going. The first stop will be at the soccer fields. They have scrimmage games all day Saturday, so I will mosey over and check out the parking. I don't need a plan B because I don't have a plan A.

I give Madeline a call as I'm about to leave and tell her of my plan. She believes I may be setting myself up for heartbreak, but she admits she would do the same thing. I have to wrestle my expectations into the firm possibility that I may not see him. Games start in a less than an hour, and I need some time to find everything. I swear over not having a printer for the map and no time to go to the office supply store. In my momentary panic, I suddenly realize I can ask almost anyone walking around campus. I gather the newspaper and a book and dash for the car.

On my way out I had to rethink the reading material. I don't want to be obvious, and that is a tip-off that I know nothing about soccer. Blending in is mandatory and being noticed is the second to last thing I want. On my way through the lobby, I buy a University sweatshirt in the gift shop. I can hide the book in my pocket. Evidently, I look like fifty percent of the players' grannies. Old habits are hard to break, and I'm talented when it comes to invisibility. Why do I worry so much? I've spent the majority of my life blending in and avoiding detection.

There is a lot of activity on campus for a summer weekend. I am not sure why I thought the campus would be quiet. Wrong! However, here I am, a woman on a mission. I find the field quickly, and as I approach the area, I'm relieved that there is a sizable crowd in the bleachers. Tucked into my pocket is the photo John gave me, of a tall, skinny 15-year-old athlete. I doubt he would change much – it has only been thirty-three years. I notice many people have programs, and I wish I had one to hide behind, but to quote Brad *If ifs and buts were candy and nuts, we all would have a nice Christmas.* I plan to stay until the end if that is what it takes. I will come back tomorrow if I don't see him, and there are more games.

I am having a fantastic time. I've settled into an end seat about ten rows up. Great view of the field and the stands are full of families. I assumed this was for high school teams, but there is an enormous variety of ages and abilities. I can't stop smiling at the intensity of the teams, and I am excited at how easy it is to follow soccer. I have caught myself cheering along with the crowd for both teams. The sun is out, and the cute factor ramps up with the peewee teams. I am thrilled that the girls play equal to the boys, and the more I watch, the more I learn. I marvel at the impressive players that come in all ages. I am charged up over a sport I don't know squat about.

Watching the action on the field, combined with the energy of the crowd, distracts me and my mind clears. I notice I have just been enjoying the day. I've seen three games and two half games with the little ones. I get up and walk around when my bones ache from the hard seats, and no one has taken my place. Brad loved sports, but only professional, or games he could bet on. Another thing I won't miss about him.

After an hour break, some of the college players take the field. I decide to walk around the campus for a while, I'm hopeful can find some other food besides the concession stand. I didn't think about bringing anything. As usual, I didn't plan past finding a parking space and a seat. I try to imagine the electricity of the campus during the regular school year.

Not far from the field is the student center and I can see a lunch counter of sorts. I trust my University sweatshirt is a badge of admittance and walk right in. Once inside, my concern of discovery dissipates. I can tell most people are too involved with their lives and insecurities to give a damn. My invisibility superpower is in full force today, exactly what I need. The University is dynamic without being intimidating, and the energy of youth is infectious. For now, I'm fed, and I start back to the soccer field with a two-handed cup of 7-up.

Upon my return I notice the family I was sitting near have left. I have to search for a new seat and end up a couple of rows up and toward the middle. I have a better view, but lose the easy exit offered at the end of a row. The little kids were talented, but the college demonstration is amazing. It is like watching a full contact ballet. Astounded by what the young bodies can do, I'm privately embarrassed that I can wake up stiff and sore from a nap. Why didn't we have this sport when I was in school?

The field clears to a round of applause, and another game is about to begin. I scan around the field and watch the two new teams run on the field. *Oh my dear God, there he is.* I would have no idea if I said that out loud. I was watching the field so intensely; I didn't look in the stands. I see him seated with a group of middle school kids just a few rows in front of me. I could recognize that balding area on the crown of his head anywhere and the laugh.

I can't breathe or move. I'm frozen in place. He is handsome and looks a little like Brad and yet at the same time he doesn't. My Andrew has a lighter feel to him; he is joking and encouraging the team. He appears to love what he is doing, and the kids look at him like a rock star. I struggle to stay seated and maintain my composure. I struggle to inhale, and I force myself to control my heart palpitations. I hope that this isn't a heart attack. I slip into the old standby of yoga breathing, as I try to take in every detail. The panic subsides as I realize he has been sitting there for a while, and it took until now to see him. I've taken negligent mother to another level.

After forty-five minutes, they rise to go to the field, and his game begins. My mind silences as I memorize every move. I watch him running back and forth on the sidelines. He gives instructions, encourages each kid, and I can only hear clips of his voice no full sentences. He makes sure every player has time on the field and within moments, it is over. He walks away with cheering children, and I exhale. I must get out of here before I am exposed. I am so proud and a little ashamed that I didn't wait for his contact.

I need to get somewhere private where I can make a phone call.

# — 38 —

"Brad, I saw him!" What the hell am I doing? Why did I automatically call him? He has no right to this man. I have to fix this and then remember how to pick up messages. I will not allow him to destroy my moment. He would be right out here, causing all kinds of trouble. I pray that he didn't change the message code. Hell, I don't think he knows that there is a code. Redial, #45 – two messages. "I'm saved."

Now to make the correct call, answer the phone, girlfriend. "Julie, I saw him! He is handsome and looks a little like Brad, same balding spot, same walk and a better laugh."

"Lizard, that is amazing. So he called you?"

"No, he didn't, but I stumbled across a summer soccer camp at the University."

"Stumbled, I'm supposed to believe that. You are a tricky one when you put your mind to it, Liz. You waited longer than I would. Are you still trying to respect the wishes of others, while you suffer? That's my martyr."

In my excitement, I barely allow her a chance to speak. As I talk, I can see everything replaying. I'm so proud of a man I only met for a moment forty-eight years ago. I tell her repeatedly how handsome he is and about his laugh.

As I fill the phone lines of soccer and his work with the team, I realize I'm crying and wipe my eyes with the sleeve of my sweatshirt.

"Oh Julie, I have missed his life, and I have so many questions, I can't begin to express them."

"Did you talk to him?"

"Oh no, I didn't. I couldn't. I can't force myself into his life when I removed myself so effortlessly."

"Effortlessly? Now, Liz, there you go again, just quit it. You know there has been nothing easy about your son. You have spent the majority of your life shaded by that decision. You did the right thing. You know this."

"You are right. But I did leave and lied. He doesn't know anything about me, and I don't want him to think I was ever ashamed of him. I will wait, but as of today, I'm satisfied."

"Calm down, Lizard. You slay me! You survived, and every decision has brought you to where you are right now; I love hearing you happy. Don't let your pooh-pooh thoughts interrupt. Quit the guilt trip and enjoy your day."

The raw emotion wracks my body; I slowly regain control as we continue the conversation. The memory of the pickle jar brings back the scent of vinegar and vengeance. I swallow the aggravation that tried to overcome my joy. "You know I never cheated on him except for stealing the money. That is probably the greater sin."

"It is not stealing if it is your money, Mata Hari. I remember how Brad took your inheritance from your dad's death and bought a cabin and a bass boat.

Just what your parents lived their lives to leave you, I'm sure."

"The first thing I did when I saw Andrew was to call Brad. Why would I do that?"

"YOU CALLED BRAD? Excuse me, was that loud? Why did you call him? What were you thinking? We both know what would happen if he found you. Nothing good can come from talking to him right now."

"Julie, I fixed it. I was able to go into the voicemail and erase it. I caught myself almost as soon as the words came out of my mouth. Has he bothered you anymore?"

"Those Donovans don't give up easily."

"I never meant to put you in the middle of this."

"You worry about you. Don't think for a moment that he intimidates me. He knows I will not take his crap. He called all charming and concerned at first. He told me he loved you so much, and you had disappeared. He was desperate and lost. He knows we are close and wants me to call if I hear from you. I told him I would not and then – *Katie, bar the door*. He accused me of sins back to the Inquisition. He even threatened me with the police, saying that he could have me implicated in your disappearance."

"I'm sorry, Julie."

"I wouldn't have missed it for the world. I would have been offended if you didn't come to me. I know that man, Sister, and our relationship is first. Just settle down and realize that Brad and Shawn are bullies who are the cowards. If they would face their shortcomings, they could be good men, but they choose not to. I have no idea what their early years must have been, but it must have been one hell of a childhood to build those two. Remember their old man, what a drunken piece of work he was. Besides, Lizzie, my life is so boring and peaceful; I live for your adventure."

We share a nervous laugh in relief. She is right; Brad has some good in him. Otherwise, I would never have stayed so long. I would have left when I still had a backbone if he didn't have something. I try to understand where the time went. Seems only weeks ago, I was tan, young and full of sass. I miss that part of me. I waited until the fear of my husband was greater than the fear of the unknown.

"I hope he doesn't bother you anymore."

"Don't worry. Brad will never get any information from me unless we agree on it. I talked to Tom; he knows to keep tight-lipped and ignorant. He isn't a big talker and decided he would feign deafness."

"You married a good man this time; you deserve him. Okay, I will take your prescription to the bookstore and see what suits my fancy. My inclination is to sit in the bathroom and replay everything in my head while looking at old photos. I think your plan is better than mine. I'll let you go for now. Thank you for being home, love you."

"Oh, golly gee, Lizard, you are getting all mushy on me. You call me at any time if you need to. I wish you were here. I have a new box of wine."

"There is another idea. Although a bottle of wine would be lovely, doubt if I will ever need 4 liters of a blended red." We drift into evening plans or lack thereof and an invitation to come back to New Jersey for a few days. My waiting for the phone call moved the conversation to a promise of reconsideration in a couple of weeks.

Julie's name shows on the display of my cell phone as we hang up. Appreciating how talking with the Diva of New Jersey helps defuse my overactive emotions. I face the evening alone.

After such a full day, I consider my stash of reading the material, and there is only a travel book left. There must be a bookstore here at the University. I scan the buildings as I walk toward the parking lot. Noticing the Community Center I expect they may have a campus map or, at least, someone I can ask. Julie is right, I must keep busy, or I will do something regrettable. I know if I talked to Brad right now, he would be in Boulder within days. He would not give a damn about Andrew's feelings. My reality is still too fragile for that conversation, and I stuff it back as I enter the front door.

# — 39 —

Whoa-Nellie, there is a job fair at the Student Center. I wonder why I didn't notice it when I was here for lunch. It can't hurt to check it out, and I'm so jazzed right now that I need to keep moving. With my Colorado University sweatshirt, they will probably think I fit in.

The second-floor conference rooms are swarming with people wandering through a large number of tables and booths. I may be the only person not carrying a resume folder and dressed for an interview. I like the crowd and blend in easily with the waves of anticipation.

I pick up business cards from temporary agencies, which is a good possibility for my immediate future. I assume they don't give a hoot about age for temp work, just skills. I had no idea decades at Accounting Associates would give me the bookkeeping and administrative skills in demand by so many companies. Hell yes, I know Excel; damn right I know PowerPoint. Thank you Mr. Offert, I had no idea you were training me for life as an itinerant clerical worker.

The University has a large booth, with a big banner and flyers. Giving the campus some of the credit for my great attitude, I decide to check into what they may offer. "Hi, are you hiring or recruiting?"

"A little of both, Ma'am. We have a few jobs and applications for attending. Are you looking to register?" Her smile is friendly and a little patronizing. "We have several older students, and they have support groups here. I'm sure we have a lot of classes you would like to take."

"You might be right, and your name is?"

"My name is Jessica."

I think my shoes are older than this girl; I'm not sure she should be out without a parent or guardian. As I flip through the brochures, and out of the corner of my eye, I detect an interesting gentleman approaching the booth. Hold it, Libby; it has been years since you paid attention to any man. Pull yourself together, he could be the last thing you need.

"Jessica, I have no idea what I'm looking for, I'm just exploring. I would like some of the brochures you have, though. How difficult is an admission?"

"Doctor Jamelson will help you with your questions. I was supposed to leave ten minutes ago. He is part of our American Lit department."

Holy cow, I didn't plan on talking to him. I can feel my face burning; just what I need is a blush. He seems slightly familiar, hell, he is talking to me, and I zoned out. Nice impression you are making, Libby old girl.

"Hi. Is there anything, in particular, you are looking for? Are you interested in attending the University, or some of the jobs?"

"I guess the jobs since it is a job fair." He has a genuine, easy smile I like that. *Jeez-Louise, Libby, get a grip.*

"You are right, Miss, I'm sorry I don't know your name."

"You can call me Libby, Libby Donovan."

"Right, Libby, Libby Donovan. Is there a particular position you are interested in?"

An initial off-color remark plays across my mind, but for once, I restrain myself. "So sorry, I have no idea what I would like. I just stumbled into your fair after leaving the soccer tournament. At this point, my options are wide open, so maybe some of your enrollment information. I'm not interested in full time, but a course may be fun. I don't care about getting a degree. Do I need to apply and find about being accepted? I'm not a resident in this area, so that will make things more difficult." Well, that was a long line of blathering.

"Well Libby, we have a lot of continuing education, non-credit classes..." I know he is still talking, but I only hear parts of the information. "... more casual, no grades and not nearly as expensive." He hands me two more brochures.

"This is my first time on campus, and I like the vibe. I have only been in Boulder a couple of days and don't know anyone. I sense considerable promise everywhere I look on this campus."

"I agree with you there. I taught here for thirty-five years and recently retired. I do some volunteer work, substitute teaching and help with an extended education class or two. I can't seem to leave the campus, but I no longer have to grade three hundred essays on the Middle Ages. Being around the kids helps me feel like I'm making a contribution to society."

"I would like an opportunity to make a contribution. I've made a recent change..." I guess that is a good thing to call it... "I have been drifting around trying to find a new direction."

Note to self: Stop blabbering, I think you are flirting, old girl.

Dr. Jamelson looks at me, and I feel like the only person in this crowded room. "A University is always a good sign post. Once you get to a certain age, the changes can be jolting whether it is by choice or fate." He looks wistful. The connection is palpable. Now I'm convinced that I must know him, but that is impossible. "Have we met before?"

He stares at my face thoughtfully and takes a moment to speak. "No, I don't think so. I used to live in Gresham, Oregon. Have you been there?"

"No, to tell you the truth, until this month I haven't been hardly anywhere except Indiana. It is a long story."

"I guess when you reach our age; every story becomes long and complicated." He unfolds that charming smile, and I notice the strong jaw and a small scar on his lower lip.

"The longer we talk, the more I feel that I know you, but I have made mistakes before." We both laugh shaking our heads in agreement thinking back to our private stories. I gather all of the information he has given me and turn to walk away.

"Libby, you should come to the counseling center on the 19th. They are having an older student get together and introduction session here at the community center."

"Do I have to be a registered student to attend? You have to remember, I have just stumbled on the grounds today, and I don't belong."

"There are no requirements, it is a meet and greet, and this helps our more mature students make connections."

"Will you be there, Dr. Jamelson?" I can't believe I asked. Who the hell am I? I know I'm blushing now, my face feels like it has caught fire.

"Yes, I will. The event is another one of my volunteer projects." I think I have embarrassed him too. Nice work, Libby. He adds, "Here, do you have enough paper now?"

"I'm going to need a box to carry everything. I will plan on the 19th." Yikes, I'm acting like a young girl with this professor, I hope he doesn't notice. There are tons of surprises left in you, old girl. "By the way, is there a bookstore nearby?"

# − 40 −

"Hey, girlfriend, bet you didn't think you would hear from me again tonight."

"What's up, Lizard?"

"What a day this has been. I am starting to think I could be a danger to polite society."

I go on to tell Julie all about the job fair and Dr. Jamelson. We have always laughed, but this time, the reaction is uproarious. I feel the heat of my flushed and tear-stained face from all of the self-discovery and surprises. Of course, she has to hear me repeat my story about incredible Andrew's soccer game.

"I'll bet you don't feel the need to call Brat, er, Brad anymore?" Julie chuckles pleased with herself.

"I haven't even thought about him since we spoke. After all of my adventure, I didn't buy a book at the University."

Julie responds quite loudly. "Sounds as if you have decided to live a book, but that was the primary task of your homework assignment, so get on it."

I slip my shoes back on and decide to get my sorry cheap ass to a bookstore before it gets any later. I need several things and make a mental note, a novel, self-help and anything new by David Sedaris.

Parking in the dark lot was a snap, and the store is almost empty. I went immediately to the humor section and found I have already read all of David Sedaris selections and notice a display for Christopher Moore; the covers are cartoonish yet kind of dark. As I scan the book jackets, I decide that providence has brought these books to me for a reason. The descriptions are outrageous, so I pick two. Next, I put a Nora Ephron in the shopping basket and wander to the self-help. Within a half hour, I have books, a new bookmark, potato chips and am on my way back to the room.

I congratulate myself concluding it takes countless funny books and movies to heal and join the living. Walking through the lobby back to the elevator, I notice the Psychic Fair only had a few more minutes. Some booths were closing down and no time to shop. I am on a mission and rush to the jewelry table I had visited earlier. The woman was packing the earrings into padded boxes. "I'm sorry to be late. Is it possible to buy the amber beads I saw yesterday? Those beads started whispering to me while I was in the lobby."

"Yeah, that is precisely what jewelry can do; it knows your psychic cell phone. It is never too late; did you want to see any of the other amber pieces?"

"I looked yesterday. I just need these four."

"Those beads will complete the pendant you have on."

Smiling confidently I think of Hot Springs and Terry. I'll send her a photo when it is all together.

The vendor helps me slid the beads onto my golden chain, and we agree they were born for the pendant a little smaller and same rich golden color.

It looks beautiful, and I'm proud of myself. It is not my nature to buy unnecessary items, another sign of the new Libby.

Waiting for the elevator, I realized I haven't eaten since lunch at the soccer game and decide the vending machines on the second floor will satisfy my needs.

After so many emotional ups and downs, I'm finally genuinely happy. Proud of my accomplishments, I slip into a nightgown and settle into bed with the treasure trove of new books.

I settle in for a long read after writing several pages in my journal. After an hour, I push everything aside and snuggle into the blankets. Confident I will dream about my handsome son. The man I have seen today will replace the old visions of a baby. The perfect ending of a perfect day.

# — 41 —

Dear Elizabeth,

You are gone. You left me over a month ago, and I don't know what I have done that you could treat me so coldly. No calls, no letters, no explanation, I deserve better. There was one constant in my life, and it was you.

I never believed that you would ever leave. I have had many nights to think about how you said I was distant. I can now see that I expected too much and didn't show proper gratitude. I am grateful for everything you do for me. I talked to the police, but they said there is nothing they can do since you left by choice.

I promise I will change. I'll stop drinking if you want me to. I beg you to come home. I don't know how to take care of things, and the house is so empty with you away. I need you here.

I want you to know I love you. Ever since the first moment we met, I have loved you. Please don't turn your back on me now. I refuse to believe that all the years we shared were a waste. They weren't for me. At the least tell me where you are, and I will send your things, or pick you up. I forgive you for all of this, and we can move forward. Please don't make me have to find you.

Brad

Damn, damn, damn. After the best day of my life, he finds a way to claw his way back into my reality. I acknowledge the freedom of a couple of hours without him in my thoughts; I guess that was something to celebrate. I am surprised it took him so long to email, but that means he has stepped up to the new millennium. I wonder who set it up for him. Wait a minute, I don't care who set it up. Making contact will be so much easier now.

I don't buy his poor me story anymore. My sympathetic nature and drive to be his caregiver have died. Maybe I will make him a profile on Match. com. He can destroy someone else's life. Better yet, he could invest his time into his mistress and her children. I'll figure out a way to let him know he can forget about me altogether. I feel a twinge of guilt placing the curse on another woman. I refuse to think about this right now; I had a fantastic day yesterday, and he is not going to steal it. I forward his message to Julie, deciding I won't worry until I think it through.

My first reaction was physical, and that was to run, but instead I have stayed in this room for hours playing on the computer. Emails, card games, they sure can suck up time. Feeling as if I've wasted enough of my life, I turn to searching the Kokomo Herald website. As much as I hate to admit it, Brad's letter touches me, and so instead of hiding further; I make a decision, finished with secrets. At this point, I check the Boulder paper and locate a couple of rent by the month apartments. I pull on my pajama pants, shirt, shoes and necklace, ready to leave. I can't help but stroke the stones on my necklace and I can feel the energy empower me. I didn't know until now that they were a necessity. I believe the necklace is a symbol of who I can be. I make a couple of calls for addresses and take off to drive by the potential apartments. I'm excited about finding a place to nest in for a while. I have some money, but at the current daily rate of a hotel and three meals in restaurants, I see it slipping away.

I set up two for viewing and have some addresses to drive past. I start with the apartment the furthest out. I arrive early, as usual, but I can't see much from the street. It is behind a strip mall, and I see some benefit if I want a soft drink or 44 ounces of beer at night. I'm a little uncomfortable about the dark alley and garbage containers adjacent to the parking lot. I wait in the car for the owner, and he is a few minutes late. I walk over to meet taking a quick inventory. He is a large man with hands the size of tennis rackets, and I get the slightest whiff of alcohol on his breath. My internal danger alarm starts to wail.

As we chat, I learn he lives in the adjacent unit, and as we walk toward the apartment, he continues to talk. Suddenly, I can go no further. Just a couple weeks ago, I would have gone on in with him, but I have changed. Stalling I ask, "What kind of lease are you looking for?"

"I would like a one year lease and first and last month's rent. There will also be a security deposit, but we can work that out personally."

Relieved that I was able to feel the danger in advance, I respond. "Guess we don't have to go any further. I'm not able to handle a lease." I turn and walk away leaving him standing with the keys in his hands.

He calls after me, "Well what do you want? I'm sure we can come up with something."

"No, no thank you. I apologize for taking up your time." I get to the T-beast and wave as I leave. Even though I am anxious for a place and a real address, this was not it. Many years have passed since I've rented anything. I'm pleased that I won't consider the expense of a long lease. Sure that I am rushing things, just to get mail, I can always have it forwarded to a post office box.

The next one looked kind of run down and the neighborhood was shabby. I want to be near the University, but not in this area. The other two choices are a one-bedroom apartment and a studio. The manager is ready when I arrive, and she is elderly and friendly. She seems relieved to meet an older renter, not inclined to throw keggers, whatever that is. The studio is large with windows, a kitchenette, and furniture. The one bedroom is more than I want to spend right now. She is to call me tomorrow to let me know if I have the place, and then I will get a money order for the first and last tomorrow.

Still energetic when I got back to the hotel I start a resumé. Checking for examples online, I learn how much things have changed since I was last job searching. The last time I just filled out an application, and this is my first resumé. One job for almost 40 years makes for a concise document. The internet sites tell me to keep it to one page, I will need clip art to stretch it that far. I contemplate a full-time job and decide I don't need or want that much. I need to fill time more than make money. I am sure all the employers in Boulder have waited day and night to hire a sixty-six-year-old homeless runaway with office skills. Finally finished, I wonder if it is too early for bed. Realizing I haven't had a proper meal, but snacked throughout the day, hunger is not an issue. I am tired, and it is just starting to get dark. I can't help but wonder if this is old age. I justify my thoughts as eagerness for the possibilities of tomorrow. It has nothing to do with the early bird discount coupons at Denny's for everyone over sixty. *Oh, my lord! It is old age.*

I put on clean pajamas and settle into what may be my last evening in the hotel. Picking up my phone, I make my evening contact. The calls have become a comforting pattern. "Hello, Julie, I hope this is you. Sorry for calling early."

"Of course, Lizard. Do you think I have appointments other than talking to you? What the hell was that email from Brad? Did you answer him? You didn't call, did you?" Julie is emotional.

"No, I sent it to you and then put it out of my mind. He sounds different. The message was nothing I ever expected."

"Liz, you know he isn't different. He is the same old smooth-talking ass munch. All of the remarks were about him. Never have I seen so many I's in such a short message. Sure, he wants you home. You made his life easier, and you handed over a paycheck. I read his last couple sentences as veiled threats. Did you see that?"

"You are right Jules; it just threw me, and I was feeling guilty. Nevertheless, I do know him well enough not to respond hastily. I've seen those contrite apologies by the hundreds. He can be charming and loving, but one or two hours into happy hour and I would be in the headlights of his oncoming fury. I find the longer I live outside of my nagging brain, that I lose some aspect of the story. Odd how I left, but I recall the reality of our marriage. I lied for so long that I forgot how to tell the truth." I feel wistful, but the ongoing disappointment is slipping away. "I like the idea he has an email address; I can contact him if I need to and not speak to him at the same time."

Julie interrupts my meanderings. "I think you may want to avoid talking to him for a long time. Well, Liz, other than the brush with the past, what else have you been up to?"

Rehashing my adventure of the day and possible rentals, she makes me agree to avoid long-term leases. I appreciate that I'm excited about the studio apartment as I describe it to her. "I do want a residence, a place to get mail and to put my clothing in drawers. The landlord seemed to like the idea I wasn't a student."

"About time being older is a benefit. Does she know you are a drunk and debauch young men?"

Laughingly I respond. "Yeah, not yet, but I'll put that on the application, or even easier you can tell them when they call. You are my reference."

"You are in trouble now! I have the power to force you back to New Jersey. All kidding aside, Lizard, I understand your need to be there for now." Julie quietly adds, "Years ago I heard something like the best revenge is living well. It is also one hell of a reward." I settle into the comfort of my bed clutching the phone feeling warm with friendship and excited about the promise of tomorrow. "I assume Andrew didn't call. You would have led with that news."

Wistfully I respond, "I am aware the apartment and job search are filling my hours waiting for him. I know he is busy and meeting me would be a low priority."

Julie answers, "Remember when we were younger, life had so many demands and time slipped away. I will never believe it took you so many years to tell me about him."

"For once I listened to my mother and locked my baby in a vault of regret."

"Now stop whining. No one can change the past."

"Apparently I'm trying to heal the past. Maybe I'll work on the shame and accusations next. I allowed these things to mark my soul."

"Shame and sexuality are a potent mixture. That was in the 60s and thank goodness times have changed."

"I was mortified when I was a teen and on the edge of destruction. I transformed at that moment and continued to change as the time and events ticked past. Convinced he was right; I accepted that I was fat, stupid, inconsiderate and lazy before he took the first swing. I was broken and accepted the fault he offered me. I confused jealousy as love."

"You were young, too. Isn't he your one and only?" Julie said.

"Oh my God, Julie, I didn't date anyone other than Brad. The thought of my dad finding out I had sex was crippling. Disappointing my father would have broken me. I'm not letting this define me any further."

Julie added, "I remember the days, girls being thrown out of their homes virtually branded. I still don't know where they disappeared to never have I heard of a boy being thrown out for being an impregnator."

"I haven't either. They were celebrated and excused with the *boys will be boys* explanation. I didn't know how blessed I was with my parents. Now that I have seen Andrew and spoken to his father, I'm secure I did the right thing. Brad has a right to know, but he will have to wait. Besides he can take care of his kids he had with Dumbshit."

Julie was quiet and added, "I know that when Shawn and I were still together, I lived in the hope he would become who I thought he could be. I would love him into wholeness. That attitude added years to our marriage."

"I'm guilty of the same lack of insight, only longer. Neither of the brothers overcame the selfish, thirsty and violent legacy they had. The verbal abuse started early, and it progressed to viciousness. Once I was noticeably damaged, Brad stepped it up to the physical. I was almost relieved. I knew that action was wrong, but his words were so vile, and the hitting would end it. I clutched onto the good part of him believing that was the real, but it wasn't. It was just a little part of a damaged package. You know, Julie, men are lucky that women are such romantics. Otherwise, there would be a lot more bachelors."

"Or funerals." Julie breaks out laughing. "True enough, girlfriend. We have the technology to survive without them, but we live on forever hopeful."

"Lizard, I can't complain, though. I was a mess from my life with Shawn; it took a couple of years for my sweet Tom to get me to pay any attention. I see that if I didn't marry Shawn, I would not have been at the right place and the right time for Tom. Just remember you aren't dead yet."

"Ok, Dr. Julie, time to stop whining. Is this insight from what you are reading now? How much do I owe you for this counseling session? I do have to admit I'm surprised how much I have enjoyed my time alone. When I planned the escape, I didn't think about all of the hours that would be involved. I'm feeling triumphant right now, and I've seen my boy."

"Don't you mean man? Your son is forty-eight years old."

"Thank you for that slap of realization. I have no idea how time has slipped past. I should have done this decades ago."

Julie groans, "You can't live in what you shoulda-coulda-woulda. Your timing is right for now. All you have is today and the future."

"You are right again Julie." At that moment, I decide to live in truth.

Once the call ends, it is still early enough to check on Madeline. I tell her about seeing Andrew, and she is very excited for me. She fills the hole in my heart as if I'm talking with my mother. I love her so much; she is so supportive and kind. I promise to see her next week. When the call ends, I am back to my task of waiting. An exhaustion overcomes me with the weight of waiting for phone calls. I doze realizing it has only been a week since I met John.

# — 42 —

Deep in sleep, I see the young woman again, more vivid than ever before. The boy is also there and for the first time, I hear her speak. I don't understand the language she is using, but there will be more soon. The dream ends abruptly, like always. After eight hours of uninterrupted sleep, I wake up peaceful and content. Brad visits some of my dreams, but he is more of a piece of furniture, something that has always been there, silently in the background. Pondering the many dreams from last night, I decide dreams come in types, like a day-to-day business, repeating, adventure, prophetic and fantasy. I like the adventure the most.

Just as I decide to attack the day, I notice a message flashing. The landlord must have called while I was yammering on the phone last night. I'm confident it is good news because the studio needs to be mine. Once I shower and dress, it will be a reasonable hour to call and arrange to drop off a money order. I had to honor she had other appointments, but I am confident this morning.

I want to go to the second-hand store, but I shouldn't start furnishing an apartment before I have the key. I need to keep the trunk capacity of the T-beast in mind. I am trying to find excuses to leave the hotel, searching for a distraction. I disconnect from the thoughts and go for a light breakfast.

Over crispy bacon and toast, I develop a plan for the day that doesn't involve shopping. I will go to the office supply store and have some printing done, photos for Andrew and my new resumé. Instead of making a list, I will get on a few lists at the employment agencies. I enjoy the fact I don't have to accept an assignment if it doesn't sound appealing.

I am starting to have doubts about attending school and using excuses of no address, being an out of state student and the expense. Each reason is a flimsy justification to resort to my old behavior of isolation. I need to fill my days while I wait. The thought of his never calling slows me briefly, and I put the worry out of my head. Blah, blah, my usual over-thinking every detail, I make a conscious decision to remain active and soldier on.

I head back to my room and put on my one good outfit for the employment agency. As I slip on the only pair of non-athletic shoes, the phone rings. The studio apartment is mine, and I arrange to meet her in thirty minutes leaving immediately for the bank. I crumple my daily list, and I dump the constant internal dialogue of doubt.

Ms. Edna brings the lease for my signature, and I turn over the money order. I slide the key onto the keyring Madeline gave me, appreciating each addition is proof of my progress. My new home is a spacious single room with a kitchenette along the back wall. The location has everything necessary nearby, and there is a well-lit parking area. I gaze out the large bay window, and I know this is home. The best part of all is it is furnished. I pull the over-stuffed chair to face the window, and it is perfect. Today is moving day.

# — 43 —

The day I planned at breakfast has become exceptionally busy. I'm out of the motel and in my home. I call and schedule the appointment with the biggest temporary agency for tomorrow and start on the cleaning. I appreciate not carrying furniture up the stairs; my suitcases are tough enough. First, I unpack my clothes, putting them away gives me reassurance, as I stow the luggage in the back of the closet. I pop out to buy some cleaning products, sponges, and hangers, but I didn't need many. My bathroom is small, but all mine and I will clean it myself. No more daily clean towels and motel maids. I won't miss their knock on my door.

In my confusion and stalling, I ended up taking action. I didn't worry about Andrew or Brad all day, and now I have a home and possible employment tomorrow. I have to remember my address; maybe a sticky note will help.

This month has been better than most of my life. Meeting Andrew's father and reconnecting with Madeline is a fabulous gift. I tell myself that just seeing Andrew is enough, but that is a blatant lie. There was no way I could have planned these events when I plotted the escape. Instead of continuing to criticize, I credit myself with having a few things organized. I would like to live near both Madeline and Julie, but miles are blocking that possibility. I consider the weather and decide. Officially finished with the hard winters of the Midwest, it appears I am opting for the more difficult winters of the Rocky Mountains. Now that I have let winter cross my mind, I will have to do research about Boulder and New Jersey for the best choice. I am not ready for any permanent commitment and decide I'll let my next home discover me.

Here goes my head again. Thrilled with today, I resolve that instead of worrying about what will be months away, I will continue one day at a time and occasionally hour-by-hour. I make hot water for tea in my only fry pan and then whip up a two-egg sandwich. I watch the light fade from the sky while submerged in my comfy chair.

# — 44 —

Waking up early, I am still warm and cozy from last night. I look around my home and think of plans for today. The list consists of groceries, linens and, as much as I would like to deny it, television. I have to make my apartment into a home stocked for human habitation with things I want. I do a quick audit of my finances, but I will have another paycheck next week, and my Social Security deposit arrived at the bank. I haven't had to withdraw anything from the savings yet.

I resolve to go to the University for the Senior-Freshman Meet and Greet tomorrow night. I am sure I won't register for school, but I'll check into auditing a class and Dr. Jamelson mentioned the community education classes. I don't need a degree, which makes decisions more delicious. At the very least, this will provide a new community I can belong to with people close to my age.

My entire life has been a lesson in patience, and I'm tired of it. I have learned the lesson and it stops now. I spent so many years reflecting on what I thought others wanted and I slipped away. Instead of making another to-do list, I rehash my accomplishments and smile. I don't have to worry about money as long as I'm careful. I will set up the 401K payments once my paychecks finish. I have completed what may be the world's shortest resumé and have an appointment with a temporary employment agency.

I will go to the Meet and Greet, and I will check into volunteering. Yes, that's a plan.

The last thing this afternoon is to buy groceries. Ten eggs, three-day-old carry out, and a box of breakfast bars do not qualify as sustenance. I'll buy the ingredients for soup, a big bowl of something warm sounds reassuring and it can last for days. I have always focused outwardly, but now, I take care of me.

When I open the door to the perfect apartment, not too expensive and just enough room, I can't help but smile. I have no yard to mow, a big window to let in the sun and to watch the stars, topped off with access to a washing machine. This place could not be better. Ignoring the next step, I settle into Boulder, for at least the next two months. I will allow the future to map by Providence and by Andrew.

I didn't realize how much I needed until I started filling the shopping cart. Two sets of sheets, towels, bathroom supplies, clock radio and a small television. Next, to stock the kitchen, service for four (in case I have a dinner party with invisible friends), pots, a knife, silverware and a couple of glasses. I go to the grocery store for basics, ingredients for chicken vegetable soup, breakfast items, and a couple more cleaning supplies. I don't scream as my account takes the hit, but my jaw needs to be pried open from the clenched position. The cheap gene barks at every swipe of the debit card and I assure myself that these are necessities no matter where I live. It is comforting to type those four letters. The years of explaining every purchase and skimming nickels and dimes turned me into a financial master – or is that miser?

Suddenly I think of Brad and realize he has been out of my thoughts for a second day. I congratulate myself on healing. Knowing I never responded to his email, a tiny bit of remorse wells. Then it is replaced with cooking the first real meal in my home. I promise to consider it, soon.

As I watch the soup simmer, I miss my favorite soup pot and begin to laugh about running away with only underwear, money, photos and a pot on my head as I climb on the bus. I will never need to worry about this again, and I sigh with relief. For the first time, I am fully in charge and reassured by my choices. Assured I can handle my mistakes too.

I sit down at the small two-person table with my hot soup and a slice of buttered bread. Peace surrounds and comforts me. I will watch television until ten, read until 10:35. I settle into my clean sheets. I'm home.

# — 45 —

I awaken with recurring dream; it is rare to have it two nights in a row. I reflect on the transformation and make note of new details. I have never seen the woman entirely, but the boy has an innocent, sweet brown face, I believe he is seven or eight years old. I feel pure love for him. These two have been with me as long as I can remember. I have seen them stare at a brilliantly starry night sky and her gently speaking. I have grown up with them and even though it is a dream; they are family. I have always believed her to be his mother telling ancient stories. I sense she is trying to ensure he learns the importance of the night. Not fully awake, I rest quietly, not wanting to disturb them, but the dream ends abruptly as the morning light greets me.

I like waking up gently, without an alarm, one of the benefits of unemployment. Today I put on my only best outfit, again and off to my appointment with the employment service. I may drop in on the second and third agencies too. It all depends on timing; I notice Libby goes to places that Elizabeth wouldn't even consider. I gather the appointment cards and the applications I completed from the job fair.

My phone minutes ran out last night, so I invest in an innovative new telephone with all sorts of applications. I enjoy loading my street number in the GPS as home. I update my resumes with the local phone and address. It was funny when the clerk wanted to assist with transferring all of my contacts on the phone; I blushed that there are only three, and I know them by heart.

At the office supply store, I make twenty copies of the updated resumé and buy a folder to hold them. With a chuckle, the thought of twenty copies please me, but I do not know what the future may bring. With my work history of one job forever, I cannot help but be amused with my excessive preparations. I think this is the best impression I can muster.

I plan to call Madeline and Julie tonight so that they will have the new number. I'll ask Madeline to forward the information to John and Andrew. I laugh at a bonus – Brad doesn't have this number.

It is still early when I park in front of the temp agency. I take the opportunity to call Rapinder at the Mail Stop in Kokomo. I give her my forwarding address and contact information. She tells me that she needs it in writing with a signature, and I can pick the form up at the post office. She will email their address and a fax number so I can expedite the changes. Initially aggravated over the details, I decide to consider it a safety precaution. I promise a payment for another three months on my box.

Immediately after, I eat the yogurt in my bag and head into the job interview.

As I enter the agency, I am anxious. Why would I be nervous? I don't need a job I have money. I decide that after this appointment if it doesn't go well, I will apply to the next one. Someone will see my potential. Damn, no turning back or excuses. Just walk as if I own the place.

The interview goes well. They were nice and took all of my information; they seemed impressed with my experience, but they are probably kind to everyone that comes in. I do well on their examinations, and we all laugh over my last typing test that was on a real typewriter. I am politely told to start calling it keyboarding. Not easy getting with the modern times, is it, old girl?

I go for lunch and check the address for another agency. The more I think about it, the more I love the idea of temporary work. I'm too old to make any more thirty-year commitments. I can say no to a job, and they'll call me another day. I have awakened a gypsy soul, and I decide to keep rolling while I'm cleaned-up. I'd be in trouble if they sent me out tomorrow. I only have this outfit. Where is Julie when I need to buy clothes?

I've accomplished a lot in a short time. Listed with two agencies and the way they talk, I will need work clothes soon. I remember reading something in the 1980s that if you only buy two colors of clothes you can make a whole wardrobe with a few pieces. I chose to buy black, white and pink. Pink matches my suitcase and represents freedom. I buy enough to cover me for a workweek. I can shuffle and remix the clothing and voila, a wardrobe. I stopped by the cable company and arranged for television and internet service. All utilities and services will up and running by Wednesday. I didn't know how much I was saving at the motel on Wi-Fi. Last time I set up a home, I used wedding presents and the electronics consisted of a black and white television I could lift and a radio.

I call Madeline with my new number, and she reminds me I'm driving over this weekend. She promises to call John as soon as she hangs up with my new phone information and ask him to tell Andrew. I again have to block the thought that he won't call, must let it play, as it will. I've already wasted 48 years; I can wait as long as it takes. I refuse to plan so far off as winter, and I must let the next step surprise me. With no worry about the future, I will manage today, and a let tomorrow be.

I begin to greet each day with the best of expectations. Planning and remembering odd bits of advice, that is my motto. I have to be careful not to gather too many belongings, as this may not be my permanent home. I try to keep everything I own transportable in the T-beast.

My old life seems distant, like a book read years ago. Only gone a few weeks, and the past doesn't seem real. I'm in love with my life at this moment. My own place, my own choices. It is amazing how little I need to feel happy. I even have friends, two genuine friends that I can talk with honestly. I am feeling productive today, two employment agencies and tomorrow, maybe more.

I've worn my good outfit four times in a row, and it is a relief to pick up some more outfits. I didn't realize black pants and a white shirt is similar to the uniform for servers at nicer restaurants. I add the pink scarf to jazz it up and to hide my old woman neck. It is still too early to leave for the Freshman-Senior get together at the University. I begin to pack for tomorrow and the drive to see Madeline and Mr. Ed. I set out the Styrofoam cooler and the smaller suitcase. I only need a change of clothes, pajamas, and toiletries. It is surprising how busy I have been setting up my little household and looking for work. I discovered if you tell the employment agencies you have an appointment with their competition, they take you seriously. My vision of success has changed, as I reach to answer the ringing phone. I put on my best business voice just in case. I have a decent start on a new chapter.

"Hello, this is Libby Donovan."

"Hello. My name is Andrew Scortino; I understand you would like to talk to me."

# – 46 –

I'm stunned; I was moving forward as if he might never call. I can't breathe, and I can't seem to form words.

"Oh my, yes, yes. I am, I would, and I would like to talk to you. How are you? I'm sorry. I don't know what to say." Lovely, now he will know that I am a complete and utter fool.

"Well Ms. Donovan, would you like to meet tomorrow? I plan on being at Central Park, on 13th and Canyon."

"You can call me Libby, and I'll be there. What time? Whatever time you say." Shoot, now I sound goofy.

"I will be there about ten in the morning, by the band shell. I'll have on a blue soccer T-shirt, and I'm 6'2" with thinning dark blonde hair," he says nervously.

I can now calm myself. "Don't worry, I will know you. I'm a sixty-six-year-old woman, and I'll be carrying a small notebook. I'm not dangerous-looking."

He sighs quietly. "That is a relief, so I guess I'll see you tomorrow."

"I will be there, Andrew." I want to say I love you, but that would be just too much. I have to dial myself back and allow him to be in charge. I just have to sit here a moment and breathe.

My first move is to call Julie; I think she is as anxious about this meeting as I am. Oh sweet Auntie May, I'm going to meet my son.

My mind is reeling with excitement and guilt. I can't sit still so I pace the apartment. I fire up the laptop to type my life. I want to write a script so that I will have some words ready when we meet. I'm flustered sitting alone. All vocabulary seems to have escaped. I waste a couple of hours in search of a profound opening statement, and I have written a little more than *hello, how do you do* on the page. I want desperately to explain the emotion, the times, the fear, the guilt.

I search for explanations, why it took me so long to show up. How trite it is. I search the thesaurus for words that can explain the passage of time. Saddened how my life breaks down into a couple of pages. Even if I don't give it to him, I feel better that I have something to rehearse. It still seems inadequate. I'm just an excuse, nothing but a big whining pile of apologies.

I want to take gifts, money and everything I own to give to him. I know that isn't appropriate at this time. I decide to give him the folder of photos and the family genealogy that I have started. If it feels right, I will also give him my short biography. Julie made it clear that I have to call her from the parking lot right after we meet. I'll load my car for the ride to Omaha before I go and then I can leave from the park after we meet.

I turn on the radio and change my clothes, again. Listening to the woes of the world quiets my mind and brings my small life into perspective. I go to bed early, thinking the sooner I sleep the sooner it is tomorrow.

Suddenly, I remember the Freshman-Senior get together. I have to give it up; I was ready to go an hour and a half earlier. It is too late to go now.

My thought was that I would wake up with plenty of time to get ready. Wrong! I have napped most of the night and would get up and lay out different clothes. I finally decide to turn on the television and let the drone lull me.

Giving up about 6 AM, I prepare to go. I start with a light breakfast. The car is packed and gassed; my folders for Andrew are with my bag. The house is clean, and I'm too eager to sit here. Maybe I'll drive past the park, so I know where it is. I can take a book to fill the time. There is no reason that I can't sit there as easily as here.

Oh shoot another phone call; he is probably canceling. What a relief, it is the agency. I have a three-day job on Monday, at the University. I can run by and pick up a parking pass and time card. Luckily, they had the introduction letter and job description ready for me. They promise to send new timecards at the end of each workweek, so I'm prepared for what comes next.

After rushing around, I am still forty-five minutes early to the park. I confront my continued work on impatience. I spent years waiting, but this time, I am grateful for the extra time. I can hardly believe Andrew agreed to meet me. My emotions are on a rollercoaster, and I had to go pee twice already. I vow not to anticipate anything; I have to be open and honest. I can hide nothing from my son.

Oh my, here he comes. He is a half hour early; obviously, he has inherited my anxiety. I guess he would be somewhat nervous to meet the woman who left him. He walks directly toward me, and he has a smile on his handsome face.

"Ms. Donovan?"

"Libby, please call me Libby. Hi, Andrew." I can see some of Brad and a little of myself in his face. He smiles, and I reach out to shake his hand. He takes my hand and pulls me to him into a sincere hug. I have no control over my tears, but it was the most glorious moment of my life.

We sit together for two hours and talk constantly. I share the photos and my story, he seems grateful that I had written about his birth. He appears to understand and isn't angry with me at all. He brags about his childhood and shares great stories about his parents and sisters. He promises me more photos and tells me about his kids, my grandchildren, I can barely form the words of grandmother. There are two boys eighteen and sixteen. He also spoke of his present marriage and the light of his life, Lilly, who is two. Andrew says that having a child at his age is an incredible gift that robs you and blesses you with energy at the same time.

I don't know how the hours pass so quickly. There isn't enough time on a summer day to look at him and bask in his pride over his children. He was there for them, even after his divorce. He has dedicated his life to teaching and coaching kids. He is the most amazing man I ever met, not that I would have any preconceived notions. I can see the best of Brad in him, but he is not as extreme. He is much smarter than his father is. Andrew blames alcoholism for the end of his first marriage, but he found treatment and has six years of sobriety. We both nod in agreement that this is a genetic flaw. Silently, I realize his father wouldn't give up booze for anyone or anything. I am relieved he didn't want to talk very much about Brad; it was mostly about his life and his kids. I love this stranger and feel I have known him forever. I wish I had a lifetime to listen and look at him, but I don't deserve that privilege.

I can feel my heart swelling! I could drop dead right now and have no regrets. Knowing what I do about how each of our lives continued, I made the best choice for my baby. He would have been a different man raised in the house that resentment built, especially with his and his dad's fight with alcoholism.

He leaves to go home, and I sit wordlessly on the bench to regain the strength in my legs to be able to walk to the car. I know I have to get moving. It is an eight-hour drive to Madeline's. Making it to the car, I sit in the driver's seat and look back at the bench wrapping my mind around everything that just happened. I could still be there if Julie didn't call and break the reverie so I can hit the road. I call Madeline and let her know I'll be late.

# — 47 —

It was dark as I arrive and I can see a light in the kitchen with a single lamp lit in the living room. Madeline is waiting by the front window. She peeks out of the drapes and waves at me with a huge smile on her face. I start talking as I enter the front door, reporting every detail. She patiently listens to my story. The dear woman is excited and supportive, as she plies me with chamomile tea. We reminisce about the time I stayed with them, and she shares more stories of Andrew's childhood. We talk until midnight. Reaching over, she pats my hand. Her eyes sparkling she announces, "I haven't seen midnight since 1975." We call it a day and a night.

The next morning I am awake early, and I overhear Madeline on the telephone. Listening carefully I hear she is speaking to either John or Lorene. It sounds like they have already spoken to their son and are all pleased with the outcome. They arrange to meet for breakfast around ten. I struggle into the day and hit the shower.

We meet at Denny's because Lorene has a coupon. "Good morning, I'm so glad to meet you." She is a tiny woman, with very dark hair streaked with silver and all of her wrinkles curve upward. The two of them look like aged Hummel figurines. I extend my hand, and she pushes it aside and gives me an energetic hug. I see the family resemblance as she sits with Madeline and they deliberate the merits of pancakes versus waffles.

The conversation is light and easy. I feel comfortable in their presence. John tells me that Andrew called last night and was pleased with the meeting. He has been digging through the photos and read the letter to him. They all laugh about Andrew's second family and his excitement about looking like someone.

We argue over the check, and finally, I agree to use the coupon if they will let me pay. It is a great morning with good humor and shared stories. Their relationship gives me hope, not for myself but for marriage as an institution. I am amazed how they seem to accept me and move like a team. I'm not sure I could be nearly as gracious. I would probably feel threatened. I owe those two people more than breakfast and a muffin basket.

Once breakfast is over, I drive Madeline to the nursing home to see Mr. Ed. I proceed to tell him the whole story for the third time. He seems fascinated with everything I say, watching each word, but he doesn't respond. I tell him about Andrew and how difficult his life would have been if I kept him. I admit I would have left Brad years earlier to protect my boy. I thank him for the help so many years ago, as he sleeps.

We go home, and the two of us share a frozen pizza for dinner while chatting around the table in the kitchen. I am exhausted from the continued lack of sleep and excessive joy. It is nearly eight when Madeline and I both head for bed. I settle in to read, and suddenly I understand there are no ifs, there is only what is. The glow in my heart quiets my questioning brain, and I drift into a deep, exhausted sleep.

It is as if I slept through the weekend and the events were a lovely dream. I could not imagine such happiness and yet, here I am. Proudly I have acknowledged my past and wrestled my shame. Now when I go to bed, there is no fear or bone aching sadness. *Goodbye, Brad, old man. The only thoughts about you have been as if you were a poorly written story. I have no residual feelings for you.*

I leave Sunday mid-morning with a bag of cookies and excitement about going to work on Monday. I like the idea of going back to the University even if it is only for a three days gig. I am fortunate to have three days of a childhood dream, which is more than most people get. I restarted my life where truth is no longer a cliché.

# − 48 −

I arrive home with plenty of time for a carry out dinner and early to bed. I am so grateful for everything that has come my way. I awaken to a beautiful morning and feel gratitude for the pure emotion of happiness, no not happy − satisfied. I have to keep telling myself that it is only a three-day job at the registration office, yet it is part of one of those grand moments full of changes. Hell, I need to be realistic; the past month and a half has been monumental.

I decide not to pack a lunch, but stick a couple of breakfast bars in my bag, just in case. I'm off to work with plenty of time to spare. *Well, zippity doo dah, Libby is employed!*

The administration office directs me to Registration. It is a busy environment as they prepare for the fall semester. I discover several new things about myself; I can lift fifty pounds, but only once or twice a day. I can lift forty pounds repeatedly, but I prefer to lift twenty-five pounds. In addition, I can learn something new, and I am much friendlier than I ever expected. By lunchtime, I want to lie down for the half hour break, but there is no suitable nap area. I am invigorated, but every one of my sixty-six years is barking. I have enjoyed the day and all the new people, so I walk over to the Student Union. A turkey sandwich and iced tea help my recovery, and I can finish the day with enthusiasm. I drag home a little after five, completely physically exhausted and satisfied.

I'm anxious to go back tomorrow; it is empowering being appreciated and useful.

For my evening, I make my calls, while eating a bowl of reheated soup and early to bed. I am anxious to be bright-eyed for tomorrow. I certainly don't want the University to know they got the best of me in one day.

# — 49 —

Day two, I'm fifteen minutes early, a beautiful morning to wait outside in the best part of the day. The air is cleaner in Boulder, and I breathe easily. My muscles hurt, but I know it is a good pain, I am confident it will work out once I'm busy. Here they come, time to roll up my sleeves and go to work.

We finish setting up the registration workstations and stocking them. I help make the directive signs and double-check the inventories. One thing for sure — I am glad I wore different shoes because they keep me running. I expected to be sitting and pounding at a desk, but I was wrong.

The morning shoots past. I remember arriving, and now it is lunchtime. The University is certainly getting their money's worth out of me. I don't remember ever working so hard. I decide to go back to the Student Union, have a sandwich and some tea. It feels great to be off my feet for even a few minutes. I'm celebrating the shoe decision.

"Excuse me, do you mind if I join you?" he asks quietly.

"Dr. Jamelson, sure, please sit down. There is plenty of room." I wonder if he remembers me. He puts his tray down and sits in the chair directly across from me. He settles in and looks at me with a welcoming expression on his face.

"I beg your pardon, but I forgot your name. I was hoping that you would come to the Senior Student meeting the other night."

"My name is Libby Donovan. I was all set to go and then my whole evening blew up into a kerfuffle. I'm kind of a nomad at this time and decided it would be foolish to sign up for a class. So I went to all of the temporary employment agencies and picked up this three-day gig." I think I could be babbling.

"Not many kerfuffles these days, I will accept your excuse. The meeting was well worth it for someone planning to be on campus. I swear being here adds years and meaning to your life. There will be another get together right after the semester starts. Maybe then." He still seems familiar, the feeling that we had met before revisits. I'm also surprised he remembered me. "Where are you working?"

"I'm over at the administration and registration area. They sure have a lot to do for the start of the semester."

"I bet they do. It takes a lot of work to begin the fall session. That is always the biggest influx of students," he said.

"I didn't expect to see you again; I thought you were retired." I catch myself needling him for more information.

"I do a lot of volunteer things and fill in as a substitute from time to time. They keep me here more than when I was officially employed." He shakes his head as if he is in disbelief. "Ever since my wife died, I find it helpful to have some place to go every day."

"That is it! I knew I remembered you from somewhere. Didn't I meet you in a short story one time? Your name is different and yet familiar and I just remembered your story. It was about the loss of your wife and some bones. I remember now. Oh my, I'm so sorry, for your loss."

He laughs quietly. "So you read my story. I knew I liked you for a reason. I am so glad to meet my one and only reader. It has been years since it all happened. The bad days are fewer, and I get by."

"I am so sorry; I thought I had better manners than this." It quietly nags at me how I could recognize someone I've never met. "It was so touching about her disappearance and the pain of unanswered questions. It moved me deeply."

"Thank you. It is so seldom anyone reads short stories, especially mine. I would guess that mine was a bummer, but I had to write it out." He looks at me pensively; I can tell he is traveling back to those terrible days.

"Well, Dr. Jamelson, as much as I enjoyed seeing you again, I have to get back. Spring registration waits for no one." I gather my tray and personal items to head back to work.

He looks at me quickly, blushing. "William, please call me William. Wait, one more moment, would you like to go to coffee when you get off, or better yet, dinner? It is so seldom I meet anyone near my age group. Great to spend time with someone that knows that Paul McCartney was in a band."

"I know he was in a couple of bands. I would like that very much." Oh my Gawd, I said yes. I hope it isn't a date. "I get off around five."

"I don't have a plan. Why don't you just come back here and we can figure out what to do from there."

"Perfect." He kept it casual, thank goodness. I like him. He is smart and thoughtful with a little funny. No time to be wistful, I have to go to work.

The rest of the day is a blur. Arriving back at the Student Center about five-thirty, I find William waiting at the same table we shared at lunch. We sat telling stories for a couple of hours and split a tuna sandwich for dinner. Never did we leave the center, time just slipped by, and now I'm home. I had the best time, didn't feel flirtatious, and the blessing of a new friend. I've only known William for a couple of hours, but it feels like he has been someone I have known for years.

Too late to call Julie, so I'll just have more to talk about next time. She will have a hissy fit; I can almost hear her now. She will either object vehemently or have me married and honeymooning in Europe. I will disappoint her with the story of a pleasant evening with a charming person. Now I have to get ready for bed, working in the morning.

# — 50 —

My three days of work stretched into a week and then a week and a half. My organizational skills made it possible to help further into the registration process. I love being at the University. I met William at the Student Union, a couple of times for lunch. He isn't busy with the fall semester and is preparing for an off-campus trip once classes start. He describes it as the *benefits of a retired guy who won't stay home*. I like the atmosphere; everything seems so full of possibilities. Tomorrow is Friday, and I know I will miss this place.

So caught up with the work I didn't think much about anything else. I do have a missed call on my phone. It looks like a local number and then I notice the message. I should start checking my phone occasionally, now that I'm a productive member of Boulder.

"Libby, this is Andrew. I enjoyed meeting you and thank you for making contact. I have decided I would like to talk to my father. I would appreciate it if you could join us at the park Sunday, around two for a picnic. I'll have my family there; they would like to meet you too."

My first thought was to get ready, except I have two days wait before it is time to be there. I call and leave a message that I will be there, and ask what I can bring. I'll get to meet my grandchildren. How did I get so lucky, my heart is pounding? I should take gifts. Kids like gifts, right?

I know it is time to contact Brad. I need to tell him about Andrew before he gets the call. Shit, but one encouraging thing, his reach doesn't extend this far. Take care of the worst first, before I over think the situation.

"Hello Brad, this is Elizabeth. I need to speak to you about something important. I will call back in a couple of hours."

"Hello! Elizabeth, don't hang up." He sounds groggy.

"Late night last night?" What is with me, I should have let it go; I guess my secret plan was to piss him off before I drop the bomb.

"No, but then I was up late watching TV. I don't sleep much anymore. Where are you? Are you coming home? I will pick you up?"

"No Brad, I'm not coming back, but I need to talk to you when you are clear headed. I'll call back in a couple of hours."

"No Elizabeth, I'm okay now, I was just waking up. Please don't hang up."

"Well I have to talk to you about something from a long time ago, and I would prefer you sit down."

"I'm lying down, will that work? I can't imagine anything worse than what you have put me through now." He is speaking much more clearly; maybe he was just waking up. There I go giving him credit when I know better. He may have been home but so was Johnny Walker. "Your paycheck was never deposited."

There it goes, thank you for confirming my decision to leave. "Don't worry about it, I have it handled. I have one thing to talk to you about, and that will be it." Listen to me, I'm in charge here, and he quiets down. "Do you remember when we broke up in high school?"

"Yes, that was my fault; I was young and made a mistake." His voice trails off.

"I don't care about blame on this, Brad. I was young and had a bigger problem at the time. Remember when I told you I might be pregnant and you got so mad?" I can hear the nervousness in my voice.

"Yeah, but I forgave you about that. It all worked out."

"No, it was not OK. I was pregnant, and I was terrified. You accused me of terrible things, and you knew better. Sorry, I digress. When I was about seven months along, I told my mother, and she helped me." My voice cracks with the raw emotion, strangles me even now. The years and tears cover my face, and I pray that he can't hear the pain in my voice.

"What? You never said anything. What happened? Why didn't you tell me? Did you have an abortion?"

"Brad, there is so much here, and I feel terrible. It was too late for an abortion and if you recall, they were illegal then. When I left that summer, I didn't go to help my aunt. I went to a friend of my mother's and stayed with them until I had the baby."

"Baby, Elizabeth! Was it – was it a boy? Where is he?" He is certainly awake now.

"Yes, Brad it is a boy and now a man. You have to remember that was a long time ago; things were different then. You made it clear to me that you would leave me to handle everything alone, and I did the best I could. Mom helped, and she made all of the arrangements to take care of everything. I still had dreams then; I wanted to go to school, I wanted to be someone. It was all a huge mistake." I continued to cry silently, and my breath catches in my heart.

There is silence, and finally, Brad speaks. "Elizabeth, I am sorry. I thought you were just trying to manipulate me. I would have married you, we would have raised him." I can hear the guilt in his voice. "I can't believe you never told me. I have another son. Where is he? Are you with him? You are living with him, aren't you?"

"He is forty-eight, and I just met him, for a couple of hours. He is a man that will make you proud. I can see you in his face and yet he is definitely his own person."

"Who the hell are you, Elizabeth? You have had years to tell me this. Where is he? I want to see him, and I want to talk to him now. I have to meet him. Tell me where you are and I'm on my way." A hoarse sob interrupts his tirade.

"No, Brad, I am leaving all contact up to him. He has asked for your information, and I will give it to him with your permission. I don't believe we have a right to force ourselves on him or his family. I just wanted to tell you myself. I need you to be prepared and to treat him with respect."

"His family? He has children?" His voice cracks again; I can tell the past weeks have taken a toll on him. "Please, Elizabeth, say where you are, I can take it. Are you with another man?"

"No other man Bradan Donovan. You were enough. I will give Andrew your information. Finally, I need you to hear this Brad, I'm done – finished. I'm never coming back."

"Andrew. His name is Andrew?"

"Yes, Andrew Scortino. I will let him know that you are OK with a call. You both can blame all of this on me. I'm the one who kept the secrets. I have already told him that you didn't know about him. I'm sure he found it difficult to understand that I married you, and we still didn't go back for him." I can't explain to anyone why I kept this for so long. "I'm hanging up now, Brad."

"No Elizabeth, please don't go. I forgive you for the pickles. Tell me more about him. How you are doing? I feel so alone, and I regret everything I ever did to you. I will change." He is crying again; I can hear it in his voice.

"I'm all right, Brad. I have to go." I know that his vulnerable side is the hook with me, and I will not fall into the trap. "I don't plan on ever coming back, so you can move on with your life."

"Are you going to divorce me? What are your plans? I need to know, Elizabeth."

"I don't know. I haven't thought about divorce yet. I guess I will be back in touch with you when

I figure some things out, but it will be later, much later. I don't want you calling me either."

"But Elizabeth, everything is in both of our names, I need you. I can't do it." I can hear the anger creeping into his voice.

"Everything is yours; I don't want anything. I will send you my email address, and you can use that to contact me about legal issues. I have to go now, goodbye." I hung up the phone and breathed a sigh of relief. *I did it! I talked to him, and I didn't fall into the old routine we danced for years.* I'm too weak to stand. The conversation brought back all of the years, not only of the pain and shame, but also his fragility and my need to protect him. I can't do anything over, but for now, I have to compose myself and prepare for tomorrow.

# — 51 —

I wake up slumped over in the chair with the phone still in my hand a little after ten. I drag myself straight to bed and am glad I already had on pajamas. I worry about being able to sleep after dozing in the chair, but the worry was for nothing. An immense weight is gone, and I fall into a deep dreamless rest.

As usual, I am on time for another day of University life. I can't believe how free I feel, but there is also a dread of waking up still in Kokomo. It was such a short time ago that I had no hope and no future, a robot clicking off the days leading to nowhere. Everything changed with the last fight and a pickle jar.

As I walk to the University building, I click off today's gratitude. I have friends, new possibilities every day, there is enough money, and only one person to feed who isn't particular. Wishing I had walked out on Brad earlier doesn't do anything but frustrate me. Some things no one can change. I confess that the details don't matter because I'm here and not in Kokomo. He can cry and send me all the shame he desires; I have had enough for this lifetime. I consciously refuse to accept more.

This week I am refreshed and full of hope and new beginnings. Positive that there is no way Brad can re-enter my life. I hadn't thought about a divorce; I decide I don't care enough to worry about his questions and the legalities until later. Stuck in Brad's reality for so long, my newfound energy and boldness amaze me. I feel alive and almost girlish. I spent much of my life silent with my head down, waiting for something different; it was up to me all along. Two months ago, I would hardly speak, and now I meet people and do important work.

I wish that when I was young, the choices they have now were available. Women were trapped in the shame of sexuality for thousands of years. My disgrace was at the beginning of the resurrection of the women's movement. It has taken time, but I can see young women taking charge of their choices. Bless the Age of Aquarius, a few years late. How many of us gave up our babies or had illegal abortions we didn't want? How many died? I decided years ago to respect every story as unique and valid. I have viewed significant changes over the last fifty years, but progress is slow and yet not enough. I hope to be alive for the day women are credited as full adults and able to look equality in the eye. I realize girls today can never know the pain and the complicated history of their progress. I shake my head; we have this relatively wealthy, educated society and many still deny the women. Life can still difficult for young mothers, but at least, they can stay in school. There is some help available, although there is a contingent of self-appointed judges trying to take us back to the '50s, the 1850s. I can't think of any good reason to go back to those good old days. I have wondered a multitude of times about what my life would have been with different choices. I shake my head. There is no living in the *what-ifs;* some things are for the storytellers. I should take a philosophy class so I can contemplate all I want and earn college credit.

The morning of reflection brings me to a busy day. The job now extends to the middle of next week, and I have another two-day job the week after. I've had lunch with Dr. Jamelson a total of three times and dinner once. I like him; he is so smart and kind. He has traveled all over the world and has a gentle nature. Julie teases about my "boyfriend," but that seems ridiculous at our age and doesn't even consider my emotional disposition. He doesn't feel like a lover, father or brother, but a friend, someone I can spend time with and trust. I haven't told him all the ugly details of my story, but I sense I could. In such a few days, I fell into a satisfying rhythm. Staying busy quiets my mental masochism. I expected more regret over Brad, but I have mostly felt relief. For now, it is work, eat, read and television.

I struggle trying to wait until Saturday; I want to prepare for the picnic. For someone who has spent decades waiting, patience has become my challenge. I decide to take some small gifts for Andrew's family and options bounce through my mind. I have to take everything a day at a time, so I don't set myself up for disappointment. Anticipation will be banished, at least until the weekend. Just another lie I tell myself. I will keep busy, not obsess, and plan to imitate a sane person when I'm in public from now on.

# — 52 —

"Hi William, is this seat taken?" He looks up to me cheerfully.

"You know it is waiting for you, Libby."

I blush. "I'm going to miss lunches with you, William. I look forward to them. The administrative department said that if they need anyone again, they will request me from the agency. So I might be back."

He is looking at me thoughtfully "Well, you know friendships are hard to find, so I want to give you my phone number and address." He hands me a business card with a handwritten number. "I also have something I would like to talk to you about."

"Thank you for the number. I don't want our friendship to fade away. Do you have another card and I'll give you mine." As I dig through my handbag for a pen, "You mentioned something else?" I ask.

William laughs and responds, "Why yes I do have a... a proposition."

"It has been years since there has been a proposition. You are too kind, but I don't think this is that kind of friendship."

"Libby, ole gal, this is a real sort of proposal I have in mind." I can see it is William's turn to blush.

"Have we gotten off topic?" He has piqued my interest. What in the world, would he want from me?

William clears his throat and puts on a business face. "As you know I do a lot of volunteer work here at the University. We talked about some of the field trips with the Archeology and Anthropology departments that I have been on."

"I remember you are leaving for one of the trips when school starts. The reason for the number exchange, right?" I return his reserved expression and a chill run up my spine.

Slowly a knowing grin creases his face, and he continues. "With the budget cuts, there are more volunteer opportunities. We are taking a class to New Mexico on an archeological dig once the semester begins."

"That sounds outrageous. You must be excited."

"I do enjoy these trips. I've been going on one, sometimes two, a year. One of our regular volunteers has stepped down due to a sudden health issue, and we need someone that can work with the students on the cleaning and cataloging of the artifacts. That person would need to be able to leave on short notice and have clerical skills. Of course, I thought of you."

"Oh, my sweet Aunt Nellie's ghost! Damn right, you thought of me. This sounds incredible. And you said in New Mexico?" I'm surprised that I don't pee my pants; I might have to check to be sure.

He is beaming and almost aglow with the news. "Hold on, Lady, calm down. You remember this is a non-paying volunteer position. You would get housing with the students and some food, but you would have to pay your transportation and extras. I repeat there are no wages at all."

"William, I don't care. This trip is the most amazing opportunity I have ever heard. I have never even considered fantasizing something so magnificent. I have money set back and even if I didn't, I would find a way. My finances are already set up; all I pay is rent and utilities. I can pay those online. Oh, how I love technology." I silently send a little gratitude muffin basket to Bill Gates and Steve Jobs and another to all of their friends and family. "Who do I contact, what do I fill out? Do you need a check? I don't have to think about this, I want it." There is no controlling my enthusiasm as I fight the urge to dance. My childhood passion has been reignited. "I have been captivated with archeology and prehistory since I was young and even took a community college class back in the 70s. So, I'm only 99% rookie."

He is laughing now. "Whoa, Libby, I thought you might be interested in an adventure, but I had no idea you would be on the edge of a stroke. I believe you should take some time to think about it..."

We both laugh. This is a huge break; the only thinking I would do is what to pack. I've never been free for this kind of adventure, and this is in *freaking New Mexico.*

He changes back to his business tone. "OK, I did bring the application for you; I hoped you would be interested. Your background and skills could fit very well into the class. I already talked to Professor Blankenship about you, and we will see what we can put together. Do you have a passport? "

"A passport? New Mexico is in the United States, isn't it?"

"If this works out, Libby, New Mexico isn't the only dig site. There are other opportunities next summer."

He continues to chuckle, and I realize that he is teasing. I never thought about a passport before, but I think I will find out about one today when I get home. "Will you be talking with Professor Blankenship today, William? I don't want anyone else to get in front of me. Do you want me to walk you over there now?"

"Don't worry; I am already scheduled to see him once we finish lunch. Ramona called last night; her husband was diagnosed with cancer, and she has to pull out. Paul called me in a panic; it is so close to time to leave. I already know about you, and he was particularly pleased with your background. I told him you were perfect. We don't have time to do the standard search and, to top it off, we can afford you."

"William, when does this happen? What do I need to get prepared, besides the passport to New freaking Mexico?" I am amazed how life is taking care of me. I don't see a relationship with the woman running away on the side of the highway in Kokomo. Maybe the old life wasn't Karma; this new life is. I took the long, rough road to get here. If my existence had an agenda, it didn't get the memo. It all seems like magic. I am anxious to go home and make my phone calls.

I have never thought about a passport, but now I feel like it is a necessity. I need to prepare as the world opens. I'm sure Google will provide everything I need. I'm still trying to grasp this break; it answers wishes I didn't have the courage to desire.

In a little more than a week, I have met my son, and will be seeing my grandchildren next. Then it is off to New Mexico with the University. How quickly I have gone from a day-to-day numbness to a dance of adventure and learning. I have seen more of this country since I left than I had experienced in the previous sixty-six years.

I have to restrain myself from running out to buy new clothes and backpacks until I know for sure. I struggle to live in the moment and quit questioning the future. The school needs me, I know this is going to work out; I'm going to New Mexico.

# − 53 −

My weekend fills with all kinds of activity. I decide to take kites to meet my grandchildren. I can't believe how much I like saying the word grandchildren. I buy six kites because I don't know who is going to be there. My new life motto, at least for today, is you can never have too many. Kites take me back to my most cherished childhood memories. Here I am, trying not to be too early with a homemade peach cobbler. I want to bring something that shows effort and not just a bakery item. I'm nervous and very excited.

Luckily, they are already at the picnic area, and I hear Andrew's voice laughing and talking with his boys. Thank goodness, it is a small get-together, just Andrew, his kids, and I see his wife, Bonnie, over by a grill.

As I walk up to the group, I announce, "Anyone want to fly a kite?" I hear a slight quiver in my bravado. Andrew comes over, gives me a hug and introduces me to his family, as I hand out kites to everyone. The older boys seem pleased with the gift, and they take off for the field. I decide to stay behind and help Bonnie lay out the plates and food. She is lovely; I can see that there is a considerable age difference between her and Andrew. I know this not my business and I ask no questions. It appears to my untrained eye she may have too much food. Bonnie must be reading my mind as she mentions that with the two teenage stepsons, too much food is impossible. The oldest, Robert, looks just like his father and I can't help seeing my own Dad in his personality. They didn't know that Robert was my dad's name until I gave him the box of photos with my letter. The younger son, John, must look like his mother and is the clown of the family. They are beautiful children, and they truly love their father. I try to congratulate Andrew, but he says that his ex-wife deserves all of the credit. I allow him his secrets.

The baby, Lilly, is easy, she comes to me and sticks by my side for the afternoon. We fly her kitten kite and I sit in the shade with her Littlest Ponies. I can't believe the all-encompassing love I feel for this family and especially for this little banana pudding of a girl. She makes me feel as if I belong here.

Once the afternoon shadows begin to grow long, and the boys wander off to a concession stand, scavenging for more food. Holding Lilly on my lap, Andrew and Bonnie begin to tell stories. He has shared my letter with her. Bonnie is bright and eighteen years younger than Andrew. They have been married four years and Lilly is her only child. She seems sympathetic to my situation, but she must question my choices.

When Andrew picks up Lilly and starts to swing her around, Bonnie says, "Andrew is trying not to judge you, but at the same time he has some issues understanding why it took you so long."

"I don't know the answer myself. It was as if I couldn't get over the shame and humiliation of my choices. At first, it was fear and then later I was protecting him from his father. Years slipped away, and as I sit I'm shocked how much time has passed and how old I have become."

Close to sunset, we have eaten too much food and laughed even more. My grandsons are back with some questionable dietary choices, but I must admit they are very smart, polite and handsome. I would like to meet their mother someday, but for now, I am grateful for the kindness they have extended to me, and happy they have a satisfying life. I swell with pride as if my heart may explode. The boys share some of their lives, about school and sports. I tell everyone about my opportunity to go to New Mexico. They are excited for me, and Robert says he would go in a New York second, and I would be a noob to miss that chance. I'm not sure about many things, but being a noob is nothing I want to be.

We clean our picnic site, preparing to leave, when I pull Andrew aside and give him the contact information on Brad. I explain the telephone call and his father's reaction to the news. I share more of the ugly details of how I left and that Brad doesn't know where I am. I feel the familiar shame flood back; he puts his arm around me and holds me close. He utters very quietly, "Don't worry, Mom, I won't betray you. I understand him. I'm an alcoholic, too."

Mom, he called me Mom, and this is the best day of the greatest week of my life. I go home with visions of the day replaying. My heart is full, and I will carry the memory forever. I am going to send a bouquet to Lorene and John Scortino, which is inadequate, but I don't know how else to show appreciation. Once again, I am assured the decision to give Andrew up was the right choice and the Scortinos were the parents he deserved. If I had kept him, he would have lived a life with a mean man and a broken woman. There would be no way he would have been able to beat the demon alcohol in our home. I can imagine the other life, but I'm too happy to allow it to take hold of my thoughts.

# — 54 —

I am lucky I didn't have a job posting for Monday. I hang my kite on the wall, so I can see it and remember the perfect day. I can process the passport application and get the two photos and drop it all off at the post office. Nothing like two photos to demonstrate how much time has passed. The vision of myself inhabits the 80s, only with a different color of hair. The passport should be here in ten days to two weeks. Now off to meet William for lunch at the University. He will introduce me to Dr. Blankenship, and then I will learn more about the dig.

Damn, that old man always beats me here. I am ten minutes early, and there he is with his customary cup of coffee. "Hey William, good afternoon. Do you have a home, or do you live right here?"

"Hi Libby, I don't live here all the time, but it does give me access to coffee without the curse of making it." He looks genuinely happy to see me; I hadn't had that kind of reception since before my parents passed away.

"Have you already eaten?"

"No, I like to get my first cup, and then I'm ready to eat when my lovely companion arrives."

"You are so full of it, William, but thank you. Your baloney makes me feel young and girly." We settle down for food and chatter as he explains the archeology and anthropology programs and the field trips. They have other programs that are in foreign countries offered by the University. There are few volunteer spots, because once someone signs on, they stay for years. I am learning so much, and that includes the value of making new friends. I would never have this opportunity if I didn't talk to William at the job fair.

Once lunch is complete, William walks me over to meet Dr. Blankenship. He is young; I find it unnerving and feel a little decrepit. At the very least, I didn't have to show him my passport photo or lift fifty pounds. Dr. B explains how I will be part of the support team and describes more about the dig. He has given me the packing suggestions list and the other handouts provided to the students. I walk away jazzed with excitement. We will be at an Anasazi site. Anasazi means the ancient ones, which means I won't be the oldest bag of bones there. He assures me that if I like it, this can be a regular volunteer position. I like the idea of spending time with the students, and I swear I can keep up with the kids. I'm not worried. I can do this, and I have all the skills they describe from my old job. Dr. Blankenship told me last year they took classes to Portugal, the United Kingdom, and Italy. They are working on several joint excavations with other universities, including this one in New Mexico.

A life story cannot be written until it is over. This chapter doesn't quite flow with the previous ones, but for now, I will make my phone calls and start reading. I study New Mexico, the Anasazi's and archeological digs. I have much to absorb, and this will be the second-best adventure in my life. I am a new person, and I like this me much more. I have become physically incapable of allowing negative thoughts to interfere.

As I fill out the application and sign the hold harmless, I need to have an emergency contact. I give them Julie's name and number and will ask her tonight. They don't agree with my suggestion that if I stroke out, they can just push me into a hole nearby. I have to look at this seriously now that I have a son and grandchildren to consider.

# — 55 —

I receive another invite from Andrew and Bonnie; his parents are coming for dinner. It is good to see John again, but I'm especially pleased to spend more time with Lorene. As usual, I'm ten minutes early and yet the last to arrive. Lorene is playing on the floor with Lilly when I arrive. We exchange our hellos. She struggles to get up, and as I lend a hand, we both almost end up on the floor. We discuss the passage of time and all the humiliating changes our bodies force on us. We slip into stories about our son starting with the day they took him. She is wearing a rose from the flowers I had sent and points out that after fifty years, you don't often get flowers unless it is too late to appreciate them. I can't help but just watch the family interaction and relationships. Knowing I am an outsider, I appreciate the kindness of including me. I'm the only one who knows the complicated life Andrew would have had with the Donovans. I bow to the Scortinos for being the real parents my boy deserves.

After a lovely meal, Lorene and I take over the dinner clean up and let Bonnie sit down for a few minutes. She calls us *the moms* and I fight back tears. I would love to talk to Lorene well into the morning hours, but there are others around all demanding attention. I don't know if I could be as gracious with a woman blowing into town and working her way into my family. She appears to be interested in me and expresses her gratitude, but I want to know the whole story. She says that if it weren't for Andrew opening them to other options, they would never have imagined the family they built. Lorene tells of foster children and two daughters adopted from Korea. She glows with the memories and the closeness of their patchwork family. Lorene admits there have been highs and lows, but credits my misdeeds as a blessing, and a God sent opportunity for them.

John comes into the small kitchen and promises they would come back over and bring Madeline before I leave for New Mexico. I am grateful for my small part of this extraordinary family.

Before I leave, I call Andrew aside. I hand him the tattered savings book, my first account I had started before he was born.

"No, Libby. I don't want money. I just want to know you and have you in my life. I'm doing just fine; I would much rather you live well."

Tears fill my eyes, and I'm embarrassed that I tried to give money, but he doesn't seem angry. I'm touched he is the first person to wish for me to live well since my parents passed.

He goes on. "I have made contact with Brad, and we had a very pleasant conversation. He apologized for not knowing about me and wants to meet."

My warning flag immediately comes into play, "Oh, and will this happen soon?"

"When we spoke, Brad was pushing to visit here, but I understand how this could be touchy with your relationship and all."

I stand quietly and decide on the truth. "I worry about his finding me; my leaving was not an amicable situation. I'm not afraid like when I left, but I don't want to see him. It is up to you. I can deal with whatever comes."

"Don't worry, I didn't tell him where we live, and we only mentioned you briefly. I offered to visit him in Indiana over a weekend."

Now that I have people, the crippling fear of him has begun to dissipate. "Since you so gallantly rejected the savings account, how about if I pay for your ticket, if that is alright with you?"

"OK, deal, Libby." We shake hands. "Now I can afford to take Robert with me. I want to go before school starts and raising kids doesn't always make money available. Thank you."

"Then I'll buy two tickets; let's do this tonight or tomorrow if it is OK with you. I can give you some walking around money too."

"No, that is too much, and he hasn't agreed to my visit yet. He is pushing to come here, and I am sure he can figure out by the area code on the phone number that we are in Boulder. I will call him with a date and let you know."

It is overwhelming and yet astonishing that I had no idea how empty my life has always been. The laughter, noise, and activity of family and children fill the rest of the evening.

The night starts to wind down at Lilly's bedtime. She is fighting sleep, wanting to stay at the party. The boys slip away to their room and video games. Lilly, my heart, calls for a story from her room. Lorene waves for me to go to her. I would read to that child for a year if she asked.

On my way home, I'm exhausted from all of the activity and chatter. I make an overdue resolution. Every day has made me stronger, but it is time I finish talking with Brad. There are other people involved, and it is time. I applaud myself that he controls less of my thoughts, and I no longer live exclusively in the past. If he can stall just for two weeks, I'll be in New Mexico, and he can visit all he wants.

# — 56 —

I work a two-day job at an insurance office in Boulder and Andrew goes to Indiana the next weekend. Upon his return, he calls to let me know it went well. He was very proud to take Robert and have proof of his worthy family. Brad took them around Kokomo and made sure they didn't miss any of the sights. He sweetly told me that Brad looked a lot older than I do, which I accept as a compliment. Andrew added that a one-day visit was enough time. It was clear Brad could compromise his sobriety. He took them to the Hitching Post for dinner and kept running back and forth from the bar, bringing friends to meet them in the dining room. Andrew voices gratitude for Robert being too young for the bar. Andrew doesn't want to talk too much more about the visit, but indicates he understands more now. There is no plan to go back to Indiana any time soon. Sheepishly he adds Brad might visit Colorado over the holidays.

I am sure at some point; he will know where I am and realize my anxiety is nearly gone. I'll be in a different state before he gets it organized. With a relieved sigh, I move my focus to packing for New Mexico.

I buy digging clothes, loose jeans, long sleeved shirts, hats and a huge backpack. I learn from Dr.

Blankenship not to take very much; there is a limited area for storage, and I have to carry all of my things. I learn everything will be full of dirt in short order. I work on the list and don't add anything except mascara. Each item confirms my transformation.

I did much of the student's assigned reading about the ancient history, Anasazi and Pueblos. My background is limited to one class forty some years ago and watching archeology shows on the History Channel. I elect to accept that everyone in the team is going to know more, and my position is to serve and learn. There is so much to discover, and I'm excited with every detail. I catch myself wondering about the history I learned in school. I had good grades in high school, but I think I added bad movies and half-read books into my Native American education. I visit the library multiple times to work on the humiliation of my ignorance. Maybe history changed when I wasn't watching.

Dr. Blankenship arranges a get-together with Ramona, the woman I am replacing. We meet for coffee and then lunch while she explains the bookkeeping programs and inventory spreadsheets I will need. Together we discuss double entries, and the basics. Even with all of the details, there is nothing I can't handle. She originated a computer program, and they have added to it making things cumbersome and antiquated. She explains that the software needs an update and mentions some new programs. She already made a request. We giggle knowingly over the expense and the University conveniently ignoring each requisition. Ramona gives me blank copies for the handwritten ledgers. She maintains these as a backup due to the age of the computers and erratic electricity at the dig sites. As soon as I arrived home, I slip two flash drives into the front pocket of the backpack and price a simplified bookkeeping program. I will be doubling diligence and back up the files several times a day.

In my nightly conversation with Julie, she mentions that if I am going to do these rough and tumble adventure things, I should have a will and some insurance. Then I can rest, knowing that whatever I have goes to Andrew and the kids and not to Brad. She is right again, and I understand some things cannot be repaid; we can only appreciate.

After all these years, I still feel a need to ask for permission. I admit the freedom is invigorating and yet worrisome. I don't have any trepidation about going; just feel like I'm a naughty child. As soon as we hang up, I rush to the laptop and sign on. I purchase a small life insurance policy and use a legal website to draw up a one-page will. I will have it signed and notarized tomorrow morning. I have already given Andrew and Madeline copies of my keys and talked to my landlord. I paid the rent in advance, and I'm ready to go.

Amazing how much work it is to go away for eight weeks. I send William and Dr. Blankenship an invisible gratitude muffin basket, as I finish preparations to leave. It took forty-nine years to plan my last trip; anything else feels like a rush. The days disappear in an instant. I decide I will ride in a University van as a backup driver.

William picks me up at 4:30 AM on the first Thursday after the semester starts. He is a few minutes early, driven by a desire, or maybe a need for his first cup of coffee. I load my backpack and laptop into the rear of the van and slide into the passenger seat. I flash him my passport and say, "I'm worried, I applied for a travel visa to New Mexico, and it hasn't arrived. Do you think there will be a problem getting in?"

I love it when he is flummoxed, taking me seriously. He looks blankly and finally smiles, shakes his head and mutters "Libby." Once loaded, we drive straight to the Dunkin Donut's drive through, and William joins the living. We reach the University by five, and I meet the four students riding with us and fall in line with three other vans of volunteers, students, and supplies. I'm not sure how William found the second cup, but his coffee consumption gives me comfort knowing we will have bathroom breaks.

The students are excited, just like I am. There is an ongoing conversation in the rear seats, about history and technology. The vans stay connected by radios and the morning hours are full of youthful possibilities. Within a couple of hours, the snoozing begins, and they settle into the reality of the long ride to New Mexico.

# — 57 —

It is early, there isn't enough light to check my watch, I know it isn't quite five. Like every morning, since we arrived a week ago, it is still dark and quiet in the dormitory when I awaken. My first thought is a prayer of appreciation and my good fortune to be here. I stay in the women's dorm, which is a metal Quonset hut. I don't fit with the students, but they are kind enough to ignore the almost fifty-year age gap. They make me feel like a team mascot in a tight community. I adore the way they tease and make an effort to include me. I bask in the warmth of the students. Quickly they stop calling me Mrs. Donovan, and now it is Ms. Libby. I love it.

I learn to ignore the nagging worries about keeping up with the dig team's energy; I search for my tube of Ben Gay – thank you, William, for that secret piece of advice. Dad's words run through my head a couple of times a day, *If it don't hurt, it ain't working*. This morning it all hurts, but once I get going, I can count on the pain melting away. The kids do the heavy, dirtiest work, and I am envious. No denying my job is also physically demanding. The majority of the finds are small, but often in groups, so they supply me with an assistant for part of each day. Each of the students will take turns on Libby duty, giving me a chance to spend personal time with everyone. I would like to be sitting in the dirt with them, making significant discoveries, but so much could be lost if I wasn't here to bag and tag. Each discovery must be cleaned, photographed, labeled, and cataloged and that is where I am the queen.

I'm not immune to the mud and filth; it has become part of the thrill of the search. I can barely stifle a chuckle remembering the girls' competition last night about the places they found dirt after the showers. With the blessing of age and the body changes, I won the contest; none of them has a wattle – yet.

Within two days, I stop being concerned about my flabby arms sticking out of the second-hand T-shirts. Every inch and crevice of my body is swathed in the red sand and dust.

I work from dawn to exhaustion like everyone else. The biggest difference in age, besides appearance, is noticeable in the evenings when I doze off while they are still laughing. I appreciate the luxury of each sunrise while they try to sleep until the heat takes over. The predawn is mine, and I cherish it. I've never been a writer, but in these quiet hours, I find it necessary just to think and scribble the disjointed thoughts in my journal. Silently I celebrate the spirit and potential of each student, but I know how life can serve up surprises. I worry about them and at the same time, I'm exhilarated. They will always have this adventure. I keep silent about my concern for them sacrificing their incredible possibilities to build someone else's dreams. I know it happens too many times, usually to the girls. I slip on today's cleanest clothes and creep to the latrine, and then I quietly take up my morning guard post on the stone outcropping and wait for the sun as I drift into scattered fantasies.

I replace much of my silent contemplations as the astonishing amount of information bombards me. I turn to a clean page in my notebook and scribble questions and ideas. I trust answers will come later. Appalled by the inadequate image of Native Americans I had believed was history. I feel foolish that I didn't know the variety and complexity of the many tribes. Number one, they all didn't wear massive eagle feather headdresses and eat nothing but buffalo. I'm embarrassed by my lack of knowledge and insight. In the evening conversations, I learn of the multitudes of large and small communities all over the Americas each with a diverse culture. I have learned to keep quiet and take mental notes.

By the end of the first week, I start to prepare for each day, writing in the quiet morning, making sense of the day before. Learning from the gathering of young and educated minds, I appreciate that I still have life and health enough for this experience. A special bonus, my heritage becomes richer too.

The dream is with me almost every night now, and I am no longer a spectator, but a participant. She has been with me for so long I accept her as my guardian angel. I have shared much of my life with this woman, and we both have a love for the boy. I miss him on the nights they don't appear. I gaze at the promontory just outside of the pueblo and Kiva dig site. This area is similar to the dream. At least, I tell myself it is; they are always around sandstone and on a cliff above a sleeping village. I feel her presence strongly in the early morning when I wait to welcome the day. I doze, and the dream replays showing more details and at the darkest moment of the vision, there is a noise, a throbbing ache, and it ends. It has always ended suddenly, but this time, it is different with the noise and pain. I have studied the details over the decades, but it has become an emotional dream with a knowing dread.

So begins my favorite part of the day as the sun kisses the night sky and gradually lights the ancient one's pueblos with a warm golden glow. I feel the original energy as the previous inhabitants' commune in the coolness of the morning. Their power permeates the camp, and all of my senses attune to the lives that came before. They slowly give up scraps of a very real existence. In each item I touch, I feel the energy, knowing an actual person used this over a millennium ago. It is hard work, but I'm determined to soldier through and not complain. I crave the teasing and will break a hip to avoid their pity. This morning, after a generous helping of muscle cream, I stretch and flex my achy hands. I rub to energize this dependable old body and get ready for the others to join the morning.

I'm beginning to hear mumbling from the men's building; I appreciate that it is their turn to cook, and it brings a smile. I smell the coffee, knowing that William is moving about, and the aroma is the precursor to the rolls and fruit to start another day. I sit in my dirty jeans, Walter Mondale T-shirt, hand-washed underwear, and silently I watch the modern day struggle to awaken and take control of the ancient site. Deep in my bones I know today is going to be extraordinary, although I have this feeling every morning. I wasn't this excited at my wedding, but I remember the joy as tainted with guilt and foreboding.

I send subliminal messages to the sleeping teams: you are missing the best part of the day, chuckleheads, and the peace of the canyon. I overlook the same little clearing just above the rocks feeling I could stay there forever and find peace. "Come on everyone. Get up; there are pots, tools, and lives to be unearthed!"

Once the sun shows its face, I slip over to the cook tent. I watch the bleary-eyed advisors and students stumble in, and the chatter begins. We are a family of brilliant minds and baggy pants. They have no idea how honored I am to be part of it. Fingering the comfort of my necklace, I listen to the conversations among the professors.

"Good morning, Star Shine, nice to see you down from your hidey-hole."

"Nice to see you too, stranger. Sit down, William, and share the exciting stories from the men's dorm."

"You know how those kids are, going to sleep late and getting up slow. At what point does your biological clock reverse itself? I'm sure the men's dorm is not a whole lot different from the women's. I've noticed you up early, and since the first morning, you have been at the same spot, gazing at the horizon. Why? The girls put you out?"

"No, William, they are very patient with me. Do you remember that recurring dream I told you about that evening at dinner?"

"Sure, Libby, the one you had since you were a child?"

"Exactly, that one. They are with me every night now."

"The woman and the boy?"

"Exactly, the dream belongs here. Every night it becomes more detailed and intense. On our first morning, I knew where to sit so I could view the promontory. I feel the spirit of the place when I sit there and yet it is peaceful. As if the spot has been waiting for me and I was slow at finding it. I am the guardian of the promontory."

"Well, Libby, old girl, have you gone up to the outcrop you are watching? I notice you there every morning, but never felt right about approaching. It seemed like an intrusion."

"I have thought about climbing, but it is pretty high, and we stay busy here in the camp." I fail to mention my fear of that spot overlooking everything.

The noise picks up as the teams arrive. They are laying out the plans and assignments for the day. Slowly with the trickle of students, excitement fills the room. I top off my thermos with tea, and a take an extra muffin to the cataloging area. It is time to set up for another day of dirt, heat, and adrenaline. I help fill the water bottles to take to my work area. Once there, I begin to lay out my tools, and I can hear the joviality spread as they leave for their assignments; the morning quiets down quickly as they become engaged in the exploration, and I wait. I never wait very long.

By the second week, the teams have developed a rhythm to the work. Not as many questions, just quiet scratching and searching with an occasional shout out. Students come in and out of my area regularly, bringing in finds and picking up more water.

Today I notice several move to a new test pit away from the main dig. I overhear that it is a short distance from the pueblos and not at the primary site. William is immersed in conversation with the mapping team, and I was unaware of this new location. We spent more time together when we were lunching in Boulder. William is always a part of the ongoing debates about the new technology and the expansion of the science. Late one evening, he found some satellite images and researched for additional detail. There was a shadow of a disturbance, and since this area is away from the main community section. William took the printouts to Dr. Blankenship. They went over it with magnifying glasses and decided it warranted further research. He mentioned a new area, but there were no particular details. William and Dr. B are the only ones involved in the decision. William takes a couple of students today, as the main site is a little slow. The area has been a very active site with multiple excavations and universities. They were unsure what the satellite image is showing, and William wouldn't let it go. Dr. B isn't partial to the location, but there are enough questions to warrant a look-see.

My day is quieter than usual, and my aches are grateful for a break. I'm able to get some labeling set up for the next big rush and catch up on yesterday's inventory photographs and spreadsheet. I finally have a chance to write the update for the University newsletter. I try to keep things organized at all times because I never know when it will get crazy. They seldom find one item, as the discoveries come in groups and occasionally piles. I watch the teams head out for their assignments, with the majority staying in the main work area. Two of the men go with William for a test pit in his new location. My day drags with very few visitors and nothing new brought in for cataloging. I do another backup on the laptop and decide I might walk down and watch them work.

"Ms. Libby, what's up?"

Hearing my name draws my attention as Belinda enters the tent. I'm probably closest to her. She is a self-admitted dirt nerd, and she checks on me through the day. She is the one who makes sure I'm not too hot, have water and nags me about meals. I probably remind her of a grandmother, or two, and I cherish the extra attention.

"You won't believe what they are finding at the new site." She reveals some of the other teams have started gathering there. She fills her backpack with additional water, twine, markers and the backup camera. She doesn't stay and rushes back out. I walk outside and don't see any of the teams; I am curious on what is causing the excitement. I consider going to the chow tent for more tea, but realize my thermos is still full from breakfast. I'm eager to learn what they are finding. I prepare the conservation tables and make a bundle of envelopes and containers ready. The day bleeds into the afternoon when Tyler stops in. He tells me a couple from his team are taking a break and walking over to the new site. "New site? Where is this new site?"

He gathers some envelopes and answers, "It is in a new area, and it is hard to explain. I'll be back." He leaves without providing any information. My curiosity is getting the better of me. This morning, I assumed that I would find out in time, and it didn't worry anymore. Now I'm wondering how I could have missed the new mapping. I stroll around the abandoned camp and finally walk over to my sunrise perch and scan the dig sites from the raised cliff. I observe a group at the pinnacle where I watch the rising sun. It is common knowledge about my spot and morning ritual of gazing at the same outcrop. I understand I don't have any scientific information to share, at least, nothing they would believe. I wave at the diggers, and no one notices, everyone fixated on the excavation. I'm not used to quiet, and I wait for the proverbial shoe to drop. I am the only one in the cafeteria at lunch, and I take the time to make a couple of extra sandwiches. I put them in the cooler for whoever comes in next. Taking my salad back to my workroom for a solitary lunch I wonder how many of these kids will stay vegetarian once they leave. I'm eating healthier because of them.

As I settle in front of the fan to eat, Belinda comes rushing in. She knocks the screen door into the wall. "Ms. Libby! You have to come."

"Why, Belinda? Is someone hurt?"

Belinda's face is burning red, and her eyes are indescribable. "No, Libby, you have to come and now."

I keep asking questions, and she continues repeating that I just have to follow her. I grab my floppy hat, the first aid kit, satellite phone and toss a water bottle to her. Belinda looks at me with an odd look of disbelief, tears the cap off the water and chugs the whole thing. She grabs my arm and tells me "Haul ass, old lady," and off we go. There is no more conversation as we run. I realize I should hush and keep moving, but the excitement is palpable as she pulls me toward the new area.

In no time, I'm sucking air as I try to keep up. It is a tough climb to the outcrop, and the loose rock slows me down. Belinda has a whole lot of hurry up and more stamina that I do. She reaches back to help me in a hazardous area; she mutters, "If it wasn't for you and the satellite pictures, we would have missed all of this." There is no way I can keep up with a twenty-year-old college student; she will have to wait as I stop again with a gasp. I can see a canvas covering the dig just over the rise, and it looks like everyone is there. I pray no one is hurt.

As I reach the top of the rise, I hear hushed conversations and see William is right in the middle of the group. They have stacked rock, which blocks my view of the people in the pit. The mood is hushed and is almost religious. As I walk over to the group, a couple of the young men stop talking, pat my shoulder and move aside for me to see what is going on. I am unprepared for the diffidence and unspoken questions. William comes over and touches my arm, moving me forward to the string marking the margin.

I see two small bodies; the desert dryness has mummified them. Todd tells me "These are the only complete bodies discovered in this dig. We occasionally find a few odd bones in the middens, but nothing like this."

The two bodies are dark and shrunken, the clothing engulfs them; I look at their faces, and the intertwining of their hands transfixes me. I have a palpable feeling of sadness and déjà vu. My legs become weak as I continue to stare.

Dr. B speaks, "Do you see it? Look closer, Libby." I know this is important he called me by my first name. I see the faces and then I see it. I'm speechless; around the larger mummy is my amber necklace. Mine is on a chain, and hers is on a cord, but the stones are identical, and the largest pendant also has an insect embedded near the center.

I stare into her darkened face and listen in the silence of the moment. After a few minutes, I feel all the eyes on me, and then the silence breaks. William asks, "Well Libby, what do you think?" Everyone waits for an answer; there is no joking or laughter.

They wait and finally through my soundless tears I respond, "I know them."

After the excitement of the day, everyone stays up late in the cook tent talking about the discovery and speculating with fanciful stories. They also found ceremonial items and the depth of the discussion is difficult for me to absorb.

When we return to the women's sleeping quarters, I sit around a little while longer with them. Finally, Belinda asks, "How do you know them?"

The women sit in silence as I repeat the details of the dream, and we dissect the details trying to come up with a plausible explanation. Finally, I begin to fall asleep while still sitting up. My head is swirling, I need time to think about it all. I usually love the chatter. I learn from these kids, but tonight I'm done.

I rise after dawn, struggle out of bed and see a message next to my cosmetic bag. It is from Dr. B. They want to meet me for breakfast with the supervisors of the other University's archeologists.

I slept in my clothes, so I grab a clean T-shirt and underwear to rush off to the latrine. Most of the students are still sleeping, but Brenda gives me thumbs up as I leave for the cook tent. When I enter, I smell food and coffee, and there is a lot of activity for so early. I grab an empty cup and head over to the group of middle-aged scholars with laptops, notebooks and papers spread over the table. William gets up from his spot next to the coffee pot and greets me with a smile and a hug.

I'm glad; he saved me a seat next to him. I notice the archeologists are in frenzy, with little conversation. They are examining photos of the site, the mummies, and her necklace. The whole group turns as one to look at my pendant. I remove it and allow them to study it; they are taking photos and measurements. I answer different queries about the facts of my vigil over the site. The scientists discount my *being called* to sit there at sunrise. Dr. B diverts a question assuring them I had no access to the site until after the mummies were unearthed. Most of the doctors look skeptical, but they are generating piles of notes. Most appear to be trying to digest the extraordinary circumstances of the discovery. One of the doctors questions the possibility that I have perpetrated a sophisticated hoax. I remind myself that they are scientists, who deal with questions and absolutes, my possible involvement tangles with everything they believe.

Almost in unison, the students swarm into the mess hall. They grab anything and everything to eat and stand around the periphery of the meeting waiting for the day's assignments. One by one, they return to the projects from two days ago. The doctors rise as one to go to the site for further inspections. They finish with me for now, and I'm dismissed to my daily duties. In an almost universal sigh, none of the student teams are directed to the new dig. The conversation from the women's dorm last night races through the encampment like a stage whisper.

Later in the morning, the scholarly assemblage returns to the cook tent and they call for me. When I arrive, the energy heightens, and they all talk at once. I wait patiently and watch while they enthusiastically download photos, email departments, and search the internet. Multiple heads are scratched as they discuss diverse theories for the location and details of the two mummies. I allow them to re-inspect my necklace but insist on its return. Questions and speculations regarding the necklaces are bandied around. None of them likes the suggestion of coincidence. I provide the web page for Golden Leaves, although I have no idea who sold the four additional beads. I think they want to check to see if I was buying amber in bulk.

Most stay in the conference into early evening, planning the next steps. It is interesting to watch the multiple universities work collectively on decisions for the moving of mummies. Dr. B is pushing for Colorado, as we are the discovering school, but it becomes a toss-up between Harvard and the Smithsonian. There is no Smithsonian representative, and there will be a joint inquiry sent by email. The decision comes down to facilities and money. Always comes down to money.

The mummies are coming to me first, and I will do additional photos, minor cleaning and pack them for shipping. They will have representatives from other schools helping. I never thought I would be packaging my dream in bubble wrap. It is late when I return to the cataloging tent to prepare. I'm fatigued, but I need to work. My whole life was to receive and take care of them. I am the guardian, and my effort is like a prayer. Stunned by the details of my journey, and the vision of her necklace brings back my sentimental tears. On an emotional level, I know they need me to protect them, but the area is restricted, and brilliant scholars wish to be involved. Slipping away from the hubbub and the students' constant chatter, I cry again. Gut wrenching sobs for their lost futures a thousand years ago. My usual spot calls me back, and I gaze toward the pinnacle. I see the panoramic view of the excavation and the massive eastern sky. I have greeted the sunrise almost every morning, but never sat at the end of the day. I turn my back to the main canyon and watch the light fade quickly. Leaning against a boulder, I listen to the last of the crew securing for the night. This day has been more astounding than anything I could have imagined.

William comes over and sits on the edge of the rock. He is dirty and visibly exhausted; he begins to tease me about my isolated place separated from the excavations and the giggling kids.

"William, I ache to guard the mother and the area high above the excavation."

"I can't imagine what you are feeling. I promise we will honor your intuition more, especially when you have the verification of satellite photos and jewelry." He sighed, staring at the horizon and puts his arm around my hunched shoulders.

I look toward William in the orange glow of the end of the day. "You have known all along that I have superpowers."

"That I have, I just didn't understand accurately what your powers were until now." He sighs with fatigue.

"It was your keen eye that found the evidence of disturbance. So we are in this together." We both turn toward the east waiting for the full moon.

I hear William catch his breath and say, "This is amazing. I don't know how you found this place; it is stunning."

"I don't know either. When we arrived, I walked to it and sat. William, if you are interested, I will tell you her story."

He looks at me with a puzzled face. "Now, Libby, I have heard about the dream and I see the necklace, but she is older than we are. What more could you know?"

"It isn't that simple. I have dreamed of them since I was a girl. Today was the first time I've seen her face. She was young, and the boy next to her is the son. Her husband is gone, probably dead, and she takes her boy to this place under brilliant starry skies. It is her responsibility to train him with the traditional stories. It has to do with the child's birthright and his responsibilities in the community. They stare at the night sky when it always ends abruptly."

He is silent for a moment and looks as if he is sleeping. He opens his eyes and responds, "Luckily, my degree is in literature, and I'm more open to flights of fancy than the professors. It must have been a landslide of some sort from the evidence where we found them."

I sit up with an expression of disbelief. "Well, Dr. Jamelson, you are listening to my fairy tale?"

William stares at me in and finally said, "Old girl, you have gone round the bend, but I have to tell you that is a great story, and it makes some sense. You need to write it, especially now that we will have more to offer."

"After everything, you give me homework? I'm going to need a new notebook."

William harrumphs and rises slowly, patting me on the head and leaves.

For nearly 50 years, I have felt worthless and small, but everything has changed. After the hours of sweat, dirt and awe, I ache as the heat dissipates in the dusk. The teams have gone to dinner for hours of discussion and William relays the details of my story. They initially laugh, but slowly it evolves to a hypothesis.

Tonight, I have no need for food and try to silence my mind. I recognize how I have felt myself on the outside and now for my first time I am part of something. I watch a harvest moon dominate the darkening blue sky. The brilliant glow illuminates my face and the shadows of time and space; the spirit of a city silenced while time surrounds me. Every step I ever took, every decision I have made brought me here at this moment.

I slip off my sun hat feeling the grit and sweat on my neck. Then I recline to bask in the buttery light of the moon in an unexpected peace. I blindly stare at the area beyond my understanding. I watch a small young woman, heavy with child approach and stand nearby. Silently the two of us watch an ancient story unwind as if projected on the enormous moon. The narrative unfolds with a shared knowing. She was not more than a girl when she wed the one who measures the sky. He left her too soon, and the young mother felt the weight of the grandfathers as she teaches her son the legends and responsibilities born of his blood. Our shadows quietly blend into one bathed in the light of a single celestial witness.

I hear my name, and jerk out of the reverie feeling the gentle touch of Belinda. She tells me the girls are worrying over the past two days, and when I didn't show up for dinner, she came searching. Three of the others follow with a sandwich and iced tea. I try to explain that I wasn't asleep, but researching. They all join in a hearty laugh, as my vision is common knowledge.

"We are all grateful that you didn't roll off the ledge in that meditative state you were in." They begin to chatter, helping me up from my rocky pew and escort me back to the dormitory. Once back, washed and fed, I share the details of the new vision. Analisa takes notes; she is the youngest and has a contemplative quality. She is the one that accepts my story as fact. I adore her as she promises to share the notes with Dr. B.

# – 58 –

The site is abuzz with students and advisors come to inspect the site, phones and cameras clicking. Our team is giving me some credit for finding the area. Questions and doubts bubble in an undertow of discussion that transform into an odd form of respect. They continue to probe and reconstruct the little patch of rock that drew me with a silent voice. I can see disbelief mixed with confirmation in their eyes as they whisper the story of my dream and subsequent visit. Most everyone wants to touch my necklace for luck.

Dr. B explains that he has an issue with the dream, but admits it is interesting and adds that it has undoubtedly engaged the students. He describes my responsibility with the supervision of the preparation of the mummies for shipment. He asks if I could travel with the bodies during shipping. I will have to leave early. As much as I don't want the experience of the past weeks to end, this is my calling.

The first time I touch them, a frightening familiarity surge through body, chilling my bones in the heat of the New Mexican desert. No matter how gentle the handling, it feels invasive. I whisper an almost continuous apology. Finally, the mummies are packed in the specialized, climate-controlled crates that were shipped in for transport.

It is before sunrise when we prepare the van for the trip. William is there for the transfer. I am traveling in the University van with Dr. David Roberts, the Archeologist from UC-Denver. With the early departure, we should be in Denver by late afternoon. The number of people there to see us off surprises me. I throw my backpack onto the rear seat, William holds the front door, and as I begin to climb in, he pulls me back and kisses me tenderly. There is a universal reaction from the spectators, and we pull away in a round of applause.

The miles glide by the conversation continues. He shares the scheduling for my mummies and explains the initial examinations and MRIs. We chat about the details of the assessments and of other recent discoveries. I find him remarkable and yet a quiet man. There are periods of silence as I gaze out of the window soaking in the wonder of this country. There are few towns, but we stop when possible to walk around and re-energize. I tell Dr. Roberts I have no problem taking a shift, but he stays at the wheel, deep in thought. Luckily, the girls at the camp have packed us a generous bag of snacks, as restaurants are infrequent. We wind our way through desert, forests, mountains and plains as I drink in the scenery. I had missed much of the grandeur on the trip down since the vans were full of talkative students and anticipation.

He expresses concern about the wait for direction from the Smithsonian. It is clear he isn't fond of their procedures and involvement. He doesn't want this discovery in storage with many other astounding discoveries. The rest of our teams will be back in Denver and Boulder by the first of next week. I make a personal decision to stay in Denver for the MRI and initial assessments. Thanks to ten hours in a van building a relationship with Dr. Roberts, he arranges for me to have a guest room.

Once we arrive, I sign my charges over to the director of the Archeology and Anthropology departments and reluctantly sign the chain of custody form. I'm exhausted and just want to relax in a real bed. There will be no clocks or predawn creeping about tomorrow.

After rising and having a real shower with hot water, my cell phone rings. "Libby, this is Dr. Roberts. The Smithsonian has called, and they are sending a representative, and we have to delay on all examinations until the expert arrives."

"Okay, Dr. Roberts. I will catch a bus and head back to Boulder, but keep me posted I will come back. Where is the bus station?" Without much more conversation, he sends his teaching assistant over in an aged Toyota, and I score a ride home. They promise to stay in contact with the testing schedule. I walk up the steps and unlock the door feeling a comforting release of home.

# — 59 —

Dr. B calls on Monday morning. "Libby, I wanted to contact you directly to let you know the pregnancy is confirmed. I just couldn't let William have all the fun of keeping you informed." I hear an inhibited laugh as he goes on. "You make it difficult for the scientific mind with your dreams and visions. Don't tell anyone that you have me questioning some of the things I have based my entire career on." I am sure I've never heard him laugh before.

"I'm not worried about you Dr. B, I haven't had any more apparitions, and she has been absent since the visit on the overlook."

"There you go again. Your stories are problematic for me." He promises to keep me updated and thanks me for my involvement. He also asks for permission to give out my information for possible interviews as he is getting many inquiries from the press. He did give me a quick course on our discovery and the information we can release.

Since the call, I have been busy with telephone interviews and a variety of doctors from universities all over the world. This discovery is getting more attention because of the human-interest involvement with the bizarre story of the necklaces. We didn't know who leaked it to the press. There have been inquiries from news outlets, but I am careful to keep all press in conjunction with Dr. B and William. They have also been very visible with interviews and television shows. They both publically express gratitude for my involvement, and they have no idea how this makes me feel. Dr. B let me know that this has been great for department funding, adding most archeological discoveries gather little attention until they get a special on the History Channel.

Dr. B plays it scientifically and avoids the dream scenario as best he can. He diverts to the scientific hypothesis developed for the mummification. He then passes off to William, who shares the coincidence of the dream and allows the audience to draw their conclusions. As close as they are, it is charming seeing the difference in their areas of scholarship.

Over the next weeks, the experts agree: the two people had been on a promontory lookout for the village when it collapsed in a landslide, which was possibly triggered by an earthquake. They are acknowledging my story of the mummies watching the celestial seasons and moon phases, as a theory. Further exploration at the site finds more artifacts and a variety of experts study the carved and marked stones. The great minds of archeology and Native culture are developing a collection of hypotheses. I presume they will slowly agree with the truth I shared.

The public delights with the lack of explanation for the amber adornment on the young mother and the matching necklace gracing the throat of the dreamer. Terry at Golden Leaves did a story about the discovery and the store's involvement in her newsletter. The Hot Springs paper picked it up, and she emailed to tell me business has been crazy. All amber sold out, and Terry had had to make emergency calls borrowing from other stores while waiting for a rush shipment. She didn't know a gift of the pendant would be a successful advertising ploy. We discussed the reading and share how the details fit together. Bless her; she believes every bit of my story.

It has been difficult to settle back into the day-to-day of my little apartment. I slept for a couple of days, and now I am back into my rhythm of calling Julie and Madeline. This week I reactivated my status with the temporary employment agencies. Julie has taken to calling the mummy Lebwana Moon Goddess and her little boy Drew. Her fanciful stories tickle me, some of them make more sense than I like.

I read that Dr. Blankenship has the honor of naming the mummies. The Native tribes are petitioning for burial at the site. I agree entirely, it feels wrong with her lying on examination tables in oxygen-controlled storage bins. They need to be together and at peace.

Andrew and his family are so excited about all of this. They have watched the news about the discovery and insist on dinner. He relays that the boys would be over tomorrow evening, and they have heard my name on the news and are excited to hear everything.

When I arrive, they have a welcome for me all arranged. The boys had helped Lilly make a sign and a macaroni necklace for me. Now I have two quality pieces of jewelry. It is wonderful to be back at their warm, noisy home.

John is the most excited as his science class discussed the discovery. John became a respected scholar because he had personally seen the necklace. He gave a report on my dream, even though I had never discussed it with him.

"John, would you like to take the necklace to school to share? I will let you do that if you are careful." My heart leaps at the thought of parting with it.

"No, Looney, I wouldn't trust me with it. But, if you wouldn't mind, can you to visit our class?"

"Certainly, John, I would be thrilled. I can bring a bunch of the photos and slides from the dig. Would you rather have one of the professors present?"

"I want you to do it. Photos would be great, and then they can see the necklace and meet you too."

"I would be honored. Just clear it with your teacher and let me know when and where. I have connections now, and I'll go ahead and get the slide show from the University." I'm feeling ever so slightly like a movie star who cries easily.

When Bonnie calls us for dinner, John asks to sit next to me, continuing the conversation, asking a thousand questions. He doesn't know how this touches an old woman's heart.

While cleaning up the dinner mess, I have a chance to speak with Andrew. He tells me Brad is coming for a four-day visit at Christmas. He doesn't want me to worry. I'm surprised that I haven't thought about Brad since my life changed. I know there is nothing for me to worry about with this visit.

I realize that the old man has probably seen the news, so my location is no longer classified. Andrew adds that he is proud of me. I hold most of the tears until I am on the way home. I still don't want my husband to find me, which even I am beginning to see as silly.

A pleasant thing about nightlife with children is that I am home early. There is enough time to send some emails and request the slide show. I make an addendum to my will that Lilly will inherit the necklace.

Now that I'm back, I see Andrew and his family more frequently. They start letting me babysit Lilly. She has stayed overnight, and I tell her stories of my childhood and the woman and her boy. We go to the used bookstore to buy puzzles and things to read together. She calls me Looney and the family follow suit; I am thrilled I have my personal grandma name.

# – 60 –

It has been over a week since William and I have spent any time together. He calls for a lunch date today, and I throw on acceptable pants and dash over to the school. I must admit I miss him. He has been busy with helping write up Dr. B's research and the demands of the press. He is doing many of the interviews, as Dr. B is uncomfortable trying to be engaging. The discovery is hyped as a major development in the history of the Anasazi. Since it was our school team that made the discovery, it is has been big news in Boulder. I allow them to use my name, but I do not want any interviews without one of them.

"Hey, Dr. Jamelson how is your brilliant self today?"

"Libby, my girl. I've missed you."

"OMG, are you blushing? OMG, I said OMG, I was with the students too long." We both laugh and settle at our corner table in the student union.

"I saw you and Dr. B on the Today show. Kind of an odd turn of events for a retired American Literature professor, isn't it?"

He shakes his head and tries to hide a devilish grin. He loves the attention. "I've been working on the press releases and the less scientific reports."

They make one heck of a team – every scientist needs a lit professor for back up.

We chat about the students and the experience of the dig. He lets me know that he and Dr. B are going to a conference in Washington DC and will be making a major presentation. They will take along the two students who had uncovered the mummies, and I may go if I wish. The University will pay for transportation and room. After the presentation, the Smithsonian will pick them up for further research. He is hopeful to have the DNA tests results before then. His excitement is mutual, and yet I see the toll it has taken, he looks older.

"Do you need a sample of my DNA for comparison?"

He looks puzzled "How would that help?"

"Oh, you science wannabes, no respect for reincarnation." My sass sends him to pondering things he hasn't thought about recently. However, in the weeks that have passed, I have come to know what is true.

William almost chokes and then looks at me earnestly. "You have already messed with the scientific community enough. I wanted to tell you, that the marked stones appear to be celestial measurement tools."

"YES! Just like I thought." I know that I gave him my full story and my means of information gathering were beyond the scientific.

"Libby, I find this hard to say, but I believe your dream. I have since you first told me. When surrounded by science geniuses it becomes difficult to accept the supernatural. Everything we have discovered supports your explanation. I'm sorry for doubting you."

"Sorry? How could you be sorry? I have had the experience of a lifetime, maybe two. I had the recurring dream since I was old enough to remember and this adventure has given me answers. They haven't returned since the night of the harvest moon, and I miss her." I get teary-eyed. "Please tell me that they will be returned to the village."

"We are getting inquiries and claims and legal action from the Navaho, Hopi, and the Zuni tribes. They wish to claim her and have her buried according to ancient custom. We hope to learn from the DNA, which tribe she is closest too. Then we will honor the primary claim. So if your DNA matched, that would let the appropriate tribe control you."

"You certainly know how to settle me down, don't you? Although most of the bones we have found were in the garbage pits, hope they maybe ignore some of the ancient customs and bury them with honor."

"Paul has procured permission for you to name the mummies. He suggests you consider using your name as a base. He and the university bigwigs want to respect your involvement."

I'm stunned for only a moment; I have thought of names for years, "I don't need time at all. I want to respect her with a tribute, *She who walks in dreams* and for the son *Gazes at stars*. Should we check the names in Zuni or something? I think they should be translated by whichever tribe they may belong to."

"I will take these back to Paul, and there will be another press release. I'm stunned with the interest for your little family. Have you done your assigned homework and start writing the story about them?"

"You damn American Lit professors, you never quit do you? I have been journaling, but I haven't written any stories. What are you going to do, flunk me?"

"No, my dear woman, you could never fail. I accept your excuse, but it is one hell of a story."

"I am sure I won't write it, so why don't you? Yes, there is a plan; you need a project to keep yourself out of the coffee shops."

He quietly shakes his head to the affirmative. "Only if you work with me. By the way, do you have any dreams about Portugal? We are looking at the Celtic sites in that area for next summer."

When I call Julie that night, she feigns disappointment that I didn't name them Lebwana and Drew. She admits to watching William and Dr. B on the news and saw the pictures of the dig. She continues to tease about my boyfriend being a well-seasoned cutie pie. Julie is sorely disappointed we haven't kissed more. When I tell her about a trip to Portugal, she threatens to leave Tom and move in with me. I love her enthusiasm and support. I owe her another muffin basket for just being.

We plan she will visit for two weeks the beginning of February. I'm anxious; I miss her even though we talk several times a week. She wants to meet my family and get away from the New Jersey winter for a Colorado mountain winter.

# – 61 –

"Hello, Brad? Why are you calling? Do you know what time it is? It is the middle of the night. Speak up. What is so important?"

"No, this is Denise."

"Denise? Is there something wrong?" It is hours before dawn and I suddenly feel very cloudy and wonder if this is another dream. I have never spoken to my husband's mistress. I don't want to call accidently her any of the names I have for her.

Denise quietly gasps for air and then in a quiet sob "He's dead. Brad is dead. He called yesterday afternoon and was fine. When he called last night, it was just a gurgled on the phone. I rushed over; he was gone."

"Oh Denise, I'm sorry. How are you and the kids?"

"We are stunned; I don't know what I am supposed to do. I could have expected it; he had a minor heart attack the day you left. He never recovered and was consumed with your leaving. You know how he can be. I mean, you know how he was. There was nothing I could do to get him to take care of himself, and now he is gone." The words just flow out of her and then silence.

There is an almost indistinguishable whimper on the line as Denise struggles for composure. "I don't know what to do; there is so much to take care of, and I don't have any legal rights. I won't be able to get his body moved out of the morgue. I know I don't have a right to ask you, but can you help? There is nothing I can do, and I don't trust his brother, Shawn."

"I'll be there as soon as possible. How can I call you?" I feel this incredible power surge as if I am called to make things right. She gives me her cell phone number and email address, and I try to comfort her a little longer.

Once we are off the phone, I call the airline and me there are flights in the morning, but I can't make those. To go that quickly is expensive. I check the train schedule, and I can leave sooner, but it takes a day and a half. I finally buck up and call Denise back.

"Denise, this is Libby, I mean, Elizabeth. Do you have a death certificate or anything I can give the airlines?"

"I'm still at the hospital; let me ask if they can do something for you. Do you have a fax number?"

"I don't." Momentarily I am unsure and then realize they can email everything. I have her connect me with the clerk, and we work out the details.

Once handed back to Denise, I assure her that I am on my way. Once there is more information, I will call. I gave verbal permission to the hospital for her to handle immediate decisions. I can hear the stress in her voice release ever so slightly.

I turn on my computer and check email. There is nothing yet. I call the airline explaining the situation and book a seat. They assure me that once I have proof of the emergency, they will issue a credit. I'm embarrassed about how at a time like this; I try to save money.

I throw a few things back into the pink suitcase, one of the few things I left with and the only thing I will take back. I only pack a few necessities, after all; my clothes should still be at the house. I set the alarm and try to sleep a little longer. It is fruitless, so I get up, and as soon as the sun rises, I call Julie.

She responds with an enormous snort of relief, expressing what I feel. She adds that she feared that man would be vengeful and would tie me up in court for years. She is the only person that can understand my lack of grief.

I call Bonnie, and she will tell Andrew when he comes home. She will also call Madeline for me later in the morning. Dearly, she extends condolences, and I accept on behalf of Denise and her children. Minutes later Andrew calls back, "Looney, do you need me? I can find a substitute to cover my classes. Then I could make the funeral."

"You don't need to do this for me. I'm not sure there will be a funeral. Only come if it matters to you."

"I truthfully don't know him, but I will come if you need me."

"No, darling, I'm good. Don't worry about it, and I'll keep in contact."

Upon arrival at the airport, I wrangle a break on the price with the death certificate. Moving quickly through security, I make it to the gate with time to spare. While waiting to board, I call William. He agrees to cover the high school presentation for John. He will contact Andrew to get into my place for the power point and video I made.

Then I call Madeline and bring her up to speed. I let her know that Bonnie will be calling with details. Madeline points out that Andrew was lucky to meet him a couple of months ago. She worries about how I'm taking the loss, but I have no connection with Brad anymore. I feel no grief, only release.

I appreciate the simplicity and flexibility of my life. Just before my flight, I call Denise.

"Denise, this is Elizabeth. I'm on my way. I will be in Indianapolis at 3:30 this afternoon."

"Can I pick you up at the airport?"

"Yes, Denise that will be great. It is about time we met."

"I've taken vacation time, so I don't have to work, and my aunt has the kids. I don't know how to thank you for coming. I didn't suppose you would help after the things Brad said about you. I didn't know who else to call."

"No apology needed. I guess this is our chance to get to know each other without outside influence. I won't bother you with the other side of the relationship. See you in a couple of hours." Surprised by my lack of emotion, I spent fifty years either loving or hating that man, and now he is gone. I recognize I'm about to clean up his last mess, I'm still the dutiful co-dependent. I try not to anticipate the multitude of things I will have to decide. I shut down my phone as they call group one to board. I expect this to be a short trip.

# – 62 –

When I arrive at baggage, Denise is standing there. She looks broken; not the confident, younger woman she was when she came into our lives. It appears that Denise has aged twenty years, exaggerated by her disheveled appearance. Obviously worn down by grief and fear, she smiles at me tentatively as I walk over and embrace her. After holding her for just a moment, Denise seems to relax and then gather strength, and we speak our hellos. At this moment, I take over the responsibility, and she willingly releases it.

Our first stop is Brad's house. I look around, and it seems like an old friend, but it is no longer my home. I had time to plan while at the airport and I scheduled an appointment with an attorney for Wednesday morning. Today, it is housework. Denise is not going to be much help, and I don't want to discuss the plan that is forming in my mind.

"Is that someone at the door, Denise?"

"Sure is, I'll get it."

I hear talking and now a familiar snort. It is Julie; what the hell is she doing here?

"Lizard, where are you? I came for the funeral." She has the uncanny ability to surprise and make things possible. Even Denise is smiling. "You know damn well I wouldn't miss putting one of the bastard

Donovan boys in the ground. No offense, Denise."
Her boisterous nature has energized both of us.

"Oh, my Aunt Hattie's cat!" There is no stopping
this woman. "Call the police – someone let the crazy
out on the street." With this, we all breathe a sigh
of relief.

"Ok, you two, you can cry at the memorial but
today and tomorrow we have things to do. Stop
pussyfooting around, you two are sisters and have
been for a long time. We are the Donovan sorority,
and we have things to do." She puts a bucket of
chicken and a box of tacos on the table with two liters
of diet Coke. "Ladies, the Volunteers of America will
be here with a truck tomorrow at three." I can see the
pain begin to soften from Denise's face.

"You always have a plan, not always a great idea,
but action none the less." I take off my shoes and
sweater and roll up my sleeves.

Denise smiles. I love how Julie includes her.
She is a beautiful woman; I'm pleased that Brad has
one person grieving his death. I owe her more than
she could imagine. Their affair stopped much of the
violence and empowered my escape. Denise asked
shyly, "Are you going to move back to the house?"

"Honey, I am not. I left this life behind, and I will
never come back." Hope I didn't say that too loud.
"All I want is my soup pot."

"Oh, and the rest of the photos, jewelry, my
clothes and the mementos from my mother. I want
nothing else, and my car, and maybe the boat. In
fact, Denise, if you want to live here you may move
right in."

"Elizabeth? That wouldn't be right. Do you mean it?"

"I do mean it. I don't know where you live, or your situation, but you can move in here. A couple of years ago we had it insulated, put in better windows and the roof is new, too." Julie looks at me, and I can see the approval in the curl of her lip. "We have mortgage insurance that pays off the note. Denise, you have earned it. I don't know exactly how long you two were together, but you have his kids. I don't know what he did legally, or if there is a new will. Your kids deserve the best he has. They lost their father."

"Don't throw away anything you want to keep or sell. You don't have to decide right now, take an hour." From this point, all three of us dig in tossing and saving. I reserve a U-Haul trailer, but cancel an hour later. I will load the boat; after all, he bought it with the inheritance from my parents.

By time, the charity truck is here on Tuesday; we have pulled furniture and clothes to the street. Denise has decided to keep a few things, but not many. She saves his high school trophies and letter jacket for her son. We worked with the motto *when in doubt – throw it out.*

As the volunteers load the truck, Denise leaves to pick up her kids and visit the funeral home for the cremation. We have too many things for the volunteers, and they promise to return late tomorrow afternoon. Julie and I work into the evening. She goes to pick up some hamburgers and comes back with the mandatory box of wine. With wine glasses in hand, we work a little more plowing through years of two lives.

I hate to admit it felt good sleeping in my bed, but since I hadn't slept the night before and then worked from arrival to exhaustion may have played a part. I am happy he died in his chair and not on the other side of our bed. That may have been bothersome.

Next morning I go to the hospital as soon as the business office opens to sign a folder of documents. They already have his insurance and Medicare cards and take my address for any additional billing. I take my magical signature to the funeral home that Denise contracted, and they will pick up the remains today. I sign another permission authorizing the cremation. Denise and her children will be here to say good-bye. I execute a limited power of attorney to Denise so she can handle final decisions and chose an urn if she wishes. Before leaving, I provide his insurance information and our debit card to pay for everything.

I return early, and the house is still quiet, calling through the hall for my sidekick. "Come out, old girl, we have places to go and breakfast to eat."

After brunch, I have an appointment with the attorney I found online. Julie laughs at my legal counsel. She believes that I had searched the internet for the youngest, most inexperienced lawyer in the phone book. He has an office that could pass for a closet and no waiting. The no waiting was a primary determination. I brought the metal box from the back of the cupboard, and I tell him we have work to do and little time to do it.

Going through the documents, we find Brad's life insurance policy for the kids and nothing for Denise. He has a rudimentary will that we had drawn up too many years ago. I have the rights to his pension and another life policy, plus co-ownership of all of the property. This appointment won't take as long as we thought.

"Mr. Appleton, my wants are simple. I want to be sure Brad Donovan takes care of his children. We had a homeowner policy that pays off the house with either of our deaths, and I want to quit claim the house to Denise Jacobs. I want his pension from Chrysler to go into an account for Denise Jacobs and code it as child support." I provide a paper with her address and phone number.

"Mrs. Donovan, I will need the insurance policies, account numbers and address information."

"I think I have everything. Here are the policies." I place a bulging blue folder on his desk. "I will have Ms. Jacobs come by in the next couple days." I feel like the CEO of getting things done.

"I will take the other life insurance policy and have it put into trust accounts for Robert, John, and Lilly Scortino equally. Robert will be 21 in March, so we can make him signatory right away. I don't want to hand over cash, that is just too tempting at twenty-one. The other two can have the money at twenty-one or for education at eighteen." Mr. Appleton writes down the instructions on a legal pad. "I will take our joint savings account to pay you and any outstanding bills. I want the lake cabin in Minnesota, but I want it deeded to Andrew Scortino, the same address as the Scortino children."

I hear no argument from anyone; he just sits taking copious notes and Julie is stunned into silence. She leans over and whispers, "I love you. Isn't there anything that you want, you have earned it?"

"My life is stripped down to the perfect size. Julie, I'm happy with the things in the boat and the soup pot. I know that Brad was a total ass, but he understands now. I will see to it that his last action on this earth will be to act right. I want nothing other than to take care of all of our children. He owes them much more than money."

My rosy-cheeked lawyer gathers everything, and I give him the contact information and a check. "When can you draw up the necessary papers?"

"We can get everything moving today, and we will call with any problems." We? Who are we? I see an empty desk where a secretary could be. "I'll have a couple of things for you to sign tomorrow and don't worry about anything else; we will figure it out." I'm feeling good about my choice of representation as I write a check.

We leave as quickly as we had arrived, hit a drive-thru restaurant and go back to the house. Denise is already there digging through the two upstairs bedrooms. "Hey sister, I'll bet you are happy we didn't use those rooms very much."

"Once I get the sports memorabilia out, I'm going to paint."

I smile broadly, "Some of that crap might be valuable so try eBay. Have you decided to take the house?"

"It was such a surprise when you offered. I talked it over with the kids, and we decided this is so much bigger, and it is better for them. Daisy is ecstatic to have a whole room of her own. Once I get things moved, I'll sell the condo and send you the money."

Julie and I laugh in unison; she has no idea about the attorney appointment. "The hell you will – not! You keep it, and open savings accounts for yourself and the kids. I'm a long-time believer in saving."

"Elizabeth, I didn't want anything when I called. I don't want you to think..." and she begins to cry.

"It is about time you called me Libby; no one calls me Elizabeth anymore. I know, you needed help, but this helps me too. I have the chance to clean out old connections."

I can't stop the smile as we load my clothing into the trunk of the car. As a group, we consider burning a couple of wall hangings trying to imitate art but agree to donate them in a third charity truckload. There is nothing like moving to have your questionable decorating ideas exposed to the world.

"Hey, anyone need a pickup, or do we sell it?" There were no takers on the truck, and I add another item to my list.

Thursday we meet Denise at the Hitching Post at seven, a perfect location for this spur of the moment memorial. She brings the old man's urn. We take a moment to honor her loss, giving her and the kids heartfelt hugs and encouragement.

It feels strange to walk in here. I'm sure everyone knows how I abandoned poor, good buddy, Brad. He spent more evenings here than in his home with me. I must admit, I spent many nights at this bar myself, but quit coming in about ten years ago. I recognize many of the faces; all look familiar and older with no other noticeable changes.

Julie has been nervous about seeing Shawn again, and he is front and center of the bar when she walks in. Instead of being intimidated, Julie announces, "Heads up you drunks, the ones that *got away* from Donovans have arrived." The she orders a round for the house.

I am so grateful that Julie is here; I owe her more than a muffin basket this time. I know that if I were alone, I would feel guilty by the empty outpouring of sympathy. Brenda, Stephanie, and Mr. Offert came from my office, and I am touched to see them. They don't stay long, and I am tickled to learn they followed the mummy news. Brenda gives me a bouquet of mums, and the play on words is as delicious as the flowers are beautiful.

I feel the heartfelt emotions belong to Denise and her kids, directing many to their attention. Then I buy a round for the house.

I've never seen his children before. The boy, Tyler, looks just like a young Andrew, and I see Robert on his face too. I hope Brad knows he has left something of himself behind. As for the girl, Daisy, she is eight and every bit as beautiful as her mother is. I can see the intelligence and bewilderment in her eyes. I never thought about how their parents' relationship has written on their souls.

Earlier today, I arranged a caterer to work with the kitchen, and we have food for everyone. The evening fills with funny stories and poignant memories. I don't disparage his name and share some amusing stories of our lives together. Denise buys a round and leaves with her kids. As the festivities begin to wrap up, the three of us have become everyone's good friends. Free drinks can work miracles.

I ask Doug, the bartender, for the tabs, both Brad's and mine. He smiles. "I wasn't sure how to ask about his. I should have known Ms. Elizabeth wouldn't miss anything." I give him a $200 tip and a wink.

As the night fades, Julie and Shawn continue talking. He is obviously grieving over the loss of his only brother. I feel awkward breaking up the tête-à-tête, but it is almost closing time. "Julie, you about ready to leave?"

"Sure, Lizard, I'm ready when you are. Let me hit the ladies room first."

I am left face to face with Shawn; we were never close and didn't get along. He always thought I was the reason his brother didn't finish college. "Shawn, I'm so sorry for your loss. I know how close you two have been. I caught myself avoiding you, and I apologize. If you ever need to contact me, I have given my information to Denise."

"Denise? Why her?"

"No reason, but this will be goodbye, I'm going back to Colorado."

"You aren't moving back into the house?"

"No, it has been left to Denise and his kids."

"Guess that is best. He would want that."

I'm surprised; the Shawn I used to know wanted everything for himself. At this point Julie comes back, picks up her bag and gives him a kiss on the cheek. "Goodbye, Shawn, thanks for the memories."

At this point, I put the signed title and keys to the pickup truck in front of him on the bar. Shawn looks stunned, and the room is silent as I strut out the door and leave the old life.

Julie whispers, "You are getting good with the ambush-and-go."

We sleep in the next morning, as everything is done. Julie wakes me up, dressed and ready to eat. I struggle out of bed, and I notice that Shawn has already picked up the truck. While at breakfast, Julie confirms her flight for tonight and I receive a text from my grandson Robert. He is on his way and will be here around seven to help me drive back.

Julie and I pick up Denise around two for the attorney appointment. I think Julie is developing a crush on young Mr. Appleton. On this visit, he has a secretary; I think it could be his mother. "OK, Mr. Appleton where do you need signatures? I have a life to catch."

He has the paperwork for the house transfer, and we conclude the largest transactions. The formal power of attorney is completed, and other paperwork signed. He has set up three interest-bearing money market accounts in trust for my kids, and a signature card for Robert to sign. I explain that I am leaving in the morning, and he assures me everything else can be by email and mail for any other documents as the need arises.

Two hours later, the three of us leave arm in arm. Denise's aunt picks up the kids from school, so we go straight to the nicest restaurant in Kokomo. We have a fabulous dinner and a good red wine on the money Brad had left in his wallet. We toast the survival and strength of the women we are. I assure Denise I will keep in touch, we talk about her kids and their new cousins in Colorado, and she asks if they can visit for vacation. I have no hesitation confirming an ongoing relationship.

We rush back to the house just before seven, and Robert arrives within minutes. Julie convinces the shuttle driver to take her back to the airport. I don't think I have ever had a day in my life that moved so efficiently. Everything fell into place, almost as if there was a divine choreographer planning each step.

Once the other women leave, Robert and I go through some of the sports memorabilia. He isn't interested in much, as he a Denver Bronco's fan, and Brad had nothing for them or soccer. The two of us prepare the couch for Robert and watch television together. I can't stop looking at him seeing glimpses of my dad around his eyes. It is still early when I begin to get tired, and hand him the remote; he is young and still on the Mountain Time zone.

I set the alarm to ensure an early start, making a mental note to take the clock. My things are packed, loaded and the boat is secured to the car. There is a full tank of gas, and the car is pointed west. Robert and I will learn how to tow a boat tomorrow morning.

Through the night, I bask in the dreams of the good memories of my life. As the light filters through the drapes, She Who Walks in Dreams materializes. She looks directly into my face; for the first time I see her beauty, and she smiles and then disappears into *the light of* the sunrise.

I bow *my head knowing this closes* chapters of insecurity, and I will drive toward my genuine life full of family, friends, and adventure. A text from William wakes me up.

Are you OK?
Leaving for home.
Cool – your turn to buy lunch.

Robert is up and showered by the time I walk into the kitchen. He has a plate of toast and is ready to go, and I am too. I'll drive the first leg of the trip, out of Kokomo. As he buckles his seatbelt, Robert says, "Get ready to hear the story of my life."

"I can't imagine anything better."

# About the Author

A child of the 60s, Midwestern by birth, Northwestern by choice, Toni challenges the boundaries for women of a certain age. After a long career as an insurance adjuster, she fell into writing through a challenge from a friend. Toni never dated Mick Jagger, but marched for civil rights, shared bread with icons of politics and art. She is spending her retirement, gathering stories prime for embellishment. Writing has taught her inspiration without perspiration is just a good idea.

Sharing more information and short stories at www.tonikief.com.